RAVEN'S MARK

MARK

An absolutely gripping crime thriller with a massive twist

CHRISTIE J. NEWPORT

Winner of the Joffe Books Prize 2021

JOFFE
BOOKS

Joffe Books, London
www.joffebooks.com

First published in Great Britain in 2022

Cover art by The Brewster Project

ISBN: 978-1-80405-539-7

FSC
www.fsc.org

MIX
Paper | Supporting
responsible forestry
FSC® C171272

*To my lovely Nanna, Olive Newport. I always said
I would dedicate my first book to you — so here it is.
Our letters were part of what started my love of writing.
You always believed in my writing, and you passed that baton
to my wife, Amy Newport. So, this book is dedicated to you both.*

Nanna and Amy — I love you.

PROLOGUE

I'm sitting in the restaurant holding a dead raven and it's ticking. He'd told me to meet him here and like a desperate fool I came. The chance to catch him, to stop all this once and for all had been too enticing. I've always felt the pressure to haul him in, but now I know who he is I'm not sure there's a line I won't cross to end this. I look around and note a few glances in my direction, ranging from intrigue to disgust. A waitress had brought the brown cardboard box to my table smiling, no doubt imagining it to be something romantic or perhaps a birthday surprise. There was a white card attached to the top bearing my name — *Detective Chief Inspector Bethany Fellows*. I opened the flaps and hesitantly peered inside. The frozen face of a taxidermy raven stared up at me. My heart almost stopped, a clenched fist in my chest, and I struggled to breathe. Gingerly, I pulled it from the box and saw it was wearing a necklace, the word *BOOM* written on a homemade pendant. Then I heard the ticking.

The table is laid for two but I'm alone. The muffled threat of the bird's tick-tock rhythm rings in my ears. A quick headcount and I know there's in excess of ten people here drinking, eating, chatting, all blissfully ignorant of what's about to happen. I received the text moments before

1

the parcel, warning me not to attempt any heroics. I hadn't understood until I saw the raven. The text said he was watching, waiting for me to make a move, do the right thing and try to evacuate the restaurant. I gaze around and know I won't do that. I can't. The faces of everyone I love pass before my mind's eye. I'll do whatever it takes to save them — yes, even let this bomb explode.

Because if I choose to save myself and these strangers, I sign the death warrant of someone close to me. After the recent devastating events, I know it's no bluff. I look at the stuffed beast with revulsion. If I'd known the personal cost of heading the Brander investigation I would have walked away. No, I would have run as fast as I could and never looked back. Now, it's far too late.

CHAPTER ONE

Present day

As I drive my car into Balfour Street, a typical northern council estate, I spot a yellow Labrador, its muzzle soddened with blood. He's zigzagging under the fluttering blue-and-white tape. A couple of red-faced uniformed police officers unsuccessfully lunge for him. I swerve into a space beside a row of grey-doored garages, slam on my brakes and get out. The garages are opposite four dilapidated terraced bungalows with weed-infested gardens. One of them is my crime scene.

I make a grab for the dog but miss by a hair's breadth. His paws are leaving a winding trail, scattering evidence. Another copper appears out of nowhere. Moving like lightning, he throws himself to the ground flat on his stomach and with his outstretched hand hooks the collar and pulls the dog up short. The dog whips around, growling, lips back, teeth bared, eyes bugging with fear. The officer puts on a brave face, whispering sweet nothings, attempting to soothe him. His shaking hand somewhat undermines his show of bravery.

'Get that dog secured now,' I snap, avoiding the stares of the onlookers. The copper's face deepens to almost scarlet

3

and I feel instantly guilty. It probably wasn't his fault but it hardly looks professional, and I'm very aware of the many mobile phones capturing our comedy sketch of errors. The press will have a field day, and my boss will have my guts for garters. Even though I wasn't here until the finale, it's my rodeo after all.

I take a little time to observe the space, along with the people occupying it. You only get one opportunity to take in a crime scene for the first time. To note the shifty-looking observer, absorb the moments before the chaos ensues. The scene of crime officers (SOCOs) are already inside, they'll have their part covered. My job is to attempt to put the pieces of the jigsaw together.

I look around and notice that two of the bungalows' front doors are thrown wide open. All four gardens are separated by low red-brick walls, mounted by metal fences painted black. Their matching gates open onto tarmacked pathways running up to identical brown wood front doors, all of which have little slanted slate roofs above them. The paint on the fences and gates are flaking, the iron now visible encrusted with rust.

An elderly woman wearing a blue apron over a floral nightdress stands on her front step, a cigarette dangling precariously from her lips. She reaches into the front pocket of her apron and retrieves a gold Zippo lighter. In a practised fluid motion, she cups one hand around the cigarette and flicks the lighter. She takes a drag, blows smoke upwards and squints, craning her neck for a better view, her narrowed eyes sparkling with intrigue. I'd bet my last tenner she doesn't miss a thing around here.

Next door to her a middle-aged couple stands in the centre of a scruffy front garden. The bloke is wearing a yellowing sleeveless white vest bearing a smattering of food and drink stains. The vest is barely winning the battle against his bursting beer gut, and a good couple of inches of flab hangs below the hem. His once white sport socks appear to be soaking up last night's rainfall.

The woman beside him has at least had the sense to wear boots — the patent leather high-heeled ankle boots don't pair well with the slinky red silk dressing gown she is wearing, only just covering her tiny matching shorts. Above her skinny legs, she has a top half as wide as the average Range cooker. She wears her blonde hair in curlers, the old-fashioned kind that you only see in old episodes of *Coronation Street*. The two of them stare unashamedly in our direction. It's human nature to be intrigued by drama, especially of the criminal variety, we wouldn't all be addicted to the crap we watch on television otherwise. Regardless, staging a performance for them is not my idea of fun.

The third bungalow has its curtains drawn, the flicker of a television just about visible through the heavy fabric. I wonder whether it's respect, a purposeful avoidance of us, or they just don't care. Lastly, I focus on the bungalow beyond the police cordons. The one with a dead teenager in situ. Detective Superintendent Dillon West's words ring in my ears. I'd been nearby, on my way into work, the phone call too brief to give me more than the basics. Nonetheless, it had been enough to make my stomach drop.

Two years ago, I'd been working cold cases and had dragged a four-year-old box out of the doldrums of our back office. This was the case everyone wanted to solve. I'd been so damn arrogant, so sure that I was the cop who would finally make sense of his twisted clues that I made promises to a devastated family, reopening their wounds and infecting them with gangrene. I can't forgive myself for failing them.

He'd struck four years before I opened the casefile, launching his attack and vanishing into thin air. He hadn't hurt anyone since, and we'd assumed it to have been a one-off. The body inside tells me we were wrong. Not only is he back, but this time he's killed. Dillon had said enough to tell me it was him, the Brander.

I approach the uniformed police officer standing beside the outer cordon. The officer looks grim, his face white. The victim was a teenager. A kid. No wonder he is pale. I take a breath and introduce myself. I show my identification card. 'Detective Chief Inspector Bethany Fellows. I've been appointed Deputy Senior Investigating Officer.'

After my previous failure, I feel responsible. If I fall short again, the cost will continue to rise.

'Yes, ma'am. PC Dom Harvey.' He nods. I can hear his teeth chattering. His sparse hair lifts in the breeze. 'Bloody freezing.' He uses his teeth to uncap a biro. 'Reason for entry?'

'Detective Superintendent Dillon West informed me that the crime scene manager, Hannah Edwards, has requested my presence.'

Harvey shoves his sleeve up and checks his watch. '8.22 a.m. Please suit and boot up and make sure you log out.'

'No problem. Thanks, Dom. I'll have an officer attend to take over as soon as I can. Once they're here, I'll need you to hand your boots in at the station so we can rule them out of any shoe prints we're lucky enough to find, okay?'

'Course, ma'am.'

I pull on a blue Tyvek suit and snap on a pair of matching shoe covers. Next, a face mask and hairnet before pulling up the hood of the Tyvek and double-gloving. I lift the tape and duck beneath it, turning to glance back into the early morning sunlight and the people who have begun to gather. The sky is, briefly, a blazing red, bringing to mind the old saying about a 'shepherd's warning', something my Aunt Margie always says. As usual, their phones are lifted. Modern humanity terrifies me.

The sun disappears, the street is dismal, the wind sends litter tumbling down the dank grey pavement. The night's rainfall has left a puddle running the length of the gutter. A blocked drain bubbles every so often, a tang of rotten eggs rising from it. If there's a weapon to search for, this will be one of the primary places to consider.

Dillon informs me that PC Dom Harvey has been inside. He was first on the scene after the 999 call came through. A paramedic attended to confirm the poor kid was gone. Now it's my arena. I head across the overgrown

6

front garden, mindful to follow the common approach path, clearly demarcated so that everyone treads the same route, where there is least likely to be evidence to disturb. In the garden, dog turds lie uncollected. The place is lacklustre and unkempt. I'm guessing the inside won't be any better.

I duck under the red-and-white tape of the inner cordon that stretches across the front door of the rundown bungalow. The paint on the windowsill is chipped and discoloured, the letter box half hanging off. I know from my brief conversation with Dillon that the man living here is a tenant. The owner clearly doesn't feel the need to keep on top of things.

No murder scene is ever an agreeable sight, but when it's a youngster, it bares its teeth at you like a beast. There's no preparing for this. I take a last gulp of fresh air and go inside.

The front door leads directly into the lounge, which has a threadbare brown carpet besmirched with bloodied pawprints. I hear the buzz of forensic worker bees busy gathering evidence. SOCOs balancing on see-through plastic stepping plates are leaving yellow numbered markers beside possible evidence and bagging items. Everything is about preserving the integrity of the scene. The plastic stepping plates will have been chosen because the floor is carpeted — they tend to skid about on hard wood or laminate. In a way, the dank brown carpet is a blessing. The only drawback is that the plastic plates aren't as strong as the silver ones, something we're all well aware of and which adds further trepidation to our already cautious movements.

There it is, the sickly, ripe, metallic tang of blood. The cream walls bear the odd red-brown smudge, denoted by more yellow markers. There are a few old movie posters in black frames dotted around the walls: *Back to the Future*, *Die Hard*, *Gremlins*, slightly smaller versions of the posters you would have seen on the walls of cinemas back in the day.

An ugly brown armchair faces away from me. Using the stepping plates I walk over to it. It's always a trial in these damn shoe covers — they're as slippery as sandals on an ice rink. If I fall, I'll mess with the evidence and piss everyone off. I step with the cautiousness of a kid on a balancing beam, carefully edging around to the front and swallow, hard.

The victim is slouched in the chair, long wavy brown hair falling against her bare shoulders. She's wearing a short denim skirt and a red slinky top. Her white arms hang down on either side of the chair. Her eyes are cloudy, shot through with small, ruby lightning bursts. Her neck is split open in the raw, wide grin of death.

Poor kid. What she had to endure. I lean closer, noting the frothy remnants of dog saliva, the telling cleanliness of the wound. Pets running amok in a murder scene are a real problem. Evidence lost, licked up and gone for good.

The house is pervaded by the dank stench of stale alcohol, teenage sweat, old cheese and excrement. I don't need to ask why I can smell shit and piss, most people in the throes of violent death lose control of their bodily functions, and I can't imagine a young girl being an exception.

Hannah Edwards, the crime scene manager, is crouched at the other side of the armchair. Her face pops up above the arm. 'Oh, hi, Beth.'

'Have you identified her yet?' I ask. The house is a known hangout for local kids. The police patrol the area, regularly kicking them out. It's home to a man with severe learning disabilities. The poor bloke's clearly lonely and ripe for the picking, and there are plenty of assholes willing to take advantage.

'She was carrying a fake ID. There's no way she was nineteen, but according to this—' Hannah holds out a plastic evidence bag containing a photographic ID card, the picture unmistakably the kid slumped in the armchair — 'she's nineteen-year-old Rose Danes.'

I reach out to take the bag and stare at the image of a smiling girl, who at one time had been very much alive and full of promise. Some might write a kid like this off. Not me. I'd been a pain in the arse myself. If it hadn't been for my Aunt Margie's perseverance, I could have ended up just like Rose. My mum had been murdered when I was four and

I'd been there to see it. A stranger had come into our home, strangled my mother to death and left me sitting alone with her for the next five hours. The man responsible took on the guise of a monster, folklore-like in my imagination. What happened to my mum, to me, has been the driving force behind every major decision I've made, including joining the police force and my determination to rise to detective.

I hand the evidence bag back to Hannah. It will need to be logged and stored along with the rest. 'I'll run the name, see if we get a hit with MISPER. If it's her real name, I reckon she'll be easy enough to find on TikTok, Instagram and the like. All kids have socials these days. Do we have an approximate time of death?'

Hannah stands up, balancing precariously on a stepping plate. 'Well, rigor has more than begun to set in, it's working its way down her body. That, coupled with the discolouration starting around her lower area, I'd say we're looking at an approximate time frame of between six and eight hours, give or take. The house is cold, so that's a factor. Lividity hasn't fully set in, though it is consistent with her having not been moved.'

'Not?'

Hannah shakes her head. 'Lividity is around the areas I would expect if she'd been sitting here since death. Don't get me wrong, she could have been positioned in the chair straight after she was killed, but I doubt it. Then again, you never know. Especially with this perp.'

'So, it's really him? The Brander?' I shudder, see Hannah notice and feel embarrassed. As Deputy SIO I don't relish showing weakness.

To her credit, Hannah sidesteps the awkward moment. 'Well, that's why I called you here. I thought it best to show you.'

'Where is it?'

Hannah uses a gloved finger to hold away a few strands of our victim's hair. On her shoulder is the image of a raven — a painful-looking red welt. I wince, imagining the agony of having shaped boiling metal stamped onto the skin until the image was seared in place. I have seen that brand before, on another young girl, and I still can't figure out what it means. Ravens represent so many different things, and without knowing who the perpetrator is, I can't make sense of its meaning in this context. On our previous investigation, we had concluded that the image was created using some sort of homemade brand. It only took a quick Google search to find ways of making them, but then again, he could have practised with lots of different items until he achieved his desired result — a heated and shaped coat hanger, a long piece of manipulated metal, or even a potato masher reconfigured into the outline of a raven. The possibilities were endless, and our guesswork had brought us no nearer to catching him.

Celine Wilson had been just fourteen years old. She had survived, but not in any meaningful way. She's a living doll now, a girl frozen in time by the act of a monster who, by the looks of things, has spent the past six years with his sickness bubbling inside him like a vat of acid. This kid has paid the price for our lack of success. We didn't catch him when he hurt Celine Wilson, and now he's killed someone else.

He's back. The victimology, her gender, age, where she's been killed, the strange brand in the same area of her body, it all convinces me that we are right — this is the work of the Brander. 'Oh, fuck.'

I squeeze my eyes shut until they water.

CHAPTER TWO

Superintendent Dillon West had set up the Major Incident Room while I was at the crime scene. The next steps are imprinted in my brain. Time is everything, and now is when we have the best opportunity to get results. We call it the 'golden hour', though it's a turn of phrase to be used relatively loosely, lasting anything from mere moments to several hours, sometimes longer. But it's essential we move fast — evidence and witnesses weaken or disappear over time.

I stand facing the semicircle of tables under the eager gaze of my colleagues. 'Okay, first of all, thanks for being here. We have a preliminary identification — Rose Danes, fifteen years old.' I point to the image downloaded from her Instagram page. She's a smiling, beautiful young girl. She has huge eyes, false lashes and a flirtatious air about her.

'The bungalow she was found in is rented by a Mr Barry Knultz, a local man with severe learning disabilities. He is somewhat of a friend, or, perhaps more appropriately, prey to the kids around the area. They use his home as a gathering place, which is what appears to have been the case last night. Barry couldn't sleep so he went to his mum's. When he returned this morning, he found Rose Danes' body and dialled 999. Paramedic John Hayhurst attended the scene and declared life extinct. PC Dom Harvey was in attendance with Hayhurst. He subsequently cordoned off the scene and called it in. There was a dog present, it's being checked over and any forensic evidence we can get from the fur is being taken. You never know what that dog may have come into contact with — the killer him or herself, but certainly the victim. Transference of evidence is a real possibility. How strong that evidence will be, well, that's to be determined by our science guys and gals. It's worth checking. Now, I have Uniform carrying out door-to-door enquiries as we speak. We have Forensics at the primary scenes, scene one and two, namely the vic herself and the place of discovery, and scene three being the blood trail left by the dog as it made a run for it.'

There's a few sniggers at this point. 'Yes, yes, very amusing, wasn't it? There's a number of officers out combing the area attempting to establish any further scenes. I need not tell you that it is paramount we figure out any possible route the killer may have taken in a timely fashion and secure it. Rose's throat was cut and—' I swallow, '—she was branded.'

I pick up a photo from the table in front of me and pin it to the whiteboard. There's a collective intake of breath.

'The Brander?' Detective Inspector Amer Anwar leans forward in his seat. 'Celine wasn't a one-off then. Fucking hell. Why would he wait six years? It doesn't make sense.'

'Could be anything. Maybe he was in prison or indisposed in some other way. Whatever the reason and whoever is doing this, it's unlikely they'll stop at Celine and Rose. We never figured out what this meant.' I jab a finger at the image of the brand. A raven. 'It's important to our perp, it means something to them. We need to know what that something is. We have to get ahead of this bastard before there's another kid laid out on a slab.' I slam the desk so hard it hurts.

'I want any leads that arise from the door-to-doors followed up asap. Amer and I—' I nod at DI Anwar — 'will visit the family. Millie—' I indicate Detective Constable Millicent Reid, an expert in the human psyche, body language, interview techniques and my best friend in the world — 'I want you to act as family liaison officer on this one.'

Millie gives a double thumbs up. 'No problem.'

'Thanks, Mills, I appreciate it.' I cast my eyes over the rest of the team. 'Antonio, I want you to find out whether there's any active CCTV in the area — dashcam footage, video doorbells, you know the drill. Any passive data generators at all could have something, so any ANPRs and the like.' Ant nods eagerly.

'Aaliyah, I need the telephone records of everyone present. This is a murder inquiry. I need everything and I need it yesterday. We are going to be very reliant on witnesses at this stage. I want to know who was at 10 Balfour Street last night. And I want to know what this fucking raven means.' I prod the image of the brand, setting the whiteboard quivering on its stand. 'Okay?'

A murmur of assent passes around the room. I divide out the rest of the roles, grab my leather jacket and leave with Amer and Millie. I always dread this next part of the job. I might have been four when my mum was murdered in front of me, but I have felt the ramifications throughout my entire life. My Aunt Margie tried to shield me as best she could, but she'd been in pain too. Her mum was left a shadow of herself, shattered by the loss of her youngest daughter. Aunt Margie became a carer and mother overnight and while she did her best, they were roles she hadn't planned for.

Aunt Margie is something of a hippie, a throwback to the seventies. She never met anyone special, had no children of her own, but she remains the constant in my life, especially since my grandmother died. Aunt Margie understands that being a homicide detective is oxygen to me. At the same time, she insists I am breathing poison and that one day it will be the death of me.

The station is based in the newest addition to Northern Policing, a purpose-built building three stories high directly alongside the River Ribble. It had been little more than waste ground before. Now it houses a glass-fronted, modern-looking establishment with a balcony on the second floor running the length of it. Beside the station is a Costa Coffee, a Greggs and a lounge bar with riverside seating.

The Major and Serious Crimes Northwest Division offers us the chance to work serious cases from a unique standpoint. Before the introduction of the MSCNW Division, I would have been desk-surfing in the Hutton office. Now, I am pretty much heading up my own team on what might be the most important case of my career. Dillon is of course overseeing everything — she's nothing if not attentive and tenacious — but she also trusts me to lead the investigation to its conclusion and finally put the Brander behind bars. I made it clear I wanted a challenge and Dillon's stepped back and allowed me the room to prove myself. I'm determined to succeed this time.

CHAPTER THREE

I hurry down the stone steps and into the car park with Millie and Amer in tow. I nod at Amer. 'We'll take mine. See you there, Mills.'

Millie will need to take her own vehicle since she may be staying on to support the family. In this role, she will be our eyes and ears after we have given Rose's family the worst news possible. Millie is the best person for the job — she is intuitive, kind, and can read people like no one else I've ever known. She'll keep the family apprised of the investigation and relay any pertinent information to us.

We get into our respective cars and set off across Preston, crossing the river then passing the outskirts of the town centre. The car park at B&M is filling up with early morning shoppers. The large metal gates of Moor Park are open, welcoming music and media students to Park School. My pulse quickens as we near Fulwood, where the Danes live.

When we arrive, I see curtains being pulled open. The family is in the throes of waking up. A woman's face appears at the front-room window and she stares out, blinking at the winter sun. We get out of our cars and walk to the front door. Even from this distance I can see that her face has turned pale. Her eyes widen. She vanishes from the window and within seconds, the front door is thrown wide.

She's standing in the doorway wearing a red Mickey Mouse nightdress. Her pale blue dressing gown is open, and she pulls it around her, hands shaking.

'Felicity Danes?'

She swallows hard and nods. 'Is it Rose? Where is she?' Her voice shakes almost as much as her hands. She peers around us, her eyes searching the empty street. 'Where is she?'

'Can we come in, please?' I ask softly.

She backs away from the door. A young girl of about five or six is standing on the stairs behind her. 'Mummy?'

Felicity nods towards the little girl. 'Inset day,' she says.

'Please, Mrs Danes, we really do need to come in.'

'Mummy?' The child's voice has gone up an octave. 'Where's Rose?' She clutches at her mother's dressing gown, peering round her at us.

I step inside, Amer and Millie close behind. Millie takes a step towards Rose's mother and reaches out to her but she twists away.

'Oh God. No.' Suddenly, she looks as translucent as a ghost.

'Where's Rose, Mummy?' The little girl asks again, staring up at her mother with big watery eyes. It's all I can do not to scoop her up myself.

Felicity takes the child's hand and we follow her past the bottom of the stairs and through a glass door into the lounge. Millie sits on a worn leather armchair and Felicity perches on the edge of the matching three-seater. Her young daughter curls up beside her.

I sit in the remaining armchair while Amer stands in the doorway. 'May I ask where your husband is?'

'Mark's in bed, he worked the night shift,' Felicity whispers.

The little girl keeps asking what's wrong.

Felicity pulls her close but says nothing. She appears to be going into shock, even before the news has officially been broken. I wonder briefly whether it was the same for my grandmother all those years ago.

I dismiss the thought and show my ID. 'I'm Detective Chief Inspector Bethany Fellows and this is Detective Inspector Amer Anwar and Detective Constable Millicent Reid. I think it would be best if we woke Mark. And perhaps—' I smile gently at the little girl — 'you could help Amer make some tea?'

'Her name's Sally.' Felicity clasps her trembling hands together. 'Where is my Rose? Please, where is she? Where's my baby?'

I look to little Sally, who is clinging to her mother. She shouldn't be here for this.

'Please, Sal. It's okay, go on now,' Felicity says.

Amer opens the double doors leading to the kitchen. I see a table, set with a child's plastic dish and a mug on the opposite side. Had the mug been for Rose?

'I could really use your help,' Amer says. 'I make an awful brew.'

Finally, Sally stands up and makes her way reluctantly to Amer.

'I'll get Mark,' Millie says, and hurries up the stairs. We hear her footfalls, followed by a knock, and after a couple of minutes Millie and Mark come into the room, Mark rubbing his eyes. His receding dark hair is tousled. He's wearing lounge pants and a T-shirt. 'What is this? What's going on?'

I introduce myself and Millie again, explaining that Amer is making drinks with Sally and that he'll keep her distracted until we finish talking.

'Maybe you should sit down,' I suggest to Mark.

'I'm fine standing. What's going on?'

'We have some very difficult news. A young girl was found deceased in a house on Balfour Street this morning—' Felicity howls like an animal in agony. Mark's mouth sets in a grim line, his anguished eyes on me. 'I am afraid we have reason to believe it's your daughter, Rose.'

'No. No way. It's not true. It can't be,' says Mark.

'I'm very sorry.'

'Not Rose. She's in bed.' He turns to look at Felicity. 'Isn't she?'

'She's not here,' she says, sobbing. Her hands grip her hair, yanking as she writhes. 'Oh God, she's not here.' Millie goes to her and pulls her close, rocking her like a child. Felicity melts into Millie's arms, her body heaving with sobs.

Mark stabs his finger towards me. 'You've got it wrong.'

I say nothing.

He picks up the television and throws it against the wall. The screen shatters, littering the carpet with shards of glass. Mark falls back onto the couch, sobbing.

One of the double doors bursts open and Sally runs into the room, Amer hot on her heels. 'Sorry. I couldn't stop her.'

I shoot my arm out. 'Watch her feet, the TV—'

Amer reaches, but she dodges him and slings herself onto the floor beside her mother.

Mark gathers himself. '*Detectives*? Why detectives? Did someone . . . did someone hurt my baby?'

I nod. 'I'm so sorry, but yes, someone did. We want to catch the person responsible, and you can help us to do that. There are some questions we need to ask you. And when the time is right, we will need you to officially identify her.'

'So, you don't know?' Felicity says. 'This could all be wrong? It mightn't be my Rosie?'

'I'm so sorry but we're certain,' I say quickly. 'It's the procedure we have to follow. For the record. But there's no question. I'm so very sorry.'

Felicity cries louder, while Sally clings to her.

I look desperately at Amer. 'Could you please take Sally into the kitchen or to see her bedroom?'

Mark says, 'Sal, go show him your doll's house, there's a good girl.' His voice is thick with grief.

Sally goes to the glass door, stops and holds out her hand. Amer takes it and closes the door behind them.

'How can you be sure that it's her?' Felicity says.

18

I show her the printout of Rose's profile picture. 'This is Rose?'

She squeezes her eyes shut and nods her head.

Mark sniffs. 'The official identification . . . How do we . . . ? I can't let her—' He looks at Felicity, who is now staring into space. 'What do I have to do? I mean, do I have to go and . . . ?'

'There will be a post-mortem to ascertain exactly what happened,' I say. 'We don't yet know the circumstances or who was responsible, which is why we need to ask some very important questions. What we do now, the information we gather, could well make all the difference.'

'Make the difference?' Felicity croaks. 'What difference? My daughter's dead.'

'The difference between whether or not we catch the person who hurt her. Whether we put them in prison.'

Mark takes his wife's hand. 'Come on, Felicity. Sit with me. We need to do this. For Rose.'

I allow them both a moment to gather themselves before I begin. It's a cruel fact of a murder investigation that the bereaved have no time to mourn. They're thrown into the depths of grief and shock, then asked to play recall. 'Firstly, I need to ask if you can think of anyone, anyone at all, who might have wanted to hurt her.'

Mark's eyes narrow. 'You seriously expect us to have a clue? You think I'd be sitting here now if I had the slightest fuckin' inklin' of who might've done it? I'd kill them with my bare hands. I find out who hurt my baby and you'd better hope you get to them first.' His face is contorted with rage. 'I will kill them. I swear.'

'I have to warn you that taking the law into your own hands would have consequences, Mark.' I take a breath. 'I really do understand—' I begin.

'Like hell you do. You understand shit.'

'I'm sorry to have to ask these questions now, I really am. I know it might seem—'

'Just ask your questions,' Felicity whimpers.

'Thank you.'

'No, we don't know of anyone really, but . . .' She falters, her eyes dart towards Mark nervously.

'Go on,' Millie says. 'Anything, anyone. It could be important.'

Felicity squeezes Mark's hand, glances at him and back at me. 'Her friend, Jenny Lambert. Her best friend.'

Mark pulls his hand free of Felicity's. 'I warned you about that little bitch, didn't I? What did I tell you? I said she'd lead Rose into trouble.'

'Tell us about Jenny Lambert,' I say.

Mark's eyes are almost slits now, his face set. 'She started in Rose's class about six months ago. Rose has trouble making friends, she's too soft, too kind. Well, Jenny comes along and she's exciting. A bit different, dresses like a slag, rolling her skirt up to her thighs, hanging around with older boys. She has a brother who's college age, not that he goes. Not that he does anything as far as I'm aware. They hang around with him and his mates. I've been telling Rose to steer clear for weeks, months. She says Jenny's her only friend — you know what kids are like. Anyway, Jenny's been round here, stinking of weed, booze on her breath. She's been in and out of foster care and her mum's rumoured to be a fuckin' prossie. Dad's nowhere to be seen. Stepdad's a scumbag. That family, it's them. Has to be. Before they arrived on the scene our Rosie was a good girl. No sneaking out and shit like that. Now we're lucky to find her in her own bed come morning.' His eyes widen. He's trying to stop the tears. 'We won't again though, will we? Not ever.'

'We'll look at them, of course we will. Anyone else you can think of?'

Felicity shakes her head. 'No, no one. I stopped knowing my own daughter some time ago. I don't know what she's been up to. We tried, we did, honestly. We did everything we could, but she wouldn't listen. I didn't want her to hate me. Oh, God, this is my fault.'

Mark puts his arm around Felicity's shoulders. 'I'm sorry I said what I did. It's not your fault. It isn't, babe.

20

You're a good mum. Rose is . . . *was* lucky.' His bottom lip quivers and he runs from the room. The sound of retching carries from the kitchen.

Felicity struggles to get up.

'I'll go.' Millie leaves.

'Did you know Rose was out last night?' I ask Felicity.

'No, not until I went to wake her up this morning. I — I normally double-check when I wake up for the loo during the night. But last night I slept right through. When I went into her room this morning she wasn't there. I thought she'd be home. I didn't expect—'

'Has Rose got a boyfriend? Girlfriend?' I ask.

Felicity looks shocked at the suggestion. 'She isn't gay. Not that I'd have cared. She was my first, my baby girl. She is such a good big sister. Some kids have no time for their younger siblings. Not our Rose, she always makes time for Sal. Takes her to the swings and that. She saves up her pocket money, cleans houses, washes cars, you know. She's a right little entrepreneur. She had her own business cards made in town and handed them out, put a notice up in the post office. Sorted it all out by herself, and at fourteen too. How many kids do you know who'd do something like that? She makes time for people as well. Stays and has a brew and a natter with the elderly folk who hire her. A lot of them are Mum's friends from the bingo. This is gonna kill my mum, they're so close. Oh my God, my poor baby.' While she speaks, her eyes travel the photographs on the walls and shelves. One shows a younger Rose, about nine years old, holding her new baby sister. Rose's face is alight and she's gazing at Sally in awe.

Felicity falters. 'Rose is a good kid. I *need* you to know that. I *need* you to care.'

I lean forwards. 'I promise you, Felicity, I do care. We all do.'

She closes her eyes and sighs deeply. 'I've let her have more leeway recently *because* she's such a good kid, so responsible. Too responsible for her age. She's not the kind of child anyone would want to hurt. I honestly do not understand why anyone would ever want to hurt her.' Felicity's tears fall thick and fast. She has been talking about Rose in the present tense, which is completely normal. It isn't real to her yet.

'Did Rose have a boyfriend that you knew of?' I ask again.

She sniffles. 'No, she's never really . . . I don't think so. She hasn't mentioned any boys. She spends all her time with Jenny, her brother — Jenny's brother I mean — and his mates.' Felicity puts her hand to her mouth. 'Oh Christ. You don't think? I mean they're like seventeen and eighteen, they're much too old. It didn't even occur to me. I must be a flaming idiot. How could I not see this coming? How could I let this happen?'

'You're *not* an idiot and you did *not* let this happen,' I say. 'We don't know that there was anything untoward with them yet. We're just covering all bases.'

Millie and Mark come back into the room. Mark's face is streaked with tears. He sits down and grabs his wife's hand. 'Sorry.'

'Please don't apologise. Did Rose drink alcohol or take drugs? These are routine questions,' I clarify quickly.

Felicity sounds distant. 'I hope not. We had the talk after smelling weed on her and Jenny. Rose insisted she doesn't do drugs. She admitted to drinking a little, but not much, according to her. We thought it best to trust her. She's coming up sixteen, and she's always been so good. She didn't have much of a life before Jenny came on the scene. It was all work and responsibility. I felt bad about it. I was—' she glances at Mark — 'pleased, okay. I wanted her to live a bit. To just be a kid for once.'

Mark blows out an exasperated breath.

'Can you please walk us through what happened yesterday? What time did you wake up?' I ask.

Felicity seems to search her memory. I know Millie will be paying close attention. She'll know if Felicity starts to fabricate. She'll be able to detect the slightest shift in her body language. Millie is the best person to be here with the family. She'll be able to comfort them while figuring them out. There was no favouritism in my decision to appoint her FLO, despite the rumours I know will be circulating.

Felicity looks directly at me. 'Sally woke me up at about seven. I took her downstairs and sorted some breakfast.'

'What did you eat?'

'Does it matter?' Felicity's lip trembles.

'It's vital we get a complete picture of everything,' Millie answers. 'It helps us to be clear.'

Witnesses tend to recall better and more accurately if they follow the details of their day. Like looking for a lost item, the best bet is usually to retrace your steps. Having Felicity and Mark relate their time with Rose in sequence also helps us to detect any deviations, omissions, blatant lies. Then if we note any irregularities, we have the option of questioning them out of order, which will usually throw up any inconsistencies for us to investigate.

'Weetabix.'

'Hot or cold milk?' I ask quickly.

Mark frowns, annoyed. 'Seriously?'

'Yes,' I say.

'Warm,' Felicity answers. 'I had a tea with two sweeteners and semi-skimmed milk — if that really matters. Then at about seven thirty, I went to wake Rose.'

'Where was Mark?' I ask.

He answers for her. 'I did a night shift, got in just after 6 a.m., went straight to bed. I was asleep.'

I look at Felicity. 'Did Sally go upstairs with you to wake Rose?'

'No, she put the telly on. She was watching some cartoon or other in the lounge. I woke Rose. She was . . .' Her tears well up. 'Her arm was up above her head, she was lying on her stomach, facing away from me. Her other arm was straight by her side, one leg hanging over the edge. She always sleeps like that, never fully covered. She kicks the quilt off in the night. She sleeps at a million miles an hour, that's what I always say to her.' Tears fall down her cheeks. 'She took a while to wake. She turned over and I thought for a moment . . .'

'What?' I prod.

'It looked like she'd been crying in her sleep. I asked if anything was wrong, and she nearly bit my head off. Told me not to be stupid. I told her she was a cheeky mare and to get up. It isn't like her to be like that, she's started with a bit of an attitude recently. I just thought it was a phase, that she'd grow out of it. She's always been such a breeze, I kind of thought she'd earned a bit of a teenage moment or two.'

'What happened next?'

'I went back down to Sal. I was mad at Rose. I should have asked more questions. I should have made her tell me what was wrong.'

Millie moves forward in her seat. 'You couldn't have known.'

'I should have. I'm her mum.'

A clatter resounds from upstairs. I'd almost forgotten Amer was up there with Sally. All eyes rise towards the ceiling.

'Sorry,' Amer calls. 'Some books fell off the shelf. I got it.'

'How are we gonna tell her? She won't understand. *I* don't understand.' Felicity stares at the ceiling.

'I can help you talk to her if you want,' Millie offers.

Felicity shrugs. 'No matter who tells her or how, she's gonna be in pieces. She idolises her sister.' She shakes her head. 'This is not survivable. Our family is never gonna be what it was. Never. Not without Rose.'

I need to keep them on track. 'How long did it take for Rose to come downstairs?'

Felicity thinks. 'About half an hour. She was washed and dressed when she came down. She walked up behind me and put her arms around my waist. She hugged me, like she used to. For just a moment it was like before, like we'd always been.'

'Where were you?' I ask.

'Washing up. I was at the sink. I didn't ask what was up again because we had a lovely moment. I didn't want to ruin it.'

24

'That's understandable,' Millie interjects.

'What happened next?' I ask.

'I put some toast in for her.' She smiles, weakly. 'Marmite. Her favourite. Rose made more tea. Sally watched TV for a bit longer, then I told her to get ready for school. I gave Rose some lunch money. She wanted to have a hot dinner so she could sit with Jenny. Jenny gets free meals. Rose is normally on packed lunches, and she never complains. I gave her the last fiver out of my purse and told her not to spend it on junk. I made sure she didn't see in my purse, though she wouldn't have taken it if she had. I handed Sally her uniform and had to be on her to get her teeth brushed. She's hard work in the mornings. Rose was never like that at her age, she was an easy kid. I was putting Sal's shoes on when Rose popped her head round and said goodbye. She was smiling. Then she was gone. I heard the front door a minute later.'

'How did she get to school?'

'She caught the school bus at the top of the street. Well, that's what she normally does. I'm assuming she did then too. She has a bus pass.'

'Does she usually catch it with anyone?'

'No. Jenny walks from her house. It's near the school. They meet in the playground.'

'Does she usually sit with anyone that you know of?'

'Not that she's ever mentioned. She's always been a bit of a loner apart from Jenny. Jenny was the first friend she ever really talked about enthusiastically. With the other kids it would be the odd passing remark, whereas with Jenny, it's "Jenny this" and "Jenny that". She looks up to her, I think. She was bouncing around most of the time, itching to go off to school, to hang out with Jenny at weekends. It was good to see her being a *normal* teenager. Being happy.'

'Did you hear from her at all during the day? Phone call, text?'

'No. She has a phone, but she has to leave it in her locker. She doesn't even turn it on until she's on her way home.'

'She doesn't check in at lunch or breaks?' I ask.

25

'No, never. Well, she never contacts *me*. Maybe she does use her phone during school hours, I don't know.'

'What time did she come home?'

'She came straight from school. Jenny was with her. They came in and went upstairs. They were listening to music. I heard Sal go in and get kicked out pretty sharpish by Jenny.' Her face darkens slightly. 'She doesn't really have time for Sal, not like Rose.'

'Did Jenny leave?'

'Yes, Jenny went home when I called Rose down for tea.'

'What time?' I ask.

'Erm . . . it was just after five thirty. I made spag bol.'

'What happened afterwards? Did Rose get any texts? Phone calls?'

'Her phone didn't stop buzzing with notifications and whatnot. I don't know if they were texts, social media, or what. Before Jenny she didn't even bother with top-ups, she never used it. She's been kind of excitable all the time lately, a kid being a kid, not weighed down with responsibilities she shouldn't have. It's refreshing to see her that way, even if she's a little moody with us.'

'Did she seem agitated or upset at all?'

'No. I mean, I don't think so.'

Rose's mobile phone is with Forensics, I'll soon know what's on it. A kid's entire life is lived on their phone these days. 'What happened after dinner?'

'The usual. The girls went into the lounge to argue over the remote while I cleaned up. It was all so *regular*. They bickered a bit, like they do. It was irritating but it also sounded kind of nice to me, listening to them being sisters. Then I went through, and we watched *Hollyoaks*.'

'So that would make it what? About 7 p.m.?'

'Yeah, I suppose. I had a brew and did some ironing in the kitchen before I went in. I had a headache, so I took some paracetamol. My head was pounding by then and I couldn't be doing with their squabbling, so ironing seemed

26

like an escape. I'd give anything, *anything* to hear them have a row right now.'

'When Rose came down for tea, was she still in her uniform?'

'No, she was in her pyjamas and dressing gown.'

'Was that the norm?'

'Sometimes.'

'Where were you?' I look at Mark.

'Work. I started at 6 p.m. I set off early, stopped by me mum's with some bits, shopping and that. Had a brew with her then went to work. I left here at about three-ish, went to the shops and then Mum's, left Mum's at five thirty-ish. That's it. My sad, boring life.'

'If you have any receipts, it will help us.' His face darkens. 'It's all procedure. We have to establish timelines for everyone. It's standard for any investigation.'

'I'll look,' he says grudgingly.

'Thank you.' I look back at Felicity. 'Was Rose still getting messages or notifications?'

'They never stopped. I made her mute it.'

'How did she seem?'

'The same as always. Nothing stood out, at least I don't think so. I suppose I wasn't paying that much attention.' Felicity's tears start again.

'What happened during the rest of the evening?'

Felicity stops crying. 'I've just remembered. She went to bed early — it was only nine o'clock. Sal went up and Rose said she'd go too. I didn't think much of it, I was distracted. My mate, Tamara, had texted to say she needed a chat. I thought it was good timing. I could call Tammy and then go up myself. I still had a headache.'

'Is that what happened?'

'Yes.'

'What did Tammy want?'

'She'd had an argument with her fella. We talked on the phone for about half an hour then I went to bed. I practically

27

passed out straight away. Next thing I knew it was morning and Rose was gone. Then you guys came and now . . .'

'What time did you get home, Mark?'

'Around 6 a.m. I told you, always the same time. I went straight to bed. I didn't know Rose wasn't home.'

'So you didn't check on the kids when you got home?' I ask.

'Are you saying you think it's my fault? That if I'd checked it would have made a difference? Are you trying to blame me? Catch me out?'

'No, no. Not at all. It's just that Felicity had taken to checking because of Rose sometimes sneaking out, and I wondered whether you were doing the same.'

His eyes search the room. 'It is, isn't it? It's my fault. I should have checked. I should have been a better dad. I should have protected my kids.'

Millie sits forward. 'It isn't your fault, Mark. You couldn't have foreseen this. Neither of you could. What's happened is down to the person who hurt Rose, and no one else. Okay? Now, I can stay here with you or give you some time. I am here to support and guide you through this. Here's my card. Contact me whenever you want.'

'We need time,' Mark says. He takes the card and places it beside him on the couch. 'We need to be alone.'

'I understand. But I'm here, day or night.'

I lean forward. 'Before we leave, would it be okay for us to have a look at Rose's room? It could help.'

Mark nods, his jaw clenched. Millie and I head up the stairs.

'It's the second room on the left,' Mark calls after us, his voice trembling. 'It, erm, it has her name on it.' His voice cracks.

Millie and I take gloves from our pockets and snap them on. The door has *Rose* across the front, in pink-and-yellow letters. I push it open and look at the thick beige carpet, the pink curtains, the single wooden-framed bed dressed in pink-and-yellow bed sheets. There's a bedside unit with a pink ET-style lamp and an exercise book lying alongside it. I pick it up and begin flicking through the pages. Some of them have been torn out. Maybe she was trying to hide something.

Millie opens the wardrobe and pushes the clothes from one end to the other, looking for anything hidden inside. There's nothing obvious. We'll have the room thoroughly searched soon enough. I kneel and peer beneath the bed and pull out a shoebox. There's nothing of obvious significance inside, just a few odds and ends. By the time we've finished, the only thing we've found of interest is the exercise book, which I place in an evidence bag.

Out on the landing, I call to Amer.

'Yeah?'

'Time to go. Everything okay?'

'Yeah, won't be a tick. Just let me put these books back.'

Downstairs, I look in on Mark and Felicity, who are huddled together on the couch. 'Is it okay with you if I take this?' I hold out the exercise book in its evidence bag.

Felicity's eyes narrow. 'What is it? Does it mean something? Did she write something in there?'

I shake my head. 'Sorry. There are some pages missing. I think it's worth having our guys see if they can make out what was on them.'

Mark sighs. 'How're they gonna do that?'

I shrug. 'It's worth trying.'

'Take whatever you need,' Felicity whispers.

'A couple of forensic officers are going to come by, have a proper look through her room. We really need you not to go in there until they've been, okay?' Asking if they mind is a courtesy. No matter what they say, Rose's room will need to be searched. No crime has taken place there, but that doesn't mean there won't be evidence of what was to come.

Sally runs downstairs and bursts into the lounge. Felicity and Mark pull her towards them.

'Can you please leave now?' Felicity says over Sally's head, while hiccupping on a sob. Their faces are drawn and wet with tears. Sally keeps looking up at them, worried, confused. 'We need to be alone as a family.'

CHAPTER FOUR

We're all subdued as we set off back to the station, not least because both Millie and I know we aren't any further along. We need to speak to Jenny Lambert. If Rose had any secrets that she was keeping from her parents, the likelihood is that her best friend will know.

We meet back up in the Major Incident Room. Some of the team are at base, the rest still out information gathering. I make a quick call to Hannah Edwards and am informed that there is now a scene four, which is likely the point of exit. They've found a few signs of disturbance in the tiny stone backyard and the gate was open, swinging against the wall in the wind. They've secured it and are searching for fibres and whatever else they can find. The route into the house will be scene five.

The whole house will be kept in our possession for the time being. Barry Knultz, the tenant, is waiting to be spoken to. He'd been brought straight to the station to have his clothes taken by Forensics and his elderly mother summoned with a change of outfit. She'd forgotten his shoes so had to be driven home again. By the time she returned, he was a nervous wreck, sitting with his socked feet tapping the floor incessantly. His mum had taken him home to calm him down and now he's back, an appropriate adult has arrived and he's ready to talk.

In Interview Room Three, Amer and I find Barry Knultz dressed in a grey sweatshirt, matching trousers and white trainers that look starched. His grey hair is scraped to one side. His pupils dance about the room and a finger tugs at the corner of his mouth. The on-call appropriate adult, Sharon Holten, is an older woman with permed white hair and a kindly face. She looks the maternal type, and I wonder absently whether she got into this gig so she can look after someone now her own kids have no doubt long flown the nest.

Barry has his back to the wall, Sharon sitting beside him. There's a small table in the middle.

'Thanks for coming back, Barry,' I begin, deciding to go with his first name. 'I know this must be very upsetting for you. We do have to tell you that this interview will be filmed and recorded.' I indicate the recorder on the table and press record. 'Okay, so this interview is being recorded by closed-circuit television and audio tape. The date is Friday the nineteenth of February 2021, and the time is 10.55 a.m. Present are myself, Detective Chief Inspector Bethany Fellows.' I look to Amer.

'Detective Inspector Amer Anwar.'

'Mr Barry Knultz,' I say, and look to Sharon Holten.

'And appropriate adult, Sharon Ann Holten,' she says.

'Am I being arrested? I didn't do nothing.' Barry's shaking almost sends his knees into orbit. Sharon places a gentle hand on his arm.

'No, you aren't under arrest, Barry,' I explain. 'We just need to find out what happened. You found Rose Danes.'

'She was hurt.'

'I know.'

'Her neck was all funny. A big cut.' He slides a finger across his throat. 'And bent weird.' He angles his neck to demonstrate. 'She wouldn't talk to me. I think she was dead. Is she?'

'Is she what?'

'Dead. Is she dead?'

'I'm afraid so, Barry. It would appear someone hurt her.'

'I didn't do it. It wasn't me. I want me mum. Where's me dog?'

'Nemo is fine, he'll be back with you very soon. He's getting lots of cuddles and treats. Try not to worry about him. And your mum is in the waiting room. No one's saying you did anything wrong, Barry. We want to find out who hurt Rose, and you can help us do that. Will you help us?'

'I don't know who did it. I went to me mum's. They were buggin' me. Bein' nasty an' that. They drank all me cider, made a mess. I told 'em I wanted to go to sleep but they wouldn't leave. Nemo was in his bed asleep, so I left him behind.'

'Who was at your house last night, Barry?'

'The lads.' His shaking subsides a little.

'Who are the lads?'

He counts them off on his fingers. 'Peter Lambert, Daniel Mint, Simon . . . I can't remember his surname, and Tony Wall.' He smiles. 'They're me mates.'

'And what time did they come round?' I ask.

'About seven, I think. The girls came later.'

'The girls?'

'Yeah, Peter's sister and her friend. The dead one.'

'Did they arrange to come or just show up?'

'They're me mates, they come whenever they want. Mum don't like 'em.'

'Why not?'

'She reckons they aren't proper friends. But they are. They like me. They come round to see me, you know, hang out.'

'Did the lads all arrive together?' I ask.

'Yeah, apart from Simon. He came after.'

'After what?'

'After the girls. He was boring, didn't do anything, just stood around. The dead one got all sleepy, but in a weird way.'

'What do you mean?'

'She was sleeping, but kinda not because her eyes were open, but they were up high in her head, like this.' He rolls his eyes upwards. 'She looked weird.'

Barry pushes his bottom lip out and makes a sort of kissing noise, self-soothing perhaps.

'Where was Peter's sister, Jenny, at that time?'

'I dunno.' He starts flicking one fingernail against the other. He'll have had his nails scraped and samples taken. We'll also have to determine whether there has been any transference of fibres from him to the scene, or vice versa. As he found Rose, we need to officially rule him out as a suspect.

'Who was there when it was happening? What time was it?'

He starts rocking back and forth. Sharon attempts to steady him by rubbing his forearm.

'Too many questions.' His eyes angle up towards a corner of the ceiling. I'm beginning to lose him. I need to slow down, backtrack to something less confronting. I glance at the clock.

'Let's talk about something else for a bit.' I say. 'When you stay at your mum's, where do you sleep?'

He looks back at me. I've thrown him a raft and he gratefully climbs in. 'My bedroom. Mum says I always have a place. She makes it smell like lavender to help me sleep. I have Batman covers and feathers in me pillow. It's warm and nice.'

'Was your mum awake when you got there?'

'She was in bed. I have me key. I used it nice and quiet so I wouldn't wake her up. Then I went to bed. I was tired.'

'What time did you wake up?'

'When the sun came in.'

'What time was that?'

He starts rocking again. 'I don't know.' His voice rises, he's getting agitated. If I don't tread carefully, we'll be forced to take a break and right now the last thing I need is more wasted time.

'Okay. So, you woke up. Was your mum awake?'

'She was in the kitchen boiling eggs. She did us eggs with soldiers and she made me a hot chocolate. A healthy one. What are they called? High . . . lights, yeah that's it, Highlights. Cadbury's.'

I'll find out from his mum what time she made breakfast. There's always more than one way to narrow things down. 'So, you had breakfast and then what happened?'

'Mum got angry about the lads coming round again. It upset me so I went home, and that's when I found her — dead.'

'Do you remember what time it was?'

'After breakfast.'

I decide not to push him on times. 'What did you find?'

'A dead girl.'

'Tell me how you got inside.'

He stares at me as though I'm stupid. 'With me key. I live there.'

'Okay, and then what?' I'm walking him through it, trying to tap into anything he may have noticed. I've also established that the front door had been locked. I know from Forensics that it's the self-locking type — you let it close, and it locks. It doesn't mean much but it does indicate that either the killer closed it or he went out the back way.

'There was a big mess. Bottles and cans on the floor. I was mad 'cause it would take me ages to clean it up. Mum would get all shouty if I told her, so I knew I'd have to do it meself. The lads were gone. I went into the lounge and saw her. At first I thought she were asleep. Nemo was licking her, giving her lots of sloppy kisses. I told him to get away — he shouldn't lick faces and things, you know—' he smirks — ''cause he licks his backside. I told her to wake up but she wouldn't. She didn't say anything back. So I tapped her, and her head fell forward more. I pushed it back again, her head, so she would look at me. There was a hole in her neck.' He pulls a face. 'She felt really cold, like ice. I didn't like it. I didn't know what to do, so I called 999 like you should when something scary or bad happens.'

'You did the right thing.'

Barry glows with the compliment and his rocking ceases completely. 'I'm sorry she's dead.'

I watch his eyes fall and know he's telling the truth. Barry Knultz is not the man we're looking for, nor had I ever believed he was. It does mean that the killer's out there, ready to strike again. As far as I can determine he's already attacked and branded two victims. Right now, he'll be watching us chasing our tails. He'll feel invincible. The race is on.

CHAPTER FIVE

Once we leave the interview room, I find Millie, pull her aside and give her a quick rundown of what Barry had to say. 'Do me a favour, corroborate Knultz's timeline with his mum. She's sitting in reception. Once that's been done, he can go.' Amer and I then go straight into Interview Room Four, where Jenny Lambert is waiting. The other members of the group are being questioned simultaneously by fellow officers.

The interview rooms are unvaried, bland. All have white walls and grey office-style furniture. Jenny is sitting beside her mum. Nancy Lambert does not look happy to be here. At fifteen, Jenny needs to have someone with her to ensure her needs are met and that the interview is conducted sensitively. I would have preferred an appropriate adult, but Nancy had been insistent.

When I walk in, Jenny stares at me defiantly, looking me up and down with huge chestnut eyes. She has dyed shoulder-length red hair, fake eyelashes and glossy lips. She sits with one ankle crossed over the other, her hands hanging over the arms of the chair. Nancy has a ginger bob with a severe fringe that hangs down over her eyes. She is wearing a denim miniskirt and cropped brown jumper, revealing a sagging, stretch-marked stomach. She's painfully thin, while her lips are plumped with too much filler.

'Hi, Jenny. My name is Detective Chief Inspector Bethany Fellows.' I sit in the chair opposite, close enough to be in her space. Amer sits beside me.

Nancy snarls. 'Kept us waiting long enough. What's happening with my son? You lot best not try and pin owt on 'im, that's all I can say. I don't understand why you needed to bring in both my kids. Anyone'd think this were a flamin' witch hunt. And what the fuck for? Fuckin' five-O, you're always pickin' on people like us.' She's using American slang to refer to us, like so many people around Lancashire do. I can tell off the bat that this interview is unlikely to be smooth sailing.

'I apologise for the delay. I can assure you no one is looking to pin anything on anyone.'

Jenny shifts her legs out of the way. 'What's this about? I ain't done nothing.'

We begin the recording, informing Jenny of what we are doing. She seems unfazed. I'm gathering by her demeanour that she hasn't heard what's happened to Rose. 'I am afraid I have some very difficult news.'

Jenny chews the edge of a red-painted fingernail. 'Oh yeah?'

'I'm sorry to have to tell you that Rose Danes was found dead this morning at 10 Balfour Street.'

Jenny spits hard, a shard of nail flying from her mouth. She sits forward. All her cockiness evaporates. 'What? No, you're lying. That's not true.'

'I'm sorry.'

'But she . . . she was fine.'

Nancy shoots forward in her chair. 'Jesus, dead?' Her eyes are wide. 'Wait, ya not tryin' ta say my two 'ad owt to do wi' it, are ya?

I look at Nancy. 'If we could just continue with the interview, it will be over far more quickly.'

She blows out a frustrated breath.

I nod, then turn to Jenny. 'I need you to talk me through yesterday, right up until now, this moment. I want to know everything you did from the minute you woke up.'

37

'What happened to her?' Jenny narrows her eyes. She uncrosses her ankles, planting her feet flat on the ground. I'm receiving her undivided attention.

'From when you woke up,' I repeat.

'First tell me what happened to me mate.'

'I understand this is very upsetting for you and that it's a shock, but I really need your help on this. I need you to answer my questions. Talk me through yesterday. Everything, even things that might seem completely irrelevant, anything could mean something. Please, Jenny.' I lean forward. 'Can we get you anything?' I hope she'll say no, we'll have to pause the recording if one of us leaves the room.

Jenny shakes her head. 'No, this is fine.' She picks up a paper cup of water and takes a gulp. 'My mouth, it's just, it's suddenly gone really dry.'

'That's normal. You've had a shock. You're upset. Now, when you're ready, start from when you woke up yesterday. What time was it?'

Nancy's face softens. She looks at her daughter. 'Come on, love, tell 'em.'

Jenny places the cup down but keeps one hand around it. She clears her throat. 'It was like eight-ish, I suppose. I woke up 'cause I heard me brother in the bathroom. He was being really loud, banging about like. I dunno what was up with him, but he was in a right mood.'

Silence. I resist the temptation to break it. Eventually it will become heavy, uncomfortable, and Jenny will feel compelled to replace it with words. Millie taught me that. She says that people naturally hate silences. She also says that if you do something kind, they feel obligated to repay you, even if it goes against their own interests. Human nature is a wonderful thing. During questioning it can be the thing that puts cuffs on a guilty person or teases out the shred of information a witness will give up because they can't stop themselves.

Sure enough, Jenny begins again. 'I went down and had some cornflakes. There was no milk, so I ate 'em dry. Pete had probably guzzled it, always fuckin' does.' It's flowing naturally now. I take mental notes of every word. 'I walked to school like always and met up with Rose — Fuckin' hell, she really is? She's really dead?'

I nod.

'She was upset about something. I asked her what but she didn't want to talk about it. She could be right funny like that. You know, quiet like. I mean, I'll tell her anything but she just clams up and won't say a word when summat's buggin' her. So, I don't know what had upset her, but she was. Upset, I mean. She looked like she might've been crying. I told her we were gonna go to Baz's that night and to sneak out and come with us. She was afraid her dad would kick off if he found out, but in the end she said she'd come. I think she needed to get out, be away from home like. Whatever was upsetting her, I think it was at home. But if she hadn't come she wouldn't be dead, would she?' Jenny sits forward, her head in her hands. After a moment she looks up at me. 'Is it because of me? Is it my fault?'

Nancy places a hand on Jenny's shoulder. Jenny shrugs her off with an annoyed glare. 'I don't need babying, Mum. Rose is the one who's been hurt, not me.'

Nancy clenches her jaw momentarily then seems to calm herself and settles into her seat. 'Fine, if that's what ya want.'

Jenny wipes a stray tear. 'We went to class like normal. We're not in the same ones for everything but we meet up at breaks and dinner. We had our dinner together. Her mum had given her five quid to spend on food so she could eat with me. She only got chips and gravy, so she'd have some left over for you know, whatever. We drank water from the fountains, filled our bottles like. We were saving so we could get some booze. We needn't have bothered, Baz had loads in. But Pete won't let us go with 'em unless we contribute, so we gave him and the others what we had. He met us outside school before we went to Rose's. I went to hers and when her mum called her for tea, I went home. I told her I'd meet her on the corner, she just had to text and let me know she was out okay. She was gonna say she had a headache or summat and go to bed early.

39

She said she'd change into her PJs but put her other stuff on underneath, so she was ready to sneak out as soon as she got the chance. Her sister Sal came in when we were planning it. I made her leave quick, and I don't think she heard anything. That were it. Rose did what she said. We were messaging a bit while they watched some shit soap and stuff and then I got the text to say she was out, and that her mum had gone to bed. I met her and we walked to Baz's together.'

Jenny picks up the cup and takes another swig. 'The others were all there, apart from Simon. He came later, not long after we got there. So, first there was Pete, Dan, Tony, me, Rose and Baz. Then after a bit Simon came.' Her nose crinkles in distaste. 'I don't mind Baz, he's all right, but Pete and the others were takin' the piss, annoying him. It's tight. Nasty like. They were gettin' him to sing and stuff, pretending they thought he was good when they know he sounds like a bad *X Factor* reject. Dan poured a full can of cider on Baz's living room carpet, he was laughing his ass off. He did it to get Baz to kick off, he knew it would make him mad. He thinks it's funny to get him all worked up and acting nuts. It's nasty as fuck, but they all do it. The dog, Nemo, was licking it so Baz put him in his bedroom, he has one of those plastic dog beds in there. Baz put up with Dan being a dickhead for a bit, then he tried to lay into him, tried givin' him a slap but Dan dodged it and Baz fell over. He started crying and said he was going to his mum's, and he fucked off.'

Barry Knultz had left that bit out, probably too embarrassed. Kids could be wicked. I also note that Jenny hasn't yet mentioned Rose being out of it. I don't doubt that Barry had been telling the truth and at this point in Jenny's story, Barry's left, which means Jenny has chosen to omit the part where Rose was practically unconscious. As hurt as Jenny clearly is by what's happened to Rose, she's also willing to hide things from me, from the investigation. She can't be completely trusted. That much is clear.

'Jenny, I need you to really think about everything that happened yesterday right through to now. I don't want you to miss anything out, okay? Even something that doesn't seem important could be. It's vital you tell me everything, Jenny, you understand?'

Jenny's fringe is sticking to her fast-dampening forehead. Her eyes dart about the room while her feet rock against the floor. She's exhibiting the fight or flight response, something Millie goes on about. It can crop up when someone is being dishonest — unconsciously, their body gives them away. Millie had driven the point home after a few beers on more than one occasion. She's obsessed with catching people out in their deceit. It empowers her, I suppose. Jenny begins chewing the corner of her thumbnail, spitting bits of skin onto the floor.

'You don't need to guilt-trip me. As far as I'm aware Rose was my mate, not yours. I think I might give a bit more of a shit about what's happened to her than you, don't ya think?' While she speaks, she is tapping her left foot.

I lean forward, close, almost as though I'm confiding a secret. 'I know Rose was your friend.' I put my hand on Jenny's knee and the tapping ceases. 'I know you cared about her. That's why you want to help, isn't it?'

A fat tear slips from Jenny's eye, and she wipes it away with the back of her hand. She suddenly looks her age, a child rather than a cocky teenager playing at being an adult. She's a fifteen-year-old kid whose best friend has just been murdered.

'That's it. I got bored and went home. Rose was still there as far as I know.' The tears come freely now. 'I'm telling you the truth, she's my best mate, why would I lie?'

'What time did you leave, Jenny? Where was everyone else? How did Rose seem?'

She looks longingly towards the closed door. Her shoulders are shaking, her lips trembling. Even before she opens her mouth, I know she's going to lie. 'I went at about one in the morning, I went out the back way. I was just . . . I was bored. Rose was fine. She was having fun.'

'Did you close the gate behind you?'

She shakes her head. 'I don't know. I don't remember.'

'Where was Rose?'

41

'Like I told you, she was fine. She was having a great time.'

'Where were Peter, Daniel, Tony and Simon?'

'I don't know, I ain't their keeper, am I?'

'Do you know Simon's surname?'

'What? No, why would I? I think he's Dan's mate, so maybe ask him.'

'Was Rose drinking or taking drugs that you know of?'

Jenny wipes her forehead. 'She drank a couple of cans, that's it. I don't know about drugs. Maybe.' She looks at her mum. 'I'm tired. I want to go home. I'm done.' She turns back to me. 'I've told you everything. There isn't anything else. I went home, Rose stayed there. That's it.' Her lip quivers. 'What happened to her?'

'Someone hurt her.'

'How? What do you mean?'

'I can't go into the details with you. But this is a murder inquiry, Jenny. It's as serious as it gets. You need to be honest about everything.'

She nods vigorously. 'I haven't lied. It's the truth. I don't know what happened to her. What did they do? Was it drugs or summat?'

'What makes you ask that?'

Her eyes widen. 'You asked if she'd taken any.'

'No, we don't believe it was drugs.'

Jenny's shoulders slump, and she lets out a long breath. 'Can I go now?'

I'm certain she's lying about something. She's also blown a hole in Hannah's exit theory. If she did leave via the back of the house, then it could well have been her who left the gate open. This interview is closing avenues rather than opening them.

'Just a few more questions.' I hope Nancy Lambert doesn't start demanding rest breaks or worse, legal representation. They'd have the interview shut down instantly. 'How well does Daniel Mint know Simon? Where does he know him from?'

'I think he's like more of a hanger-on than a mate. They all just go where the booze is and at Baz's it's mostly free.

42

One time he just turned up with Dan and he's been back a few times. That's it really. I dunno anything else about him.'

'Was he inappropriate with you or Rose? Were any of the boys?'

'What do you mean?'

'I mean, did Simon or anyone else touch you or Rose in a sexual manner?'

'Better fuckin' not 'ave,' Nancy says.

'No. Nothing like that,' Jenny says quickly. 'For one, Pete is my brother, so, eew, and the others are like his best mates. They wouldn't dare. Not with Rose either. They call us jailbait.'

'How old would you say Simon is?'

'At least a few years older than Pete and the others. Maybe late twenties or thirties. I dunno, I'm rubbish at ages.'

'Can you describe Simon to me?'

Jenny smirks. 'He's fit. He has a six-pack. Brown skin like yours. You know, like mixed. Not Asian or Black, but like you. He's tall too, like over six feet, easy. He has a shaved head, I guess. I don't know his eye colour. He's just, like, ya know, fit.'

'Shaved head, you guess? What does that mean?'

'He's a skinhead. Bald.'

Which means there are unlikely to be any head hairs for DNA. Great. 'Do you know if he works? Where he works? Where he lives?'

Jenny's brow furrows. 'Jeez, I dunno. We don't talk about shit like that. Ah, wait. He said he does deliveries.'

'What kind of deliveries?'

She shrugs. 'How should I know? Ask Dan or Pete. Ask someone else.' She chews her lip. 'Are you gonna tell me now?'

'Tell you what?'

'What happened to Rose. Me best mate.'

This kid is a contradiction. She brings out in me a range of emotions that I can't begin to decipher. I want to mother her and slap her at the same time. However, there is still something she isn't saying, and I wish I had the power to keep her here until it spills out. Instead, I have no choice but to let her go.

CHAPTER SIX

It's getting late by the time Amer and I set off to attend the post-mortem. I leave Millie with a checklist of things to get done and messages to relay to Dillon. PMs can take hours, so we are likely to be there well into the night. The MIR will wind down and the team will clock off before we're done. We take separate cars so we can go straight home from the mortuary.

I arrive first, followed shortly by Amer, who has a coffee stain on his shirt and a harassed look on his face.

'Come on,' I say, 'let's get this over with. Everyone's here.'

'Everyone' means the forensic pathologist, forty-year-old Dr Damien Sanders, his usually slightly overenthusiastic assistant, Tara Monks, the crime scene manager, Hannah Edwards, Cath McGraw, an exhibits officer to take charge of any evidence, and the stiff-upper-lipped coroner's officer, James Mascoll-Law. They're an eclectic-looking bunch thrown together by the worst of circumstances. We've been in these very rooms many times. Me and Amer watching from the viewing room, while the others do what is needed in the PM room. Today is different. Today it's a child, a teenager. There is little chat.

Rose Danes lies naked on the silver table, her hands still bagged. Contrary to what the media would have people believe, it isn't usual to find a fifteen-year-old murder victim in a city like Preston. If it does happen, it's almost always a stabbing or a fight that got out of hand. This is a whole other ball game, one we reluctantly hold tickets to.

Everyone in the PM room is wearing the appropriate gear to prevent transferring material to or from Rose. They stand towards the back of the room observing, while Dr Damien Sanders and Tara Monks move around the body in their practised way. Having taken note of Rose's measurements, Damien Sanders begins the rape test. While he carries out the vaginal and rectal exam, I avert my eyes, offering Rose a modicum of dignity. All but James Mascoll-Law do the same.

The speaker in the viewing room crackles. 'Doesn't look like any sexual assault or interference occurred. She has no vaginal tearing or trauma, nothing noted rectally either.' He shakes his head. 'Small mercies.'

'Any semen present?' I ask. In Celine Wilson's case, the poor kid had been brutally raped without a condom. The DNA from the semen is kept on file, though we've never had a match. It would have provided us with a solid, indisputable link between Celine's attack and Rose's murder.

'No. Good for her. Bad for DNA possibilities.'

'Does she have any other wounds?'

He rolls his eyes. 'Christ, Beth, give me time, will you?' He turns back to Rose. He won't be pushed to give results before he has them officially. Silenced, I stand, watching him start the Y-incision. I should be seasoned enough by now, but the fluttering in my stomach reminds me I'm not. As Deputy SIO, I need to set an example. I'm not going to cave and leg it. Not this time.

'You doing okay in there, Beth?' Bloody Tara. Jesus.

I press the button on the intercom. 'Yes, I'm fine.' By now Rose's organs are being removed and weighed.

The post-mortem goes ahead without issue. I just about manage to hold my own. Some DSIO. I feel like a complete fool. How can I hope to give the right impression of being a strong, capable woman at the helm if I can't cope during a PM? To their credit, none of my colleagues poke fun or make light of my pallor. If anything, Tara avoids eye contact — maybe she's feeling guilty for having drawn attention to me.

The exhibits officer, Cath McGraw, has taken charge of all the evidence that's been recovered and noted. She'll take it to the appropriate place for further examination, logging and storing. Hannah Edwards says goodbye and heads back to scene one. She won't enter it, not after having been here, but she will follow up with her colleagues. It's her role to coordinate the forensic team, ensuring that no one visits more than one scene. I can't go and see the suspected point of exit for the same reason. If and when any case ends up in court, there's no way we'll want the defence claiming cross-contamination. And as Locard said, 'Every contact leaves a trace'. Our very breath is a contaminant.

Rose's body will be prepared before the family make the official identification. Millie will escort them into the mortuary, where the team will present Rose in the most considerate way possible. The idea is to minimise the trauma, but the truth is no one leaves the same as they arrive, especially not a parent.

CHAPTER SEVEN

It's mid-morning when I receive a text from Millie, a sad face emoji and the words *All done.* She's been at the mortuary with the parents, supporting them during the official identification process. Amer and I have been going over the interviews from yesterday.

We are sitting at a table in the MIR, paperwork in front of Amer, my laptop open in front of me. I close my laptop and turn to Amer. 'Jenny's hiding something. She's lying, I'm sure.' I shake my head. 'She cares, that's obvious, but I don't know . . . I get the feeling she's not being completely honest with us. What do you think?'

'I think you're right. There's something off, I have no idea what, but there's something.'

'Let's hope her conscience gets the better of her.' I clap my hands. 'Right, we can't lose momentum. I need you to gather what you can from our feet on the ground. Get everything collated. I want the recording of the crime scene from Hannah, I want the photos on the board. I want the MIR in full operation and everyone chomping at the bit to get going by the time I come back.'

Amer runs a hand through his slick dark mop. 'Yeah, sure. Where are you gonna be?'

I turn towards the closed MIR then stand. 'I'm gonna grab Mills and go to our first vic's family. I need her with me on this. You understand?'

Amer stands fiddling with his belt, an awkward movement that I know means he does understand but isn't best pleased at being side-lined.

'Yeah, I suppose it makes sense.'

'I have to do this. We need everything happening at once. I can't risk missing anything like we did the first time. The police, I mean. Celine Wilson never got justice, and essentially we let whoever attacked her stay free long enough to do this.'

Amer chews the inside of his lip. 'You really believe it's the same perp?'

'Don't you?'

'I reckon it could be. But—'

'But never start with a closed scenario. Always be open to possibilities. Yes, I know. I also know that the likelihood of a different perp branding a victim, who's almost the same age as Celine, with something akin to a raven-shaped cattle prod, with the same emblem in the same spot and leaving her in a similar property is pretty damn low. Not to mention we never revealed the details. No one knows about the brand.'

'The family knows. Celine Wilson's family, I mean. God knows who they might have told in the past six years.'

'Precisely why I'm going to speak to them. Look, I don't have time to stand around explaining this. I'm going.'

'Okay.'

I turn and begin walking away but he calls out, 'Beth? I'll get onto everything else.'

I give a small smile. 'I know. Thanks, Amer, I appreciate it.'

I open the door to leave. Behind me, the MIR is fizzing with chatter, though most of the team are out following up any potential leads highlighted by Uniform. They'll be locating and reviewing CCTV, checking ANPR cameras for any notable vehicles passing through during our window of interest. They'll be pulling the many threads together to create a case that, with any luck, will see the light of day in court. I look back at my team and close the door, then spot Millie hanging up on a call in the main office.

'You're with me, Mills.'

Millie turns to face me, understanding evident in her expression. She knows the pressure I put on myself, we're as close as any friends can be. I confide in her my darkest fears, my deepest regrets, my grief over losing my mother. Millie is the person I go to when I need someone. Next to my Aunt Margie, she's my only family — well, as good as, anyway. Meanwhile, I'm ignoring the almost constant buzz of text messages from my long-term partner, Yvette.

I don't want to face Yvette after our latest argument. I haven't been home since, opting instead to stay at Aunt Margie's. From there I was called out to Balfour Street, and since then I've been using it as an excuse not to deal with Yvette or the stress she brings. She can't understand why my work is more than a job, it's my vocation. I joined the force to become a murder detective, to catch killers like the person who walked into my home when I was four and took my mother. I was too young then to be able to give an accurate description of him. I was powerless to save my mum, but doing this job gives me some of that power back. Yvette can't understand that.

Millie looks at me. 'You okay, Beth?'

'Hmm? Oh, yeah, sorry, of course. I should be asking you that. How did it go with the Danes?'

Millie chews the side of her lip, something she does when she's upset.

'As you'd expect. They were a mess, especially Felicity. It never gets easier, witnessing people breaking. But the official ID is done.'

'Thanks, Mills. I take it they didn't want you to stay on?'

She shakes her head. 'No. They wanted to be with Sally. Just the three of them.'

'I get that. Come on, we'd best get moving.'

49

She rolls her eyes. 'Can I ask where to?'

'To see Celine Wilson's family. I want you with me. They need to hear about this from us, it's the least we can do. Plus, if there's any reading between the lines that needs doing, I know I can trust you to do it.'

We set off at a fast pace, down the steps to our respective cars. Separate vehicles again, so Millie can stay behind if necessary or go to the Danes' if they call. I lead the way, Millie almost tailgating me around a winding B road lined with fields, bushes and trees. I open my window, letting the wind whip my hair, the crisp scent of the countryside clearing the staleness from my car. My stomach grumbles loudly as I pass the Corporation Arms, spotting the 'food served' sign outside. I haven't had breakfast and can't see myself finding time for lunch either.

Within about twenty minutes we arrive in Longridge and pull up outside a modest semi-detached. The front garden has a small shrub in the centre of circular stonework, potted plants around the edge and an assortment of stone forest animals. A colourful windmill spinning wildly in the breeze is leaning from a grey ceramic pot. Red front door, golden numbers. Fourteen. The four still crooked after all these years.

They stayed on after the attack on Celine. Kept her room exactly as it had been, even though she's been in a care home ever since. Celine's older sister, Danielle, left home at eighteen, just a year after Celine's attack. I spent time with the family. I wasn't involved in the original case, but I've been here in the years since, following up, checking in. I've always had a strong sense that I'm missing something.

Danielle had been eager to get out of the house. She ended up dating a cop, who is now a detective at our station — Detective Constable Thomas Spencer. He'd been a god-send when I was working the cold case, mediating between me and a still angry Danielle until we became something approaching friends. She'd never forgiven the system for letting her sister down when she was attacked. That she'd married a cop had surprised me at first but once I got to know him, I saw why they'd been drawn to each other. Tom Spencer was the solid, dependable type that Danielle had been looking for. He also had something of a hero complex. They filled each other's needs.

Tom won't be working the case for obvious reasons, but he's a good guy and I know I can trust him to help if needed. Tom and Danielle were married and had two kids by the time she was twenty-two. She's only twenty-three now, but her life is far removed from the one she'd been leading before. The family home fell dark after Celine and became a shrine to a girl who didn't die, her photograph on every surface, every wall. Her things are strewn about in her room — pink fluffy dressing gown on the back of her door, cream cardigan over her purple dressing-table chair, socks balled up on the end of her bed. The bed is still unmade, just as it had been that day, the selection of trolls with multicoloured spikey hair on her chest of drawers. The photograph of her with Danielle, both holding up concert tickets and grinning like Cheshire cats. They had their lives ahead of them that day, but Celine's came to a sudden end. They'd thought she was dead. The paramedic had been called in the expectation of confirming her deceased. Then she'd found a pulse. There had been hope, but it was fleeting, and was stolen away completely days later, when scan after scan revealed little brain activity. She would be a shell of a person, alive but not living. She would breathe, but would be fed through a tube. She would drool because she was unable to swallow. She would be moved from bed to chair, strapped to keep her from falling. She would smile sometimes. Her parents would spend their time between their home and her care facility, managing her needs. They would age with her, watching the years go by without change, without hope of recovery. They would wait for it to end but it never did. The monster who had rendered Celine Wilson that way had walked free and is out there even now.

I knock, hear the sound of feet shuffling along a carpet, and there she is, Diana Wilson. Celine's mum has aged at least twice as fast as she should have. She is only forty-two years old but looks mid-fifties at best. Her face is lined. The dark bags beneath her eyes reveal nights spent chasing a sleep she'll never catch up on. She's stick-thin and her hair is completely grey. The bright blue eye shadow she wears seems out of place. Her lips are dry and cracked. The smell of cigarettes clings to her dressing gown. Her skin is pale, her cheeks sunken. She looks as much of a shell as Celine.

'Diana.' I duck my head slightly. She's only five feet two, and the way she holds herself cuts that to more like five feet. 'It's me, Beth, Detective Chief Inspector Bethany Fellows.'

'Oh, so you've been promoted then. Yeah, I know who you are. I remember you coming here two years ago with all your promises. Telling us you'd get the bastard. Never happened though, did it? Yeah, I remember you well enough, I ain't the one laid up without a thought in my head. That'd be my daughter. And you lot *still* haven't caught the person who did it to her, have you?' Her eyes widen. 'Wait. Have you? Is that why you're here? Have you got him?' She turns and calls, 'John! John, come here quick.'

John Wilson appears, a fed-up expression quickly transforming into one of hope. He stands beside his wife and slips his arm around her waist. 'Why are you here? What's going on?'

'Can we come in, please?'

They step aside, gesturing for me and Millie to enter. We walk into the lounge, Diana and John behind us.

'Have you?' Diana repeats. 'Did you get him?'

I pull my jacket around me. 'No, I'm sorry. I didn't mean to . . . get your hopes up. That's not why we're here. I'm sorry.'

'Then why are you here?' John steps so close to me that I instinctively move back.

I sense Millie bristling. Millie hasn't had dealings with the Wilsons, so she won't feel the same debt to them as me. We all do to some extent of course — the police are a unit, and our culpability is shared across the board. Me, though,

I spent a lot of time with the family a couple of years back. They would never know how hard I tried, how much I wished I could have solved it.

Over time, I'd become somewhat close to Celine's sister, Danielle. I'd listened to her story, heard how Celine's attack had destroyed them all. I shouldn't have made promises, but I hadn't been able to stop myself. I owe them a huge debt.

'Please sit down. This is important.' I nudge Millie towards an armchair and sit on the other, leaving the couch for Diana and John. 'There's been another attack and we have reason to believe it could be the same person who hurt Celine.'

Diana gasps. John jumps to his feet.

Millie instinctively gets to hers. I pull her back down into the armchair beside mine. 'It's okay, Mills,' I whisper, and look up to John. 'I am so, so sorry.'

John doesn't speak. I can see he's pulsing with anger.

Diana looks from her husband to me. 'Did she live?'

I shake my head. 'No. No, she didn't.'

'I knew it. Oh, Christ. What the family must be going through. You have to stop him. This time you must. John, I need them to leave now.'

John looks at me. 'Please go.'

We do as we're asked. This is becoming a habit, having grief-stricken families asking us to leave. I stop at the door. 'Can we come back? Whenever you feel able. You might be able to help us. You, and Danielle too. Please?'

Diana nods. John takes his wife's hand. They are so completely different from the Danes, but the trauma, the shock, are the same.

We have achieved nothing more than to add to the Wilsons' heartache.

CHAPTER EIGHT

At 2 p.m., I knock on Dillon's office door and, without waiting for an answer, walk in. She's sitting behind her desk eating a chicken salad sandwich. She must have nipped next door to Costa. Oh, to have the luxury of time to eat, I think unfairly. I know how dedicated Superintendent Dillon West is. She probably sleeps like a bat, hanging from her office ceiling. I aspire to be like her.

'Update?' Dillon says.

My stomach lets out an audible groan.

Dillon raises her eyebrows.

'We're trying to identify this Simon bloke that was present at Barry Knultz's. We don't have his full name yet, but I don't think it'll be long before we do.'

Dillon sits with her hands clasped on the desk in front of her. 'Anything else?'

I fill her in on Barry and Jenny's interviews. She listens intently and I feel that familiar churning in my stomach because I know we have a long way to go. Even so, I am chomping at the bit to get this bastard and nothing is going to derail me.

'So main points thus far?' Dillon sits back, wriggling in her seat until she is comfortable.

'Okay. One, we have no real ID for this Simon bloke. Two, Jenny was flippant about the possibility of Rose doing drugs but Daniel, Tony and Peter all swear blind she never would. They baulked at the mere thought of that kid taking so much as an aspirin. They did say she drank two or three cans, so that tallied.'

Dillon drums her fingers against the arm of her chair absent-mindedly, a habit I find mildly irritating. 'Forensics will clear it up, I should think. Kids can be daft, but if she's trying to hide something, science will suss her out.'

'True. Until Forensics come back to us we just don't know about the drugs. It does seem strange to me that Jenny would consider the possibility, given the boys' reactions.'

'What's your gut telling you? That maybe both girls were experimenting with drugs and Jenny is trying to hide it? Would make sense I suppose. Kids get scared. Could be scared of us, her family, repercussions.'

'It's a definite possibility.' I shrug. 'I'll have another chat with her once she's had a break — see if I can get her to open up. I'm going to get Millie out to Rose's family, to check in on them after the ID. Then I want her with me when I go back to see the Wilsons, especially Danielle. You know, I always believed she holds the key, that there was something she knows.'

'Do you really think she would have kept it from us? Celine is her sister.' Dillon finishes the last of her sandwich and slurps the dregs of her coffee.

'Not intentionally, no. But sisters talk, they communicate, even without words. I think there's at least a possibility she knows something. She probably doesn't even realise it, but I think she does. As far as I'm concerned, she's always been our best bet for sussing out Celine's state of mind back then. She'd have known whether there was anything of note going on in Celine's life. Maybe there was something the original investigators overlooked — perhaps I missed something too. Time can change a situation, we both know that. Allegiances shift, people reveal secrets they would have died to protect before. It's always worth treading old ground to look for new roads.'

Dillon smiles momentarily. 'Well, go and find out then. And have someone bring Jennifer Lambert in again later, have another crack at her once she's rested a bit.' Dillon smiles. 'Always gotta play nice and give the kiddies their nap times. But I'm with you. From what you tell me, she's not being completely open with us, and I don't like it. I don't like it one bit.'

'Yes, ma'am.' I turn and head for the door.

'And Beth?'

I face Dillon. 'Yes?'

'Bloody well eat something. Your stomach sounds like a freight train's charging through it. You can't have that thing making a racket when you're with witnesses or relatives. Go to Costa, treat yourself.'

I leave Dillon's office knowing I'll ignore her order. I have a cereal bar in my drawer. It will stop the grumbling, at least for now. I'll eat properly when I've earned the time out.

'Hey, Beth. Beth!' Amer's racing across the office with a small parcel in his hand. 'This came for you.'

I take hold of it and shake it beside my ear. 'What is it?'

Amer arches a brow. 'I didn't open it. How would I know? A courier dropped it off about half an hour ago, the front desk had it.'

'A courier? Weird. Okay, cheers. Maybe I forgot my own birthday.' I laugh.

'Wouldn't surprise me with you. Anniversary maybe?'

'Nope.'

'Come on then, don't keep me in suspenders. Open it, let's see what you got.'

I laugh. 'Nosey git. For all you know it's sexy lingerie. And, Amer?' I smirk. 'Please don't plant the image of you in suspenders in my head again.'

Amer blushes.

'Aw, come on, I'm just winding you up. I'm sure you'd look beautiful.'

Detective Constable Antonio Giovanelli waves from the other side of the office. 'Amer, I got that printout you asked for.'

'Cheers, Ant, be right with ya.' Amer pouts. 'Damn it, gotta run. Let me know what's in it, I'm curious.'

'Depends on what it is. I might want to keep it all to myself. It could be chocolates.' I smile while cuddling the small parcel as Amer pretends to wipe away tears.

'If it is chocs, they were a bit stingy,' Amer calls. He takes the printout from Antonio and holds open the door to the MIR.

'I'm gonna go and talk to Celine Wilson's sister. I'll call you when I'm done. I'll take Millie with me,' I say.

'No probs. I'll keep things ticking over here.'

'Cheers, mate. And if they are choccies, I might let you have first dibs.'

Taking a seat at the bank of computers in the main office area, I open the parcel. Inside I see a small black mobile phone. It's unsealed, nothing fancy. Just a bog standard pay-as-you-go. I take it out and press the buttons on the front. The screen comes to life immediately. The battery is full. A loose charger cable sits in the bottom of the parcel.

There's no screen lock, so I'm able to flick through the menu. No apps, nothing on it except one saved phone number. The hairs on my arms prickle and my chest tightens. The one name in the phonebook is all too familiar: *Simon*. Looking across the room towards the closed MIR, then to Dillon's office door, I'm about to call out. Before I do the phone beeps with an incoming message.

I open it. A photo of Millie leaving her house pops up. Another buzz, followed by an image of my partner, Yvette, at work. Another buzz — Aunt Margie watering the flowers outside her bungalow. One after another they appear. Amer, Amer's wife, his children. Everyone close to me. I'm being targeted, along with everyone I love.

The next message is an emoji with a finger to a pair of lips. The words that follow make my heart go cold.

You can't be everywhere. You can't save everyone. Unless you follow the rules . . . This game is just for us. It's YOU and ME, let's see who wins this time. Simon says . . . you'll find out soon enough. :)

Another picture message comes through. One that confirms this is very real, that he is who he's claiming to be. The face staring up from the mobile screen is that of Rose Danes, wide-eyed, terrified. Alive. He's letting me know he can do the same thing to any of them if he chooses to.

I'm his puppet. This is his show. He knows as well as I do that I can't put everyone into witness protection. It's impossible to protect them all. So until I know who and where he is, none of the people I love are safe.

I go to put the phone in my pocket when another message pings.

Last one for now.

A photo slowly downloads beneath the words. I'm looking at myself, right now, sitting here. I stand and look manically around the office. Up and down the rows of computer banks, out to the balcony, through the windows, at the closed doors.

He must be here somewhere.

CHAPTER NINE

I walk into the MIR and spot Millie. I drink her in, grateful for the sight of her. The mobile is tucked in my inside pocket, burning a hole. I've decided not to tell anyone about it. Not yet. I can't take the risk. The message was clear: tell a soul and someone will get hurt, or worse. Looking at Millie, I know I won't take that chance. I can't. I just hope I'm not making a grave mistake.

Someone has to know who this Simon fucker is. There has to be a way to get to him.

Millie notices me and walks over. 'You look like you've seen a ghost. You okay?' She stretches her back then cracks her finger joints.

'I'm fine. Christ, Mills, do you have to do that? It's like you're realigning your entire body or something.'

Millie winks. 'Spot on. I've been sitting too long in one position.'

I grab Millie's arm. 'Come on, don't keep me waiting. You've had time for your insights to ruminate. What you got?' I hope I'm not sounding too desperate, that I'm showing the same enthusiasm as I would for any case. My fear for those I love will be mine and mine alone.

'Nothing. Absolutely sod all. I'm not a magician, you know.'

'I know, Mills, but you are the people-reader. I just hoped—' I look up to the ceiling, sighing. 'Oh, for fuck's sake. This was never gonna be easy, was it? Fuck.'

I want to pull the damn mobile from my pocket and share my burden. I look around at the others. Could it be one of my own team? Someone must have known exactly when that phone was in my hands, the timing of the messages was too perfect. Not to mention the photo of me. Simon, or someone helping him, is here, there's no other explanation. Unmasking the monster might very well mean revealing him to be someone close.

I need to find a way to make Simon the focus of every officer. He's the Brander, but I'm the only person who knows that for certain. I can't tell anyone about the phone. All I can use is the knowledge that he's an as-yet-unidentified, mysterious older bloke hanging out with a group of kids.

I walk to the front of the room and examine the whiteboards, which are now full of crime scene photos taken from various angles. They show everyone who was present, except, of course, Simon. There are pictures of Rose Danes and Celine Wilson. Close-ups of the brand they share. There is no doubt about it, side-by-side images prove that these ravens are identical. The Brander has finally done it — the fucker has murdered someone. When I failed to catch him the first time around, I convinced myself that Celine had been a one-off and consoled myself with the belief that it wouldn't happen again. Now, not only is the Brander back, he's chosen me as some sort of opponent in a sick, twisted game.

Have I brought this on myself? I wish to Christ I'd left well alone.

When I opened the cold case file into Celine's attack, I put all I had into it. By the time I resealed the file, I had exactly nothing useful. But maybe I'd hit a nerve back then? Why else would the Brander be gunning for me personally now? There has to be something I missed.

In order to find out who killed Rose Danes, I'll first have to go back to Celine Wilson. For me to be in the Brander's cross hairs signifies that I was close before. Going back may well be what pushes us forward.

Notebook in hand, Amer hurries over. 'Beth, look what Mrs Fowler just brought in.'

'Mrs Fowler?'

He passes the book to me. 'The neighbour.'

'The old biddy from 8 Balfour Street? The chain-smoker?' I remember the elderly lady who had been watching with interest from her front garden as I'd arrived.

'That'd be the one, yeah.'

I open the book and look down at what appears to be some kind of surveillance record. Names, descriptions, activities, times of said activities — it's exceptionally detailed. 'What the hell is this?'

'She likes to people-watch, apparently. Takes her civic duties very seriously, particularly as the area has no active Neighbourhood Watch and the police and PCSOs are, in her words, "as useful as a chocolate teapot".'

'Please tell me she—'

He grins. 'She did indeed.'

'Then why the hell is she only just handing this over now? We spoke to her the day Rose's body was discovered. She claimed to know nothing.'

Amer's smile vanishes. 'She tried to cut a deal with a few newspapers before realising they couldn't print anything that would damage an active investigation. At least, that's what I read between the lines of her excuses. She "hadn't realised the significance", blah, blah, blah.'

Frantically, I leaf through the book until I reach the evening in question. There it is. The group members' arrival and departure times. She'd watched Barry Knultz walking away with his shoulders slumped. Jenny did leave around 1 a.m. as she claimed. According to Mrs Fowler's observations, she was 'stomping' down the street. The three boys left together at about 1.30 a.m., so not long afterwards. But there is no exit time for Simon. There are clear and unflattering descriptions for them all, and she refers to Simon as the 'coloured boy'.

She has eyes on the front and back of the houses. She's meticulous. She could have missed him leaving, but seeing that she noted Jenny leaving via the back gate — because she heard a noise and investigated — it seems unlikely she'd have missed him or anything else.

I turn the page, wondering why the old lady was up so late in the first place. There's a note claiming the commotion from next door was keeping her awake and she was diarising with the intention of reporting them to Environmental Health and getting the 'idiot boy' evicted. Nice lady. After the three lads left, she stayed awake for another twenty minutes to be sure it would stay quiet before taking herself off to bed. During their interviews, the lads had all claimed Simon left before them and after Jenny, so where was he? He must have been hiding somewhere in the bungalow, lying in wait until the coast was clear. Mrs Fowler is obviously painstakingly thorough — I doubt very much she misses a beat on that street, and didn't that night. At least now I have another reason to keep the team interested in Simon. But until I have an identification for him, I am chasing his shadow.

I need to talk to Danielle again. I'm convinced she knows something. I'd bet money on it. I also think that she can't possibly understand what she knows. She loves her sister. Her own life has been turned upside down and inside out by what happened. And sisters talk, they share things. Or so I hear. I've never been lucky enough to have a sibling. I have Mills and that's as close as I've ever come to that kind of bond. I'd do anything for Millie, and vice versa. Danielle must have been that for Celine at one time. She wouldn't choose to keep quiet, would she?

If she does know something, I'll get it out of her. This time I won't take no for an answer.

Millie tugs my arm. 'Beth? When was the last time you ate anything? No offence, but you look like shit.'

62

The room is spinning, flickering in and out of focus, small black dots skittering across my vision. I'm shattered, overwhelmed, scared, and yes, starving. 'Cheers, Mills. I don't know. This morning? I think.'

'You think.' Millie guides me to a chair. 'You looked like you were about to hit the deck. You need to eat. You're no good to anyone passed out cold. Sit.' I do as I'm told, resting my head on my arms on the table. 'I brought two sandwiches today. One is yours. Won't be a tick.'

My stomach tightens when Millie goes through the door and out of sight. I only breathe easily again when she comes back in. She nudges a plastic food bag containing a ham sandwich against my hand. I rip open the wrapper and devour it. It tastes of nothing, but it does the job.

Millie perches on the edge of the table, nibbling her sandwich. She smiles. 'Better?'

I wipe crumbs from my lips. 'Thanks, Mills. I needed that.'

'You don't say? You were swaying on your fuckin' feet, missus.' She shakes her head. 'I don't bloody know, you're a liability, Beth. To yourself anyway.'

'Thanks.' I poke out my tongue. 'Seriously, I think I'd fall apart without you.'

I get to my feet. 'I need you to come with me to speak with Danielle, Celine's sister. I've always felt she knows something, even if she doesn't realise it herself. Who better to have by my side than the people-reader?' And what better way to keep Millie in my sights? On the way over, I'll fire off a text to Aunt Margie, to see where she is. Just getting a reply with the standard two kisses and no words will make me feel better. At least I'll know she's safe. I'll text Yvette too. It's bound to open the proverbial can of worms, but I need to know she's okay. The Brander is right, I can't keep track of everyone all the time.

'What's her married name?' Millie asks.

'Danielle's?'

'No, Madonna's.'

I roll my eyes. 'Very funny. Spencer.'

'Not far off from Princess Di.'

'Eh?'

'Danielle. Diana. Spencer. You know.'

'Don't go into comedy will ya, chuck?'

On our way out, I see Amer stalking across the office towards the break room, no doubt going to pour himself another coffee. Like the others, he's oblivious to the danger he's in. The only person who knows, besides the Brander himself, is me. If anything happens to any of them, I'll never forgive myself.

CHAPTER TEN

We arrive at 2b Starburst House. The apartment building isn't anything special, but it does have a nice view. The Preston Docklands are a stone's throw away, along with the telltale red boat at the edge of the road. The path leads to the shops — Dunelm, Morrisons, the Odeon. Danielle and her little family have it all right on their doorstep. Luckily, they aren't able to see the murky-grey shade of the water from their second-floor balcony. I wonder whether the stagnant stench ever drifts up. It's a bonny spot but there are certainly drawbacks that I wouldn't be impressed by. Not at the prices they must be paying to live there.

Danielle works in an office at the edge of the docks from Monday to Wednesday. Her husband, Tom, has worked in the same building as me ever since his promotion to detective a year ago. Their kids are well turned-out and from what I remember, cute as buttons.

With a glance at Millie, I steel myself before I press the buzzer. I can't help feeling anxious as all the promises I made to Danielle come back to haunt me. I failed to catch the beast who hurt her sister, and here I am about to beg more answers from her.

Millie is adept at compartmentalising. We all have to be capable of it to some extent, but Millie's a pro. I know that when she's alone, Millie allows herself moments to crumble, and does so with complete abandon. But then she calls time on it, puts it back in its box and reverts to the person I rely on, Detective Constable Millicent Reid.

'Hello?' Danielle's voice sounds tinny through the little speaker, but it's still recognisable, even after two years.

'Danielle, it's Beth Fellows, Detective Chief Inspector Bethany Fellows.'

'You didn't need to clarify. I know who you are, you think I'd forget? Besides, Mum said you might come by. I suppose you'd better come up.'

The entry system buzzes. At the door to their apartment, Danielle stands with a baby girl on her hip. The baby has rosy cheeks and is sucking her thumb. Her hair is wavy and brown, just like Celine's.

Danielle has had her hair cut since I last saw her. She now has a short blonde bob. She wears stylish thick-framed glasses and has lost all her pregnancy weight. She's always been a looker but now she looks stunning. She goes back into the apartment, leaving us to follow. Little four-year-old Erin careens into her mother's legs, her face alight with the excitement of having visitors. In the kitchen, the black counter across the centre has four breakfast bar stools lined up, one out at an angle, where I imagine Danielle or Erin must have been sitting. There's a highchair at the top end.

'Ava?' I ask.

Danielle nods without turning around. She clicks the highchair straps shut, then fills the kettle and switches it on.

'I gather your mum told you?'

Danielle spins on her heel to look at me, her face pinched. 'What? That you let a kid get murdered by the same monster who attacked Celine? Yeah, she told me.'

It stings. 'Yes,' I admit, 'there has been another victim. At this stage we think it could be the same person who hurt

66

Celine, but we haven't confirmed that yet, so we really need to keep it between us. For now.'

'Killed.' She gives the child a spoonful of baby mush. It is bright yellow and smells strongly of bananas.

'Sorry?' I glance at Millie, who is silently observing, taking everything in.

'Killed. He killed Celine, he didn't just *hurt* her. She's as good as dead.' She puts another spoonful to Ava's lips. 'If we're being honest.'

I have no good response to that. Danielle's right, Celine has no life. She's skin and bones and little else. There is no true substance to a day spent being manoeuvred by doctors and nurses, incapable of feeding or toileting yourself. Saying that she has been 'hurt' doesn't do justice to what happened to Celine Wilson.

Erin is tugging on her mum's clothes, wanting attention. Danielle grabs a banana from the fruit bowl on the breakfast bar, opens the skin and hands it to her. 'I can never feed Ava without Erin wanting something too. She's only just eaten.'

The kettle has long since boiled. Millie smiles at Danielle, gesturing to it. 'Would you like me to . . ?'

Danielle nods. 'Sure. Go ahead.' She opens some milk chocolate buttons and tips them onto the baby's tray. Erin's big brown eyes stare at her mother incredulously. Her banana hits the floor a second later. Danielle relents and opens a packet for her too. I watch Ava's chunky fingers shoving the chocolate around the tray as she tries to pick them up.

'Tea or coffee?' Millie asks Danielle.

'Tea, just a dash of milk. No sugar.'

Millie makes the drinks and slides Danielle's mug across the breakfast bar.

Danielle smiles weakly. 'Thanks.'

'Do you think we could sit in the lounge?' Millie asks. I understand why — she wants Danielle to feel comfortable, so she will let her guard down.

'Okay, I suppose.'

Danielle lifts Ava out and we go into the lounge, Erin pottering behind us. She goes over to a tiny pink doll's buggy, puts a stuffed bear into the seat and begins looping around the lounge. Danielle puts Ava down on a play mat and sits on the corner couch. Millie and I move a few toys out of the way and take our seats.

I wait for Millie to take the lead. We discussed how this should go. Millie would ask the questions once it felt right for her to step in. I would do the introductions then leave her to do her thing. My presence would help put Danielle at her ease. Or so we hoped.

'You must be proud of Tom's promotion,' Millie says.

Danielle shoots her a look. 'Of course I am. It was over a year ago, though.'

'How's he liking it?' I ask.

'Tom's fine. He loves his job. He's dedicated. If they'd let him, he'd try to find Celine's attacker himself.' She glares at me.

'You know that's not possible. It would be a conflict of interest. I'm sure Tom understands that. I know he would want to help if he could but for so many reasons it's not something that can happen.'

'Well, I think her family should get a say in how the investigation is run. He didn't even know her before . . . I don't see why him being married to me now means he can't. I think it's ridiculous. I trust him far more than I trust any of you,' she snarls.

I settle back into my seat a little — it is my indication to Millie. She spots the movement and changes the subject. 'How often do you see Celine these days?'

Danielle looks at her kids. 'Not as often as I should.'

'It must be very hard, having a young family. Finding the time.'

Danielle nods. 'Yeah, you could say that.'

'How often would you say, roughly?'

'As often as I can. We all share the responsibility. My parents. Me. Tom too. He's brilliant. Always has been.' She beams.

Millie smiles. 'That's good. In what way is he brilliant?'

I watch Danielle, the pride on her face. 'He sits with her a lot. Reads to her and stuff. She used to love Enid Blyton, *Harry Potter*, you know, she loved books. He goes there and reads. Gives us all a break. He's my . . .' She smiles coyly. 'Saviour. Before we met, I was fucked up.' She looks at Erin. 'Oops. Mummy said a bad word, don't be repeating that. To be honest, I still am messed up. What happened, it was awful. Seeing my sister like she is now, it's hard. Like, really, really hard. My parents aren't the same anymore. I don't think they ever will be. Whoever did that to Celine, they ruined our whole family.'

Millie takes a sip of her tea. 'You're very lucky to have found someone to help shoulder the responsibility.'

Erin sidles up to her mum, lifts a teddy from her pram and holds it out. 'Baby needs a huggle.' Danielle takes it, cradling the teddy and smiling at her daughter.

'He gets it, you know. I mean as a cop, as a human being, he just . . . he understands. We were friends at first. I could talk to him, and I needed that so badly. My parents shut me out, they wouldn't talk to me about it, and I needed to, I really needed to talk about Celine, about what happened, about all of it. He was there when I needed someone and we grew close, then we fell in love. I don't know where I'd be if we hadn't met. I think I'd probably have given up on living to be honest.'

I glance at the wall to Danielle's right, admiring a canvas print of her, Tom and the kids. They're all lying on the floor, Ava in front, Tom and Danielle on their stomachs, and Erin on Tom's back, her hands wrapped around his neck. They're all smiling. They look like the perfect young family.

'How is your relationship with your parents now?' Millie asks, while Danielle hands back the teddy.

Danielle looks wistful. She clasps her hands together in her lap, wringing them. 'Not great. I wish it was better. They got stuck, after Celine. They can't move on. What happened to my sister was horrendous, the worst. I'll never really get over it either, but I have to live my life. I have the girls, I have Tom. I'm a person too. I'm my parents' daughter as well — there are two of us, not one.'

Millie nods.

Erin walks over to her mum, places her hands on her mother's and looks up with big, concerned eyes. 'Mummy? You 'kay?'

Danielle gives a watery smile and nods. 'Yeah, Mummy's fine, sweetheart. Here.' She reaches into her back pocket and pulls out an unopened packet of chocolate buttons. 'Look what I've got. Share them with Ava, okay? There's a good girl.'

Erin doesn't need telling twice. She's off like a shot, plonking herself on the play mat beside her sister, handing her a button while eating two.

Danielle looks at Millie. Anyone can talk to Millie, confide in her. She once told me that when she was an older teenager, she developed what she called 'bus friends', people she didn't know from Adam who would choose to sit with her for a natter. She wasn't the most popular girl at school, but put her in the real world and she's the person people feel compelled to tell their stories to. I'm hoping Danielle will do just that.

'I, erm, I feel bad just saying it,' Danielle confides. 'I get kind of angry with her. My sister, I mean. Celine went and got herself attacked and all our lives have been . . .' She looks at her girls, occupied with their treat. '*Fucked*,' she whispers. 'I know she would never have chosen it, that it's the fault of whoever did it. I know all that. But that *asshole* isn't here to blame, is he? Don't get me wrong, I love my sister, I really do. I visit her.' A moment of worry crosses her face. 'I'm never cruel to her. But she left me alone to deal with our parents. She may as well not be here at all. She doesn't know anything, does she? She's . . . she's a shell. I know I shouldn't say all this. I don't know why I am. I'm sorry. I sound like a complete bitch.' She glances at her daughters again and looks relieved when she sees them engrossed sharing their snack. She smiles, nodding towards her girls. 'They go mad for those things.'

'Do you remember much about Celine from before? Who her friends were? Boys, that kind of thing?' Millie keeps her eyes on Danielle, in a look of friendship and understanding. It works.

'Celine and boys.' Danielle laughs lightly. 'The number of times I've been asked that question. She didn't have boyfriends. Not that I ever knew of. She didn't even really have friends. She was a loner. She was only fourteen, and she was a young fourteen. Not like me. I was the one who had boyfriends at that age. Celine was too . . . good, too innocent, I suppose. Studious. She loved books. She loved her own company. She was as far from a teenage tearaway as you're likely to get. I wish I could tell you that there was some guy hanging around, someone I could point my finger at and say, "Look at him". But there's no one. No one at all.'

My disappointment comes through as a sigh, which I disguise with a well-placed cough. Are we wasting our time here? Is this straw-clutching? The phone in my inside pocket feels impossibly heavy. I can't forget its presence for one solitary moment.

Millie edges further forward in her seat. 'Celine was attacked in the evening. She was in a house that was a known hangout for drug users. It all sounds very far from who Celine was.'

Danielle nods enthusiastically.

'You say she didn't have many friends and there were no boys on the scene at the time. What about after her attack? Is there anyone who wasn't in your life before that suddenly popped up?'

Danielle frowns. 'Not really. I mean, I met my Tom of course. There were a few girls who wanted to visit her. I think they were curious or felt guilty because they weren't nice to her at school. They'd probably have posed with her for flaming selfies or something if we'd given them the chance. Mum and Dad didn't let them visit. They didn't want Celine being seen like that. They just kind of went away afterwards. The girls, I mean. The odd post goes up on Facebook every now and then, but I untag myself. We don't need or want their fake care. They weren't friends so they can bog off as far as I'm concerned. I don't know why Celine was in that house. I've always thought she must have been lured there. Dragged, maybe. She wouldn't have gone there by choice, no way. She wasn't into anything like that. No drugs, no alcohol, nothing. I used to wind her up about it, calling her a goody-two-shoes. But if she did go to that house by choice and wasn't lured there, it must have been because she was trying to help someone. There's no other reason that I can think of.'

'Help someone? Like who?'

'I don't know, just someone. She was one of those kids who give their dinner money to the homeless. She was good — too good really. She might've met someone who she thought she could help and followed them or gone to meet them. She was gullible. That sounds awful, doesn't it? What I mean is, she was soft when it came to anyone in need. I could see her walking into a trap.'

This is the first time I've heard this theory of Danielle's. She's never mentioned it before. I'd tried getting information out of her, but it had been like pulling teeth. She'd never opened up like this. Half an hour with Millie and she was spilling her guts. It galls me that Danielle is only now saying all this. Maybe if Danielle had been more forthcoming before, we wouldn't be where we are now, with Rose Danes dead and my closest people threatened. I keep my counsel and listen.

'Did Celine ever mention any particular person? Someone she thought was in trouble or who she might be able to help?'

'I've thought about it so many times,' Danielle says. 'I don't remember anyone specific. I wish I did. But there's no one I can think of. There was this one time she came home upset. I followed her to her room. She was crying into her pillow, trying to muffle the sound. I asked her what was up and she said there was so much sadness in the world, that people had problems so big it was hard for them to breathe. She was sobbing, I mean really crying. I thought she was being OTT, if I'm honest. But she was fourteen and just this really sensitive kind of person. Everything bothered Celine, everything was personal. She was a walking, talking wound even before.

'I tried to get her to tell me what had happened, why she was so upset but she wouldn't . . .' Danielle's face lights up. 'Wait, she did say something. I can't believe after all these years I'm only just remembering. This is weird, but she said something about money, she said, "*Money is so lost*". It made no sense — she never had any money. I have no idea why I'd forgotten it. Probably *because* it made no sense. That's all. That's all she said. After that we watched an episode of *Teen Wolf* together and ate from her stash.'

'Stash?'

Danielle laughs, a tinkling sound. 'Yeah, she had a drawer full of junk food — sweets, chocolate, crisps. She wasn't bulimic, before you ask.'

'How long after Celine's attack did you meet Tom? You would have been seventeen when it happened, I guess.'

'Yeah. I met Tom near the hospital, a few days after. He was there following up on something to do with work, a car accident or something. He was kind to me. He bought me a coffee and we got talking. I told him everything. He was a good listener. Still is.'

I hear a key in the lock and jump.

Erin looks up, gasps and runs to the door, her little legs going ten to the dozen. 'Daddy!'

Danielle smiles. 'Tom said he'd try to finish early, after I told him about you seeing Mum and Dad. They must've let him. Tom! Through here.'

He walks in carrying his daughter. He's handsome, tall with broad shoulders and is wearing a crisp grey suit. His dark hair is slicked back with a stylish, boyish flick at the front. His brown face is drawn, his brow sweaty. He nods to me and Millie and sits beside his wife with Erin on his knee. I can smell his expensive aftershave.

'So, Danielle tells me there's been another attack and you reckon it's the same person who attacked Celine?' His eyes dart from me to Millie and back. 'From what I hear at the station it sounds like that's what you're thinking.'

'We think so,' I admit. 'We're just here to gather as much information about Celine from Danielle as possible. Anything could help.'

'You've done all this, over and over again. I was supportive of your efforts last time. Even when John and Diana lost faith, I kept them believing, trusting. Danielle—' he looks at his wife — 'I talked into helping you as much as she could, despite the cost to her, to us. And now here we are again and honestly, I fail to see why putting my wife through this yet again will yield any more answers.' He takes one of her hands. 'And it's been six years. How can you even begin to make a connection? I mean, what makes you so sure? *I* can't see it. Of course, they won't let me into the fold at work. Maybe if they did, I could understand.'

Erin wriggles free and slides to the ground. Tom keeps his grip on Danielle.

This is new. Tom has always been on our side, he's never questioned me like this before. 'Tom, you know we can't give you access to the investigation. It would compromise us, it could mean the case falling apart in court,' I say.

'Court,' he scoffs. 'You'd have to catch the maniac first. If it's even the same guy.'

'That's why we're here,' I say. His attitude is beginning to grate. 'We have evidence that strongly suggests it *is* the same perpetrator. Something that would only be known to Celine's family and the person who attacked her has been repeated. It's unique to this perpetrator.'

Tom says nothing. He must have squeezed Danielle's hand very hard. She lets out a tiny yelp and pulls it free, giving him a look of alarm.

He shakes his head. 'Sorry, I . . . It's just — that's awful. Can't you just tell me what it is, this unique thing? I'm guessing you mean the mark, the brand?' He wipes his forehead. 'I'm sorry, I shouldn't ask you to confirm it. I know you can't. And I do understand. It's just that I don't want Danielle dragged through all this again. The stress, the upset, the hope, only for it all to come to nothing.' He glances at Danielle. 'I'm scared to death of what it will do to Dani if this falls apart too.'

'I get that, Tom, but you know we have no choice. We have to go over Celine's case again if there's any possibility it will help.' I don't need to ask him how he knows about the brand. There are few secrets between a husband and wife. I'm less irritated by him now, I can relate to that need to protect someone you love from harm. He adores Danielle and she's already been through so much. 'Look, whatever you know, or think you know, I would urge you not to repeat any of it. *Especially* not to the press.'

'What do you take me for?' Tom snaps. 'I'm not a complete idiot.'

I watch Danielle and Tom closely. 'About that brand, the one we believed was a raven. Can either of you think of any reason why someone would use that symbol?' I've given up on being allusive. We all know what has been said. I won't confirm it but there's no point denying it either.

Danielle leans forward. 'It's still there, you know. We can never get rid of it. I wanted her to get it tattooed over or something. Mum won't have anyone try anything to get shot of it. She'd rather cover her in clothes and blankets and play ignorant. But I know it's there. I can't forget it. I help wash her and I see it. It makes me feel sick that *his* mark is still on her. And, no, I don't have a clue what it means. Don't you think I've tried to research it? I've done everything I can think of. You know what they represent, ravens? Anything from fertility, wisdom, longevity, to *death*.'

Tom puts his arm protectively around Danielle, pulls her against him and narrows his eyes at me. 'See? *This* is why I came home. Why I don't want you here. Look at her — look at the state of her. I don't see why you need to be here, upsetting her. There's nothing she can tell you that she hasn't already said a thousand times over. I think you've asked enough questions for today. I want you to go. *Now.*'

Millie stands. I'm slow to follow. I'm getting tired of being asked to leave before I can get real answers, real truths. Danielle sniffs and rubs her hand. Tom is behind us, offering no chance for us to stay a moment longer. There'll be no more questions while he's standing guard over his wife. I realise he's just being protective, that for the past six years, he has been witnessing her pain. He's been there through it all. I can't really blame him.

At the front door, Millie stops and looks at Tom. 'I'm curious, what was the case you were covering when you met Danielle?'

'Excuse me?'

'At the hospital. When you met Danielle. You were there for a case.'

'Ah, right, yeah. That was years ago. I don't remember. Hardly seems important now.' He frowns. He steps past us and opens the front door, waiting silently for us to walk through.

As soon as we are over the threshold into the corridor he closes and locks the door. We listen to his footsteps retreating into the apartment and make for the stairs.

Halfway down, Millie stops. 'Well, that was weird.'

'What? Danielle suddenly remembering something new?'

'Well, yes, that, and Tom practically putting his shoe up our arses to get us out of there. Not to mention forgetting what case he was working when they met. I mean, it was the day he met his future wife. Something like that would stick, wouldn't it?'

'Yeah, I'd have thought so. Then again he's a bloke — you're lucky if they remember your birthday. But I do understand him being protective, I reckon I would be too. Not to mention I fucked up last time. I made promises I didn't keep. I never found who attacked Celine and that's on me. I can't blame Tom for being pissed. He supported me, convinced the family I was going to get to the truth, and I never did. We've come here today, upset Danielle all over again, and we're no further along. Dillon is gonna have my guts for wasting time.'

'I wouldn't call it a waste. We now know Celine was upset about something to do with money.' She shakes her head. 'I don't know, the way she said it — if Danielle is remembering right, it almost sounded like a person. A nickname?'

'You think so?'

'It's possible.'

Outside, a blast of icy air smacks us in our faces. Maybe it hasn't been such a waste of time after all. Something feels off to me. I can't quite put my finger on it but it's nudging at the periphery of my brain. Before I can think any more about it, I hear a mobile buzz. My heart hammers against my ribs, and it takes a few seconds for me to realise it's coming from my jacket. It's my own phone and not the one I've secreted away in my inside pocket.

I retrieve it and look at the caller ID. Millie peers over my shoulder, looking sideways at me as I hesitate before answering. 'Yvette? Everything okay?' I would have rejected the call, but after the Brander sent me her photo, I have no choice but to talk to her.

'I got your text. I'm at my mum's.'

At least she's with her mother.

'You didn't go home last night.'

'I stayed at Aunt Margie's. I take it you've been home then? You okay? Why aren't you at work?'

'Yes, I've been home. The bed was still made, and seeing as I'm the only one who bothers making it, I know you didn't sleep there. Anyway, I've taken a few days off work, not that you'll care. You're not gonna take time off to spend with me, are you?'

I turn away from Millie and reply under my breath, 'Of course I care, Yvette. I'm working a really big case, which is why I can't take time off. You staying with your mum today? Tonight?'

'What's it to you what I do? Yes, I'm staying here. Mum's looking after me really well.'

'Why? Is something wrong? Are you ill?'

'Oh, for God's sake, Beth. No I'm not ill, but I do have worries. I have things going on too you know. You're not the only one that matters in this relationship. I—'

I glance at Millie, who's looking away, pretending not to be listening to every word. 'Yvette, I'm working. I really have to go. Can we talk later?'

The line goes dead. I'm in the doghouse. Yvette believes jobs are a means to an end. They pay the bills but the rest is the important bit, like our lives together. She can't grasp why my career is my entire life. Aunt Margie is forever pointing out how fundamentally incompatible we are, which annoys the hell out of me. I'm determined to do everything possible to make it work. Yvette can be difficult, but she's also a lot of fun. A person like me needs an Yvette. She lightens my darkness.

I put my phone back in my pocket. 'I'll call her back in a bit, explain about the case.' I ignore Millie's knowing look. 'She'll understand when I tell her I've been made Deputy SIO.'

'You haven't told her already?'

'Come on, we need to get a move on. Forensics could have something by now. I need an ID on this fuckin' Simon bloke.' Millie has no idea just how badly I need to know who he is, how high the stakes are, and I'm biting my tongue to keep from telling her.

CHAPTER ELEVEN

I barely slept. My brain refused to switch off and I was so caught up in my thoughts I forgot to set my flaming alarm. It was a panicked rush to get ready and into work on time.

I arrive at the station and the MIR is already in full swing. Bottoms on seats, phones in hands, a sea of white paperwork littering the tables. I wish I had more to bring to the party.

Dillon must have spotted me coming in because she walks in straight after me. Her spiky blonde hair is looking slightly less gelled than usual, her face more pinched.

'Beth, I need a word. Now. My office.' Dillon turns her back and strides out. I see the relief on the faces of my colleagues, glad that they're not in the firing line. I hope she isn't about to question my commitment to the case.

I follow Dillon into her office, shut the door and sit down opposite her. 'What's up?'

'I've received a complaint.'

My mouth falls open. 'What? Who? Why?'

'Danielle Spencer called first thing.' She arches a brow and I infer she's unhappy with how fine I cut it this morning. 'She stated that she doesn't want you stopping by anymore, particularly not unannounced. She tried claiming it was harassment. I put her straight on that. You had a valid reason to speak with her in light of what's happened. Even so, I think it would be best if you gave her a wide berth for now.'

'I don't get it. She was fine with us. Did she mention Millie?'

'Not specifically.'

I'm pissed off, big time. Danielle was upset that there'd been another attack — this time a murder — so why do this? I thought she wanted to help, that we had developed some kind of understanding since my investigation two years ago. Okay, I might not have solved the case, and I let Danielle and her family down, we all did. But why this complaint to Dillon? She could have turned me away at the door.

'I'll stay away. But I don't understand this, ma'am, I really don't. I let Millie take the lead. I didn't say or do anything that would—'

'Are you saying Millie did?'

'No! Of course not. Not at all. I didn't mean it to sound like I was putting the blame on her.'

'Calm down, Beth. You aren't being reprimanded. There's no official complaint. I put paid to that. It's a friendly request is all. Nothing to get bent out of shape about. This case is bigger than Danielle Spencer. You don't need her right now. I suggest you get back in that room—' she gestures towards her door — 'and take charge. We're running out of time. Before long, any trails we have will start to fade. We are already into day three.'

As if I wasn't aware of that. Fizzing with annoyance, I make my way to the door. 'I'll keep you updated.'

Meanwhile, I'm thinking of that damn phone, willing it to ring so I can hear his voice. Maybe I'll recognise him, maybe I'll even be able to reason with him. I turn and open my mouth to speak, desperate to spill my guts, tell her the killer has picked me out, and that I've received photos, threats.

Dillon is staring at the screen of her computer, her face illuminated in its glow. 'I know you will. Thanks, Beth. Close the door behind you, please.'

I head back towards the MIR. What was behind Danielle's complaint? I'm fast deflating, like a ball someone has stuck a pin in. It feels strangely as if I've lost a friend.

At the entrance to the MIR my mobile buzzes. Again, I think it's *his* phone. I pull it from my pocket, look at the caller ID and sigh. 'Yes?'

'Oh, thanks.'

'Just a sec.' I wander along the corridor, seeking privacy. 'Sorry, I—'

'I've been calling, texting. You're ignoring me.'

'If I was ignoring you, I wouldn't have answered, would I?' I could bite my tongue. I'm being a prize asshole. I owe Yvette better than this. 'Sorry. It's been already a tough day.' I can hear the humdrum of the radio or TV in the background — Yvette's mum always has one or the other playing, regardless panic grabs me. 'Wait, you're still at your mum's, aren't you?' I ask. I have to be sure.

'Yes, I am. It's been a crap day for me too, you know, but I didn't want to leave things like we did. I wanted to talk to you, hear your voice. You don't sound pleased to hear mine though,' Yvette says. 'You're not the only person in the world to have hard days, Beth. Mine's been pretty dire too, not that you'd ask, or listen if I tried to talk to you.'

'It can't possibly be as bad as having a dead fifteen-year-old kid to deal with. It can't be as bad as telling a family you've let them down for the second time.'

'I know you have a tough job, Beth, but you choose to do it. Well, I didn't. I didn't choose this. But because I love you, because we're supposedly a couple, I got lumbered with it. Sometimes I wonder how much of a partnership this actually is. I shouldn't have to deal with your shit all the time. It isn't fair. You aren't being fair to me.'

I grit my teeth. How she can attempt to play the victim? The real victims are Rose Danes and Celine Wilson. Not Yvette fucking Donovan. 'Are you serious?'

'Deadly. I've had enough. You don't think anyone else can have problems, do you? You're not the only one who has a hard time. You're just so selfish.'

'Me? *I'm* selfish?'

'Yes. You. Oh-so-perfect Bethany Fellows. I'd called to tell you I'd changed my mind and was coming home tonight, but after what you've just said, I'd rather stay with Mum again. I don't want to see you. I don't want to hear from you. I can't deal with your crap right now. I have things going on myself. I called because I needed you. How stupid of me to think you'd care.'

In spite of myself, I feel guilty. I shouldn't feel bad for doing my job, for prioritising murdered and damaged kids. It's important, much more fucking important than giving someone a bad haircut, which is all that can possibly be wrong in Yvette's life. She's a hairdresser, for Christ's sake. What could she know about stress? It's better she stays with her mum anyway. Gives me one fewer person to worry about. 'Fine.'

As Yvette hangs up, I hear her sob. Guilt rises like bile. I have to get on top of things — this case, my life, my relationship. I'm losing control of them all.

CHAPTER TWELVE

I hit dial and my stomach lurches. Hannah Edwards picks up almost instantly, sounding out of breath. 'Hi, Beth.'

'You got something for me?'

'And greetings to you too. Give me a second, will ya? I've just legged it upstairs, my lungs are exploding.'

'Have you?'

'Eager beaver, aren't we? Actually, I was just about to call *you*, would you believe. And the reason being that we *do* have something.'

I exhale loudly. 'Thank God. What?'

'Forensics just got back to me about the cider cans we collected. They have a fair few prints. Some are understandably smudged, overlayed and whatnot, but we hit on something that could be paramount.' Her voice rises with excitement. Like the rest of us, she's completely invested. No one attends a murder scene with a dead kid at the centre of it and doesn't feel impelled to find the scumbag responsible and have them charged.

'Go on,' I say, wondering why Forensics haven't contacted me personally.

'Well, one of the cans had the dregs of cider in the bottom but there were also traces of ketamine. We have latent fingerprint matches to two people on the can.'

I hold my breath.

'One of them is Rose Danes and the other Peter Lambert.'

My heart sinks. I was hoping they were Simon's prints. Then the implication dawns on me. 'Fuck me. Ketamine? Jesus. No wonder Rose was so out of it. That fuckin' little shit drugged his sister's mate. If she hadn't been in such a state, she mightn't have . . .' The rest dies on my lips. If this was any other investigation, any other detective but me, the findings would implicate Peter Lambert.

I can't reveal what I know — that it's Simon, whoever the fuck he is. Hell, maybe Peter Lambert is involved some-how. He wasn't the killer, though, he's just a kid. Not to mention he would have been far too young when Celine Wilson was attacked. However, that doesn't mean he isn't involved at all. He could have helped, even inadvertently.

'It certainly looks like a strong possibility that Peter Lambert spiked her drink,' Hannah says.

'Strong possibility? It looks like that's exactly what the asshole did. I'll get him brought back in under caution. As soon as the pathologist gets back to me with his findings I'll have more to go on. If ketamine is in Rose's system, which I'm betting it will be, then we have him bang to rights, at least for drugging a minor. He'll cave under questioning. He has to. Thanks, Hannah. Kinda pissed that Forensics haven't called me directly, but hey.'

'You might want to check your phone. Apparently, they tried to get hold of you before they called me.'

'What? . . . Oh.' I must have accidentally switched it to silent after my to-do with Yvette. I've fucked up. I'm the DSIO of a murder investigation and I put my phone on silent. I hadn't even checked missed calls or messages before calling Hannah. Fucking hell. Even if they don't know it, everyone I care about is relying on me to stay alive.

It's getting to me. Despite the barriers I've put up I can't keep it all at bay. At some point feelings, weaknesses get to you, they get to everyone. Yvette's becoming overbearing.

The case isn't moving fast enough. I have no idea who Simon is . . .

'Beth, are you okay?'

'Sorry. Yeah, I'm fine. I just . . . Fuck, it's been on silent. I must have done it by mistake. I'm sorry, Han, I really am. I need to do better.'

'Hey, hey, hey, don't be so hard on yourself. You're doing fine. We're only three days in and we have a strong lead. We have everything under control. The science is working for us. You have boots on the ground canvassing for witnesses. The crime scene is well sealed—'

'Yeah, you're brilliant as always. You're not the one fucking everything up.'

'Beth, I was trying to say we're a team. And as a team, we're doing all right. Now go and bring Peter Lambert in. Get him spilling his guts. You're doing fine, Beth. Just remember, I'm here if you need me.'

'Thanks, Han, pep talk received with gratitude.'

'Adios, my friend.'

Hannah hangs up. I stare at my phone. I unmute it and check my missed calls. They had to call during the few minutes it was on silent, didn't they? Typical.

I see a text from Yvette. I don't open it, I'm still seething. I know it isn't fair, but I need somewhere to plant my frustrations.

I call the lab myself and apologise, blaming a technical issue with my mobile, hoping Hannah won't drop me in it. I instruct them to call Amer if they have any difficulties getting hold of me in future. I get the exact same information Hannah has just imparted.

Then I arrange for Peter Lambert to be brought back in. I find Detective Constable Aaliyah Kimathi in the main office and quiz her on her earlier interview with him. There had been no alarm bells. He'd been sweaty and nervous, but so are most people when they're cooped up in an interview room. She had the impression that his alibi was pretty strong, unless the lads undertook the murder as a group, which

Aaliyah understands is a possibility. She found no reason to hold him or take things any further.

Aaliyah seems a little put out that he'd fooled her. I know the feeling. Suspects, witnesses, people in general will lead you on a merry dance if it serves their purpose. It's Simon who is behind it all, but I need to glean from Peter Lambert whether Simon put him up to drugging Rose, whether he did so knowingly or was some sort of pawn in the sicko's game. Perhaps it was all just chance, nothing more. I need to know how Peter was involved, and fast.

He arrives wearing navy trainers, blue skinny jeans and a white Nike T-shirt straining over his muscles. His brown hair is swept back and to the side. He's a good-looking guy. He watches me approach, his cocky expression only vanishing once we're ensconced in the little room. I sit opposite him, my knees almost brushing his. I've brought Millie in with me, the people-reader.

After going through the usual business for the record, I begin. 'So, Peter — may I call you Peter?'

'Call me whatever you want, darlin'. Don't matter to me.'

I swallow the retort that springs to mind. 'I want you to look straight at me—' I point to my eyes — 'and tell me why you drugged Rose Danes.'

'I fuckin' didn't.'

'We have your prints on a can containing the drug ketamine. Rose's prints are on the very same can. Her saliva is on the rim. We *know* you did it. Now talk.'

I pray he doesn't think better of his decision not to have a solicitor with him. According to him he's innocent, and the whole thing's a farce, a fishing expedition. Fine with me. I need him to not grow a brain. The last thing I want is to be stuck in a 'no comment' interview, especially if I'm needed elsewhere.

Amer is coordinating the investigation for the time being. He'll interrupt if he needs to, but that's another thing to be avoided. This interview has to flow. I'm hoping for a swift end, a confession to drugging Rose and a full identification of Simon along with his address. I know the likelihood of that. Most guilty people don't admit to what they've done. They prefer to stick with their lies rather than condemn themselves with the truth. The probability of this kid being sophisticated enough to be a player in the game I've been forced to play is unlikely. I'm surmising that at best he doesn't realise he even has a role.

'I didn't drug her or anyone else. I was gonna take some ket meself. I didn't though. I didn't even use it.'

'Then why would your fingerprints be on the can? Come on, Peter. You can do better than that.'

'I don't know. My prints are probably on most of them. I was the mug getting 'em out the fridge, being the skivvy. I probably passed it to her. But I did *not* drug no one.'

Shit. He's just given me a plausible reason for his prints to be on the can. The only idiotic thing he's said so far is admitting he had ketamine with him. Then again, he might be smarter than I'm giving him credit for. If he was the one to buy the ketamine but denied it, then we proved it later, he would be caught out in a lie. 'Where's the ketamine now?'

'What?'

'You said you didn't use it, so where is it?' I sense Millie's eyes on me and know she'll be second-guessing me. She'll be wondering whether there's something more than the case on my mind. If only I could tell her.

For the first time Peter looks unsure of himself. He fidgets with his T-shirt, scrunching it up. 'I don't know. I honestly don't know what happened to it. I left it on the side in Baz's kitchen. I went to grab it before we left, and it was gone. I don't know who took it.'

'Did you ask your mates? Apparently, the three of you left together. Did any of them appear to be under the influence? Come on, Peter, give me *something*.'

'I wouldn't say so, and yes, course I fuckin' asked 'em. It was mine and it weren't cheap. They denied it, so I let it go. They're me mates. We don't steal from one another. Never have, and I don't see why they'd start now. To be honest, I thought it must've been that Simon fella, or me sister.' He looks panicked for a moment. 'Not that I'm suggesting she'd drug her mate. Nah. Must've been Simon.' He grins, regaining his cockiness. 'And before you start again, I don't know his surname. I don't know where he lives, works or hangs out. I don't know *him*.'

'You suspected Jenny of stealing the ketamine. Why?'

His hand is back at his T-shirt. 'I was wrong. She didn't.'

'How can you be sure?'

'Because she — Aw, shit, I dunno. She just didn't, okay? She's real cut up about her mate. She wouldn't have drugged her. I only meant she might've taken it herself or given it to that Simon bloke. She was flirting with him. That's all I meant. I didn't mean she'd put it in someone else's drink. Why would she?'

'Did you see Jenny leave?'

'No, she snuck out. Vanished. One minute she was there and the next she'd fucked off.'

'Was Jenny showing signs of having taken ketamine?'

'No.'

'Then why would you think she'd stolen it?'

'I don't know. I wasn't thinking. Like I said, she might've taken it for herself or given it to Simon to show off. I didn't mean she was high at the house. She wasn't. She'd drunk a bit, we all had. But she wasn't high. She didn't even smoke weed. She ain't an angel but she'd never harm someone on purpose. Especially not her best mate. I know she didn't hurt Rose.'

'How can you be so certain?'

'Because she's me sister.'

'Was Simon under the influence?'

'How would I know?'

'Observation, how did he look?'

'He didn't even drink.'

I glance at Millie. 'Then why would he go to the house? Why hang out with a group of kids he barely knows?'

'You'd have to ask him, but we ain't kids.'

'You're teenagers and Simon is, what? Mid-twenties?'

'At a guess, maybe a bit older than that. I'm not sure.'

'Does he normally drink when he hangs out with you?'

'It's not like he's always there. It's been a few times that's all. But no. Maybe he's an ex-alkie or summat. He just hangs.'

'You're saying he doesn't drink, you don't reckon he does drugs. If that's true and if Jenny didn't take it either, where did the ketamine go, Peter? How did any of it end up in Rose's drink?'

'I don't know, okay? If I knew, I'd tell you, but I don't.'

Simon is becoming even more of an enigma. He pops up out of nowhere and has no connections to any of them. He gives nothing away, just hangs out with a group of teenagers. He doesn't take drugs or drink alcohol. Why them? Why these kids? Why Rose Danes and Celine Wilson?

My head feels like someone's using a road drill next to my ear. I badly need paracetamol and a hot drink. I have to find out who Simon is and what the hell this is all about.

CHAPTER THIRTEEN

The MIR is a scene of frantic activity. Everyone's eyes shoot to the door when I enter. Glumly, I shake my head and stand at the front of the room.

'Right. I've heard back from Dr Sanders. He confirmed that Rose Danes had ketamine in her system. We have the can it was in, with the prints of Rose and Peter Lambert on it. We also have an annoyingly plausible reason as to why Peter Lambert's prints could be on the can. We have nothing further on Simon's identity — if Simon is even his real name. I mean, what grown man hangs around with a group of teenagers he doesn't know and doesn't even drink?'

I need them looking at Simon, I need their interest in him piqued. He is clearly at the top of our suspect list, but I don't want them focusing elsewhere even for a second. Peter Lambert is a distraction they don't need. Simon has to be our focal point; he has to be the only direction we are looking. 'Yep, you heard right. He doesn't drink or do drugs. He simply hangs out with them. There must be some pull for him. The young girls, perhaps? We need an ID on this guy. We need him here being questioned. I'm hoping we'll get a fingerprint, a DNA hit, fucking *something*, but regardless we can't rest on our laurels and wait for science to do our job for us. There must be some CCTV or dashcam footage of him in the area. He didn't flamin' fly or teleport to that house.'

I let them know that if anyone wants to put in a few hours' overtime they'd be more than welcome, but that I'll need them fresh and ready for work tomorrow, so not to push themselves too much. I myself will be working into the night. I can name the others who will be there too, along with the few who'll be out the door the moment their shift ends. It will tell me whether this is a vocation or simply a job to them, who will likely climb the ranks and who'll get the results. Unfortunately, sometimes the ass-kissers scale the ladder while the people who work their fingers to the bone and barely sleep for the duration of their careers are left clinging onto the middle rungs by their bleeding fingertips. But I'd rather work with the latter. I can count on them. The others just step on and over you on their way up.

Once the room returns to business, Amer heads my way. 'Beth, Ant thinks he might have something.'

'Ant's been checking for video footage, hasn't he?'

'Yes. There's a garage around the corner from Balfour Street which has CCTV. They've had a few incidences of vandalism, so they put it up fairly recently.'

'What's on it?'

'Don't get too excited. It's something but it isn't the best quality or the best angle.'

'Great. I wanna see it right now. Come on.'

'It's here. They let us take it. Ant's in Room Five viewing it now.'

We head there together. I'm practically running in anticipation of finally laying eyes on Simon.

Ant spins his chair towards the door as we enter. His eyes are wide, his grin wider. 'Well, hello.' He gestures to the screen. 'Meet Simon. Daniel Mint has identified him. It's definitely him.'

I peer over his shoulder at the grainy image of a tall, muscular man. It shows him from the side. There is nothing distinctive — no overly long nose, scar or tattoo. All I can see is that he is over six feet tall, a skinhead with broad shoulders. He also has brown skin very much like mine, just as Jenny Lambert said. 'Can you sharpen it up?'

Ant shakes his head. 'I can't, but there's a copy with technical. I'm hoping they can make it a bit clearer. This is the best shot. He's only in the frame for a couple of seconds as he passes the corner.'

'Let's hope the techies can get us a clearer view of the fucker. Thanks, Ant. Good work.'

'He might be a fucker, but he's a handsome fucker, ain't he?' Ant smiles.

'Jenny Lambert certainly thinks so,' I say.

'By the way, it was PC Kelvin Pritchard who came upon it. So you might wanna thank him. He had the ID verified with Daniel Mint, then brought it straight here. Good guy, Kelvin.' His smile broadens.

'Cheers, and yes, I will thank him. See, this is what we need. Teamwork and dedication.' I grin. It's something. I've seen him now. Perhaps I could even pick him out of a crowd. Maybe I could see him coming.

Ant looks me and Amer up and down. 'One of you ringing?'

Amer pats his pocket, takes his phone out and shakes his head. Panic grips me. If the Brander is calling now of all times, I can't possibly answer. I touch my pockets but there's no vibration. It isn't ringing. Maybe I missed his call. If I did, he might do something to demand my attention. I take out my own mobile and shake my head.

Ant shrugs. 'Must be imagining things.'

I bring my attention back to the grainy image on the screen. 'Okay, we have that with technical and we have Jenny being interviewed about the ketamine. They've gone out to her home address. I sent them straight away so they could speak to her before Peter gets the chance. I've had him delayed.' I smile at Amer. 'Tactics.'

'Good thinking, Beth,' he says. 'What now?'

I quickly offer up a few instructions before dashing out of the room. Round the corner, I thrust my hand into my inside pocket, pull out the mobile and check it. Then I check it again, assuring myself there's been no missed calls. Ant really must have been hearing things.

Relief washes over me. I haven't messed up with the Brander. Yet.

CHAPTER FOURTEEN

The day is wearing thin. My head feels as if it's in a clamp that's tightening with every passing second. My eyes stinging and watering, I battle to stay awake and focus on the computer screen. By the time darkness is nudging its way into the building my focus is waning.

I down three potent coffees in a row. I haven't heard from Yvette and in all honesty, it's starting to piss me off. It's pretty damn obvious that I'm up against it. And that's without her knowing the extra monumental pressure I'm under because of twisted Simon's fixation on me.

Yvette's mum, Phillipa, texted a little while ago letting me know she's there and will be staying the night. There were none of the usual kisses at the end. I'm clearly not flavour of the month with her either. At least Yvette's safe. I can't help thinking it would be better if we weren't a couple at all. It'd be safer, at least.

I've spent the past couple of hours trawling the internet researching ravens, crows, blackbirds. I've done all this before, two years ago. There's little to nothing new. I had hoped I'd missed something the first time around and have learned more about birds than I've ever wanted to know. Ravens can symbolise prophecy and insight. They can also be associated with the dead and with lost souls. Meanings range from fertility to death and everything in between.

Without knowing who Simon is, I can't tell what the raven means to him. I would imagine it to be more death than fertility, but who knows? Perhaps he just likes frigging ravens. I take the mobile from my inside pocket and check for the umpteenth time but find nothing other than the photos and the message I've already seen. His silence is terrifying.

Jenny Lambert denied touching the ketamine. She was apparently 'deeply insulted' at our suggestion that she would drug her friend. She had no idea who took it and thought our time would be better spent doing 'actual' police work. What the kid thinks police work is, I don't know. Most likely the kind of thing she last saw on telly.

Hannah has informed me in no uncertain terms that Barry Knultz's home is a forensic swamp, a challenge at best that will take an age to unpick. There's so much DNA, so many overlapping shoeprints that it looks as though they'd been having a month-long party. The only gold they've struck so far is the can with the ketamine remnants inside. They are busy counting shoeprints at the moment, working into the evening in an attempt to discern exactly how many people were present. It isn't an enviable task. It's painstaking. It can be revolting, and no doubt when it comes to Barry Knultz's home it is. Luckily, his mum seems to make an appearance every now and then, so it won't be the cesspit it could have been.

'Beth?'

I damn near jump right out of my skin. Dillon has found me staring at the whiteboard, absorbing the information we've gathered so far and becoming increasingly infuriated because it isn't nearly enough.

'Whoa.' I put my hand over my heart. 'You almost had me there. What's up?'

'It's gone eight. You're here well beyond your finishing time. I understand, but damn it, Beth, if you don't go home and get some sleep, you'll be no good to me. I was standing in the doorway for a good few minutes and you didn't even flinch. You had no idea I was watching you, did you?'

I flush. 'No.'

'That's not good, Beth. You need to be on the ball. Right now, you're flagging. Worse, you were literally swaying on your feet. You kept putting your hand to your eyes. Headache?'

I sigh. 'Killer — no pun intended.'

'Then go home. Now. I insist. This—' she waves her hand around the room, empty now apart from the two of us — 'will all still be here in the morning.'

'Okay. But, ma'am . . .'

'Yeah?'

'I can't promise I'll sleep.' I indicate the board. 'We missed something all those years ago, and because of that Rose Danes is dead.'

'I get it,' she says. 'I really do. I feel the same. We'll do it this time. We'll stop him. But there'll always be more, Beth. It's your job. It's what we signed up for — to step in when everyone else steps away, to bring the bastards down. No matter how determined you are to not let up, you can't run on empty, no one can. You have to look after yourself if you're going to be strong enough to see it through.'

'You're right, ma'am, I need to get some rest. I'll be on form tomorrow.'

On my way out, I fire off texts to Millie, Yvette, Amer and everyone else who is unknowingly at risk. I wait with bated breath for them to reply. I'm certain I won't sleep a wink if they don't.

CHAPTER FIFTEEN

I receive a stream of replies to my texts, ranging from *I'm fine, at home* to *Trying to get some sleep*, to Yvette's *I'm watching a film with Mum. Leave me alone.* It's a tenuous reprieve, which Simon can rip to shreds whenever he chooses. I despise that he has so much control. Truthfully, I want to tear *him* to shreds.

I drive to Aunt Margie's and let myself in. I no longer have a bedroom made up. Aunt Margie uses the space for exercise, meditation, painting and whatever new hobby or whim takes her fancy. Aunt Margie's house faces the north side of St Anne's seafront in Lytham. It is painted in vibrant blues and pinks, much to the disapproval of the local historical society.

We moved here when I was six and plagued by nightmares. Preston had been full of painful memories. At four years old I couldn't really process having witnessed my mother's brutal murder. My memories were much like the way a child colours in a drawing, smudging colour over the outline until the drawing is obscured. I would sleep fitfully, tossing and turning, my cries breaking Aunt Margie's heart. Finally, the only thing she could think of to help me was to up sticks and move. Lytham was the ideal destination. It was a distance for me but close enough that she could keep her job. It felt safe — safe as we would ever be while Mum's killer remained at large.

By the time I arrive at just after 10 p.m., the house is in darkness. Quietly I open her bedroom door, needing to lay my eyes on her to reassure myself that she's here, safe. Aunt Margie, a light sleeper, is wearing a pink silk eye mask and ear plugs and is snoring softly. I watch her for a while, resisting the urge to wake her for a natter, a cuddle. Then I make up a bed on the couch, settle down and pass out almost instantly.

The strains of 'Dancing Queen' blast through the room. With a groan, I roll over and feel for my phone. Jesus, it isn't even five thirty. I catch sight of a flash of brilliant yellows and pinks and Aunt Margie's mass of frizzy blonde hair just disappearing down the hall.

'Aunt Margie, forgodsake! What in the name of God are you doing?'

She dances back into the room. Her hair is piled on top of her head, her eyes bright, despite the hour. 'And what, pray, are *you* doing on my couch again, young lady? You can't sneak into my home in the dead of night and then complain when I wake you up.'

'Oh, come on, Aunt Margie, it ain't even five thirty.' I stare at the MP3 player willing it to spontaneously combust. 'Your poor neighbours. You'll wake the whole street.'

Aunt Margie's grin stretches from one ear to the other. 'Will I 'eck. In case you've forgotten, this bungalow is semi-detached, and Martyn is as deaf as a post. I reckon I'm safe as houses.'

'What *are* you doing?' I scowl at the MP3 player. 'Come on, turn it down, will ya? My head's banging.'

Aunt Margie lowers the volume to a slightly more bearable level. 'There. Happy?'

'Ecstatic. So, again. *Why?*'

'My Zumba class starts at half past.'

'Seriously? Where?'

'Online, of course.'

'At five thirty?'

'No, at nine thirty. It's in Mauritius, sugarplum. They're four hours ahead.'

I roll my eyes and shake my head. 'Only you.' I give in, drag myself from the couch and head for the kitchen, Aunt Margie dancing behind me. 'Brew?'

'So, what's up with Princess Yvette now?'

'Don't call her that, you know I hate it,' I say.

'Sorry. Go on then, do tell. You're on my couch for a reason. What is it?'

I can't tell her that I wanted to watch over her, afraid of what Simon might do. 'The usual. She thinks I'm putting work ahead of her.'

'When is that girl ever gonna get that you put work before everything? You always have, and you always will.'

'That's not fair.'

Aunt Margie grabs my hands. 'It is, sugarplum. You have a calling. There's nothing wrong with that. Quite the opposite in fact. I for one couldn't be prouder, though I do wish you would smell the roses occasionally. That is one thing me and Princ— erm, Yvette, can agree on.'

'I don't know how.' I slump into one of the little yellow kitchen chairs and look up at Aunt Margie, noticing her get-up for the first time. She's wearing a multicoloured leotard, bright pink leggings and yellow leg warmers, straight out of an eighties edition of *Smash Hits* magazine. 'What's with the eighties look?'

'It's my Zumba gear. The girls love it. They think I'm very *Ab Fab*.' She laughs and winks. 'They adore us Brits.'

I roll my eyes. 'You're nuts, Aunt Margie, anyone ever tell you that?'

'Daily.' Her guffaw drowns out the music.

'I'm Spinning Around' by Kylie comes on next. This is a headache-inducing playlist if ever I heard one. 'Christ, this music, it's making my ears bleed.'

Aunt Margie pats me on the head. 'Then sleep at home.'

I sigh dramatically. 'I'm a train wreck of a girlfriend, Aunt Margie, I really am. I don't know how to be in a healthy relationship.'

She pats my head gently. 'Ah, come on now, sugarplum. You just haven't found the right woman yet.'

'Don't be horrible.'

'If she made you happy then maybe I'd put aside that she's jealous, possessive, and ridiculously needy. I'd even try to ignore the fact she spends half her life checking her own reflection. But she doesn't make you happy, does she?'

'Wow, Aunt Margie, that's one hell of a character assassination. And she does make me happy. It isn't her. It's me.'

'Beth, darling.'

It's serious when she calls me anything but sugarplum.

'You are stringing that girl along. She isn't right for you. We both know it. She's far too flouncy.'

'How can you, of all people, call anyone out for being flouncy?'

'Well, sugarplum, *we* ain't dating. You were born serious, and, well, after what you went through — after your poor mum was killed, it set something off in you. A need.'

'A need?'

She sits down next to me. Two steaming pink flamingo-patterned mugs are on the table in front of us. 'A need to seek out justice. To catch the bad guys because the monster who hurt your mum got away. You were made to be a detective. A bloody hardworking, dedicated one. It's a part of you that will never change. Someone like Yvette, she wants to change that, and she's fighting a losing battle. Do yourself and her a favour, and . . .'

'What?'

'Cut her loose. Let her find someone like her and you, my dear, find someone with a heart just like yours. The heart of a lioness.' She pats my hand.

Maybe letting Yvette go would be the best thing for both of us. She'd be safe, and I would . . . Well, I'd be free. 'I have a big case, Aunt Margie. A really big case.'

Aunt Margie raises a brow. 'And you're sleeping on my couch? You need to be well rested. You need your own bed. Jesus, Beth, it's your house. Why the hell is it always you who has to sofa-surf whenever Yvette has a hissy fit?'

Yvette isn't at home. But if I'd gone there, I wouldn't have been able to sleep. I need the sanctuary of Aunt Margie's.

To be near her and to know she's okay. 'Aunt Margie, it's the Brander. He's back.'

Aunt Margie lets out a gasp. 'Beth, that case almost did you in when you couldn't—'

'When I couldn't solve it? Yeah, I know. He's killed someone.'

'Not that kid on the news! They didn't give a name, just that a fifteen-year-old girl was found dead, and that it's a murder investigation.'

I nod.

Her hand flies to her mouth. 'Oh no.'

'You can't breathe a word.'

She glares at me. 'As if I would.'

'Sorry. I know you wouldn't. She was just a kid, Aunt Margie.'

She scratches at a mark on the table. 'How horrible. Her poor parents.' She places her warm hand over mine. 'You'll get him, sugarplum.'

I only wish I had the same faith in myself. 'Thanks, Aunt Margie. I love you.'

'I love you too, kiddo.'

'I'm gonna go in. I need to be on this.'

'I know you do,' Aunt Margie says. 'Good luck, sugarplum. Keep me posted.'

My thoughts already on the case, a surge of adrenaline rushes through me as I dash to my old bedroom-come-gymnasium and grab some work clothes. I stay here often enough to keep things on hand. Aunt Margie's home will always be my go-to place when my world is going awry.

As I leave the bungalow, Aunt Margie is dancing like a lunatic in front of her computer screen, watching a group of women all dancing their socks off along with her. Her zest for life never fails to make others smile. While losing my mum made me darker, more serious, for Aunt Margie it had the opposite effect. She insists on living every moment to the fullest, for herself and her sister. She refuses to let bitterness drip its poison. She won't give her sister's killer that level of power. Sometimes I wish I could be a bit more like that. She and Yvette will never be on the same page where I'm concerned and I can live with that, but it would be nice if they'd stop sniping about each other.

I race down the M55 towards Preston, opening the window to let the wind tear at my hair. I arrive in less than fifty minutes, hoping a speed camera didn't catch me out, and pull up in the car park by the River Ribble. The time is 6.45 a.m.. I kill the engine and get out of the car, pulling my leather coat tight. It's Baltic, the mist billowing in clouds around me.

I look up at the Major and Serious Crimes Northwest building. The balcony is shrouded in darkness, the glass front covered in early morning frost. There's a whiff of musky river water in the air, melded with the dewy scent of dawn.

I take a breath and start up the concrete steps. Costa is still closed — what I wouldn't do for a decent coffee. The young woman at reception nods as I scan my pass. There in front of me is DS Dillon West. She has a mug in her hand, steam rising tantalisingly from it.

Her lips narrow at the sight of me. 'Oh dear. Well, I suppose I can't rightly chastise you when I'm here too.'

'Couldn't sleep?' I ask.

'No. You?'

'I got a few hours. I got woken up early by flaming "Dancing Queen" and an extra from *Ab Fab*.'

She raises her eyebrows.

'Don't ask. Needless to say, I thought I may as well come in since I was up. More use here.'

'Fair enough. Coffee and a chat?' Dillon says.

'Why not? I'll meet you in your office.'

'Okey-dokey.'

I make myself a coffee in the break room. The building is silent. I love it at times like this. It's when I can really think. I've spent hours here reading through old cases trying to find some link to my mother's murder. That, and Celine's case. Now it's years later and here I am again, both cases still unsolved.

CHAPTER SIXTEEN

My phone buzzes — a text from Yvette. At this time in the morning it's unlikely to be good. I read her words with a sinking feeling:

Nice of you to come and see me. I thought you'd show up, that you cared what I was going through more than a load of strangers. I'm never your top priority though, am I?

Shame and irritation battle for prime position in my mind. Am I being unfair in thinking that her problems are merely mundane day-to-day shit?

I'm almost at Dillon's office when she calls my name. She is poking her head out of the MIR. 'Thought we might as well be in the hub. Come on. Hurry up.'

Inside, Amer is flipping through some paperwork. He likes to print everything out, says it's easier to read in hard copy. He hates computers with a passion. He has an aversion to staring at so much artificial light, says it's like looking into the eyes of the Terminator.

He looks up. 'Oh, hey, Beth.'

'Amer.' I smile. 'You too, eh?'

'What can I say? You trained me well, Sensei.' He winks. We both turn towards the door.

Millie lifts her shoulders and pulls a cutesy face. 'Couldn't sleep.'

'Well, come and join the party.' When she is leading or observing an interview, Millie is supremely confident, but it's a different matter when she finds herself alone with us. Millie sees her route into her career as being somehow less pure than ours.

She had been a school counsellor, working with troubled children, and had been brilliant at it. The school was where kids were sent when the mainstream institutions couldn't handle them or their needs. They were all emotionally or psychologically fragile. That was where Millie came in. She built up their trust until she was able to get them to confide in her. On occasion she'd find nothing, no trauma, no abuse, no reason at all for their behaviour. Nevertheless, she helped them get their lives back on track. Others damn near broke her heart with the lives they'd endured, the things they were still attempting to survive.

Then there was that one kid, the one she got too close to. When it didn't work out, it finished her career. She wasn't asked to leave, but she was done. She went into some kind of slump or depression and kicked her heels for a while until she pulled herself together and I put her in touch with the force.

Millie and I first met when we were little more than babies. I'd started infants in St Anne's late, after moving to the area. Millie was the shy, lonely kid, and I was drawn to her instantly. At six years old we became inseparable. We grew up together like sisters. Our families almost merged into one. And now we are working side by side. I still fear that I've brought Millie into a world that will destroy her further. It's a hard world, and a violent one. I worry that it will take her apart like a Russian Doll — piece by piece until all that's left is the tiniest, most fragile version of her.

'Here.' I hand Millie my coffee. 'You look like you need it more. Did you sleep at all?'

Millie rubs her reddened eyes. 'Not really. I just couldn't seem to get it out of my head.'

'We'll solve it.' We have to. I won't find Millie like Knultz found Rose Danes. I can't let that happen.

She takes a seat beside Amer. I can hear them muttering to each other. They're here with me, safe.

I turn to the whiteboard and stare at the photographs. I visualise my friends and family staring back at me, their blood on my hands.

CHAPTER SEVENTEEN

By 8 a.m. I'm ensconced in front of a laptop reading yet more, most likely irrelevant, crap about ravens when Hannah Edwards calls my mobile.

'Beth?'

'Yep.'

'I called the lab. Sorry, I was eager. Anyway, they had an update. Those footprint impressions we took — they confirm that there are at least seven separate sets.'

'That tallies.'

'It does. What doesn't is that they are sure one set has been donated by someone wearing the wrong size shoe. The wearer was putting pressure in all the wrong places, not following the wear and tear areas — and it's trainers we're talking about here, Nike Air to be precise. Anyway, the front of the trainer was too light, the toes didn't reach the end, not nearly.'

'It was planned, wasn't it?'

'I'm not the detective here, but, well, it's definitely something.'

'Thank you so much, Han. How come you're at it so early?'

'Couldn't sleep.'

I glance around the rapidly filling MIR and sigh. 'Yeah, there's a lot of that going around.'

'I'm sure there is. This is not a stabbing in a park. It's a kid, and we all feel it. We know this branding thing is different. The similarities or connection to Celine Wilson, it hits home for us all. We understand the importance of it. I mean, don't get me wrong, all crime is important and needs to be investigated with everything we've got, but this . . . this—'

'Han?'

'Yeah?'

'You're waffling.'

'Sorry. I do that.'

I can't help but smile. 'I know you do. There's no need, you know.'

'To what, waffle?'

'No, to justify your investment in this case. We all feel the same.'

'Thank God, I just didn't want to sound like an ass.'

'Now, Han?'

'Yeah?'

'Do you have anything else? Anything at all? We're grasping here.'

'I wish I did. You know how it is.'

'Yeah, yeah. "Science is precise not fast".' I quote Hannah's own words, which she uses annoyingly often. 'I'd better go then. I need to tell the team what you've found.'

'They're there?'

'Pretty much. Like I said, we all feel the same.'

'I'll keep you updated.'

'Cheers, Han. Oh, and when do you think you'll release the scene?'

'It's a swamp, a cesspit. There's so much DNA and material it's taking us an age to gather it. We're working our arses off. Barry Knultz has lost a section of his carpet to Forensics. It's taking some time. Lucky for us he isn't a hoarder, they're even worse. Hopefully we should be done later today. Then the lab will have to analyse it all and figure out what's relevant. With any luck we'll get something out of it. I can't imagine us not. There has to be something from the killer among it. There just has to be.'

'Han?'

'Yeah?'

'Waffle.'

'Sorry. I'm just—'

'Running on coffee beans and cigarettes?'

'You got me.'

'Adios, Han.'

'Au revoir.'

I look at the expectant faces of my colleagues. 'Forensics confirm the presence of seven people, which tallies with what we already know. But they also found that one of the donors was wearing Nike Air trainers that didn't fit them. Basically, they had on someone else's shoes, or second-hand ones. Whoever did this—' I point to the whiteboard — 'planned it. He went prepared and is clearly forensically aware.'

'For fuck's sake.' DC Antonio Giovanelli isn't given to outbursts, he's usually calm as a cucumber.

'I agree.' Thanks to the media, if someone really wants to commit a murder, they have enough information at their fingertips to help them give it a good shot. A thought occurs to me. 'Fuckin' hell.'

'What?' Dillon says.

'That bastard.'

'What?'

'His head is shaved. He's completely bald.'

Dillon's eyes widen as she realises what this means. Amer speaks first. 'He shaved his head so there'd be no DNA. He wore shoes that wouldn't be traced back to him. He planned it all.'

I stare at the whiteboards. This is going to be harder than I'd hoped. At least now I won't have to convince them that Simon is our man. He might have been smart forensically, but that awareness also puts him firmly in the frame.

CHAPTER EIGHTEEN

Dillon collars me as soon as the commotion dies down. 'Be careful you don't get blinkered.'

'Meaning?'

'Meaning that you have zeroed in on this mysterious Simon fellow.' I open my mouth to speak but Dillon holds up her hand. 'I understand why. I think he's a strong possibility, but we are at the very start here. We can't afford to have the person charged go free because we missed something. Tunnel vision is not the way to go. Now, we know Simon's some kind of mystery and that he hasn't come forward. We know he was knocking about with a load of teenagers. We also know someone there was wearing shoes that didn't fit them. But the fact Simon has a shaved head could be a coincidence. Rose's murder could have nothing at all to do with him.'

My heart sinks and I'm unreasonably annoyed at Dillon for unwittingly making this more difficult for me. I need to keep the team focusing on Simon. I try to justify my reasoning that Simon must be our guy. 'But there were no other shoeprints. No one else went in afterwards. It has to be the same person. It has to be someone who was already there.

One of the group. We've eliminated the shoes of all the others. It's *Simon*. It's him. It is.'

'Beth, I'm with you. My gut is telling me it's Simon, but hunches don't hold up in court, and they don't get convictions. I'm not saying don't pursue him. Go after him by all means. Bring him in. Stick his head on the wall. But *don't* get the team baying for his blood alone. Don't have them all working under the assumption that he's the *only* possibility. Ever heard of putting all your eggs in one basket?' Dillon raises her eyebrows.

'I understand.' A swell of irritation fills my chest, but she doesn't know the same as I do. She's working with the information she has. The phone, the texts can't be a ruse. But I can't tell Dillon about those. 'I just *know* it's him.'

'Then find out who he is and prove it.'

Dillon walks away. I know what she means, and I appreciate it. She isn't hovering over my shoulder or questioning me in front of the team. However, she doesn't have all the facts.

I begin handing out my own instructions, making sure I'm covering every avenue. I've little doubt that the Simon who's contacting me is the Simon from the gathering at Knultz's, but little isn't none. 'Little' leaves room for error. I need to be certain. First of all, I have to find out if the guy from Knultz's is the person who had the phone delivered to me.

I make a beeline for Millie, who is about to visit the Danes. I have given her the unenviable task of filling them in on the minimal progress we have made so far. I touch her arm and whisper, 'Do you want me to come with you?' I need to keep her in sight. Of all the important people in my life, Aunt Margie and Millie top the list. I can't bear to leave her unprotected.

Millie gives me a small, barely there smile. 'Might help, if you have time. I know you're up against it.'

'We all are, but after all, we do it for the families. They're the heart of any case.'

'How're you holding up?' she asks.

'I'm fine, honestly. Come on, I'll get my coat.' I dart through the door ahead of Millie, avoiding her look of concern.

I catch up with Amer before I leave. He'll be in charge while I'm out. I trust him implicitly. I also know he'll be safe inside this building. Before I go, I casually mention Amer's wife, Zarah, and their kids, making sure they're accounted for. The phone sits in my inside pocket, a silent, malevolent presence.

Millie and I walk into the car park. The river beside it is dark, the sky overcast. Naturally, Millie heads for her own car since the Danes may be ready to have her stay with them. I must accept that no matter what I do, at some point, Millie, like the others, will be out of my sight.

I sit in my car and take the mobile from my pocket. No new messages. I follow Millie through Preston as closely as possible, anxiously blasting my horn at anyone who tries to get between us.

CHAPTER NINETEEN

We pull up outside the house just after 9 a.m. It's raining and Millie's standing beside her car under her black-and-white umbrella.

'Beth, what's going on with you?'

'What do you mean?'

'You've been acting weird. Is it the case? Yvette?'

'The case, I guess.' I turn to face the Danes' house, watching a wet cat jump up onto their windowsill and begin licking its paw. 'I'm fine, stop fussing.'

'I'm not trying to annoy you. I'm worried, that's all.'

'Well, don't be. I'm fine. Come on, we have a job to do.' I don't mean to sound so abrupt. Millie's only being a friend, but I can't help it. Keeping secrets from her doesn't come naturally.

I duck under her umbrella and we hurry to the front door. Next to me, Millie is giving me the side-eye.

Mark opens the door. He is dishevelled, his hair messy. His eyes are red. I'm sure he has lines on his face that weren't there before. He looks a good ten years older.

'You here to tell us you got him?'

The smell of coffee and toast drifts out of the house. They have a young child, life has to go on.

I shake my head. 'I wish we were.'

He begins to close the door. I hold it open. 'Can we come in, please?'

Felicity appears in the hallway, looking as ravaged as her husband. 'Oh, let them in, Mark, for God's sake.'

She disappears into the lounge. Mark lets go of the door and we step inside. I catch a glimpse of twitching curtains, noses pressed to windows. One neighbour is even out on her doorstep, clad in dressing gown and slippers. No wonder the Danes' home is in darkness. They're hiding from the stares.

Sally is sitting next to her mum in front of a little table on which rests a plate with a half-eaten slice of buttered toast and a pink plastic cup filled with milk. There's a new television in place of the one Mark threw. It's a school day but it doesn't look as if Sally is going in. Felicity is wearing the same blue floral-print dressing gown as on our previous visit. Mark is in sports gear, jogging bottoms and a sweatshirt, though I doubt he's off for a run.

Millie and I sit in the same armchairs as before. Mark remains on his feet, hovering. Sally stares at the television.

Felicity narrows her eyes at Millie. 'So, you got any news at all? Or are you just here to tell us the person responsible for killing my daughter is walking the streets, safe in the knowledge you're doing sod all to catch him.'

Sally looks up at her mum, her eyes wide.

Millie clears her throat. 'We have a person of interest.'

What the fuck is she doing? We haven't agreed to this. We don't have a full name or anything yet, we have nothing but a ghost.

Felicity sits forward. 'What? You have someone?'

I perch on the edge of the armchair, trying to narrow the gap between us. 'All I can say is that there's someone we want to question. But—'

'What do you mean, someone you *want* to question? Why isn't he in custody? I assume it's a he, since you haven't even told us that much.'

I silently curse Millie for landing us in this situation. 'Yes, it is a male. I'm sorry, we don't mean to keep you in the dark, we want to be as open and honest with you as possible. The problem is that it's an active investigation, so the information we have is extremely sensitive. We want to support you, and we're here to guide you through this. You are the most important people in this case, and Millie will be here whenever you need her.'

'Finding the person who did it is the only thing that matters,' Mark shoots out. 'Just get him, will you?'

'We're doing everything we can, I assure you. It will take time. We need to arrest the right person, we need to have enough evidence to charge him and we need to have everything in place so we can get it to court and achieve a conviction. We do have someone of interest.' I look from Mark to Felicity. 'Now, this mustn't leave this room, okay? The people who were at that house have all been accounted for bar one. There is a fifth male we are eager to speak to. The problem is we only have a first name at the moment. We are doing everything we can to find out who he is.'

'Doesn't Jenny know him?' Felicity asks.

I shake my head. 'I'm afraid not. None of them do.'

'Or they aren't fucking sayin', they're protecting their mate,' Mark spits, his face puce with rage.

'We have extensively questioned everyone else who was there. They have all been interviewed. As I said, we are doing everything we can.'

'But you can't make them talk, can you?' he says. 'If they're lying, you can't touch 'em, can you? If they're protecting their sicko mate, there's fuck all you can do about it.'

'Besides talking to them, we are reviewing CCTV, checking for fingerprints, DNA, whatever we can. We're conducting house-to-house enquiries. We will find out who he is eventually, and we'll speak to him.'

'Eventually? That's not good enough, he needs to be in a cell now before he does this to someone else's kid.'

'We don't know it was him yet. He's a person of interest. At this stage he isn't a suspect.'

'What's his name? You say you know his first name, so what is it?'

'I can't tell you that. I'm sorry.'

'Like fuck you can't. This is my kid we're talking about.' He jabs himself in the chest. 'Rose is my fuckin' kid.'

'I'm so sorry. If I tell you, it could harm our investigation and jeopardise the case. I wish I could, I really do.'

'Person of interest, suspect — it doesn't matter how you say it. You obviously think it's him. So go on, what is it that makes you think he did it?' Mark is shuffling on the spot while clenching and unclenching his fists.

'Let me reiterate, he's a person of interest, not a suspect. But, what I think is that the fact no one knows anything about him is suspicious.'

'That all, is it?' he snarls.

'Then, of course, there is the fact that he hasn't come forward. We need to find him to either eliminate him from our inquiries or to focus them entirely on him.' I tell myself to tread carefully. The last thing I want to do is push Simon to take action. He mustn't think I've crossed a line, even though I don't know where he's drawn it.

Mark kicks one of Sally's toys across the room. She jumps. Felicity holds her daughter closer, glaring at her husband.

'Then fuck off and *find* him.' His voice grows louder with each word.

'Jesus, Mark, would you just stop it? Sal's shaking,' Felicity says. 'It isn't just you that's at breaking point here. You're not the only one that's hurting.'

I am beginning to understand why she's so clingy. She is scared of her father. Had Rose been afraid of him too?

I stand. 'I'll leave, but Millie can stay if you like. She is here to support you. Mark, I understand that you're hurting, you're angry, but Detective Constable Reid is here to help, and I will not have her feeling threatened. Do you under-stand what I'm saying?'

Mark closes his eyes for a moment, his jaw set. He hisses air through his teeth. 'I think it'd be best if I went for a walk. If Flick wants her here, fine. But I need some air. Excuse me.'

He shoves past me and leaves the room. The front door slams.

I turn to Millie. 'I think we should have another officer here with you, just in case.' There is another reason why I don't want her to be alone, but I can't tell her about that.

'He won't hurt her.' Felicity sounds affronted. 'He isn't like that. Come on, cut him some slack, for Christ's sake. His daughter has just — Don't treat Mark like some criminal.'

Oh Christ, am I doing that? 'I'm sorry, that isn't my intention. I understand that Mark is angry. I would be too. But I have to consider the safety of my officers.'

'I'll be fine, Beth,' Millie says quietly. 'I'll let you know if there is any need for someone else to be here.'

I leave the house feeling no better about leaving Millie alone with them. It would only take one fit of rage from Mark Danes for Millie to be badly hurt. I feel responsible for her since I brought her into the force in the first place. She's my best friend. Our unit is stretched thin, it's badly understaffed, but that doesn't mean we should compromise any officer's safety. Then there's Simon and the threat he poses. I grip my keys until they almost pierce my skin as I walk to my car.

As soon as I'm back at the station, I'll look again at who I have, what they are currently tasked with, and get one of them out to the Danes'. I'm not prepared to leave Millie alone for a second longer than necessary. Despite what she says, it's my call and I'm going to make it.

I sit in my car and check both phones, my own and the burner. Nothing. After I get someone out to Millie, I'm going to see the Wilsons again. Not only should I keep them in the loop, but I feel strongly that they hold the key to catching this guy.

Simon is clearly forensically aware. Not only that, but killers escalate, they hone their craft. They aren't born with the knowledge of how to get away with murder, they learn with each victim. If Celine was his first, chances are he was less careful back then. He could have been clumsy. There was the semen of course, but there's never been a match, and we need a suspect in custody to have a hope of getting one. There has to be something else linking him to our current case.

I decide to try and talk to Danielle again. If I can just find the right question to ask, I'll have him.

CHAPTER TWENTY

I seek out DC Antonio Giovanelli and find him going through reams of CCTV with Aaliyah Kimathi. He's sitting back in his chair, brushing back the blonde hair that flops over his eyes. He sees me come in and beams. Antonio, with his invariable sunny disposition, always manages to brighten my day. All I see of Aaliyah on the other hand is the back of her head and her lustrous spirals of ebony hair. She's completely focused and barely acknowledges my presence. I ask Ant to go and join Millie at the Danes' place.

He happily jumps up from his seat, no doubt eager to get away from the screens. On his way out, he pauses by the door, suddenly looking anxious. 'How are they? The family?'

I shrug. 'How you'd expect. That's why I need you there. The husband, Mark Danes, is very angry, a bit volatile. I'll feel safer having you and Millie together.'

He nods. 'No worries. I understand. I'll head off now then.'

'Thanks, Ant.'

He can just about be spared. We need as many eyes as possible on the hundreds of hours of footage. If Simon has been in a shop, he might have paid with a bank card, which could lead us straight to his door. I doubt that he would be that stupid, but criminals never fail to surprise me. They can be extremely short-sighted, only covering their tracks in the immediate vicinity of the crime without realising how far the net will be thrown.

Now that we have the grainy side-on image of Simon as well as Jenny Lambert's description, we might just strike lucky. We can only hope, but I certainly won't be closing the door on any possibility.

I head through to check out what leads have been raised by the Home Office Large Major Enquiry System. Specialist staff in the main office put everything into the system — personal details, addresses, vehicles, exhibits, the contents of witness statements. If a lead exists, it will be in our computer records system, HOLMES 2. It stores all the details of our investigations, establishing links faster and more efficiently than humans are capable of. It's a life saver, sometimes quite literally.

The wonder of modern technology means that from wherever we are, my team and I can log in and see what enquiries have been generated: whether there is a particular witness we need to reinterview, information we have to gather and process. It is the lifeblood of any major investigation. Before the advent of the computer, investigations were run very differently. The Yorkshire Ripper was a case in point. Using index cards to correlate the enormous amounts of information that had been gathered left room for human error, oversights that allowed Peter Sutcliffe to keep killing undetected. I never take technology for granted. My job is made a great deal easier thanks to HOLMES 2.

Having looked at the enquiries thrown up by the system, I call Hannah Edwards. 'Any news?'

'Oh, hey, Beth. 'Fraid not, love. I'll call you as soon as we have anything, I promise.'

'Yeah, I know. I was just checking.'

'We're going to be done at the house soon. It's a mess though. We had to take a load of carpet in the end. There was just so much spillage, possible material. We needed it back at the lab.'

'Understood. So, Barry Knultz is going to be upset then.'

'Aren't they always? Doesn't matter to them that someone died. The state of their home is always their biggest concern. Human nature, I suppose. I reckon he'll end up moving out. I wouldn't want to stay after—'

'Han?'

'What?'

I smile. 'Waffle.' I know Hannah well enough to know she won't be offended.

'Sorry. Okay. I gotta run anyhow. Busy, busy.'

'Adios.'

'Au revoir.'

As soon as our call ends, my mobile starts vibrating in my hand. I look down and see Millie's name. My stomach tightens. Antonio won't have reached her yet. 'What is it, Mills?'

'Beth, it's Mark.' I can hear the panic in her voice. 'Shit, Beth. I . . . need you.' The line breaks up then goes dead. I press frantically at 'return call'. It won't connect.

I leg it through the office, out the security door, through reception and down the steps, attempting to call her the whole time but getting nothing.

My heart hammering, I race to my car and start the engine, scattering gravel as I speed away.

CHAPTER TWENTY-ONE

I drive like a lunatic, fuelled by panic, my phone on hands-free, to a chorus of blaring car horns.

My phone buzzes and finally I hear Millie's voice. 'Beth, are you in your car?'

'Course I'm in my car! I'm on my way to you. What has he done? What's happened to you?'

'Me? Not me, Beth. Peter Lambert.'

The thudding of my heart eases slightly. 'Peter Lambert? What? I don't understand, Mills. You said Mark—'

'I was in the backyard, I lost signal. Mark's gone after Peter Lambert. He's there now. I didn't want to call it in, I thought—'

'Where?'

'At the Lamberts'. Jenny and her mum are there. The mother, Nancy, phoned here. She didn't want Peter carted off to the station to make another statement. But it sounds heated. I think you'd better—'

'I'm on my way. You're okay though?'

'Yes, of course I am. Why wouldn't I be? Beth, you need to stop this. You can't keep worrying about me. It isn't your job to keep me safe.'

'I've gotta go.' I hang up and swing my car around.

The Lamberts' street is small and crowded with run-down cars and onlookers. This isn't the kind of place where people call the police. Here they grab the popcorn for the show or more often their knuckledusters for the immersive experience.

I abandon my car in the middle of the road — too bad if it's an inconvenience — and race towards the commotion. I can hear shouting but can't make out what is being said over the noise of the crowd. I barge my way through. In front of the house, Mark has Peter by the throat, shoved up against the wall. The kid looks as though he's struggling to breathe.

'Who the fuck is he? I won't ask you again. If you don't tell me I'll kill you, you little shit. I don't give a damn about going to prison, I'll gladly do time for you. Understand?'

Peter nods furiously, his eyes bugging. His mum is tugging at Mark's sweater. 'Get off him! Get the fuck off him! He doesn't know anything!'

Jenny stands on the doorstep, staring in mute disbelief.

I push Nancy aside and reach out to grab Mark's free arm, but he swings it back and wallops me on the side of my face. Ignoring the intense pain, this time I get hold of his arm, pull it back and twist it up behind his back.

He turns his head and sees it's me. He stares wide-eyed at what no doubt is a fast-forming bruise and black eye. 'Shit, I didn't — It was an accident.' He releases Peter, who rubs at his neck while his mum fusses over him. I let go of Mark's arm. He stares at the floor and shakes his head. 'I know I can't bring her back. I just need to know who did it.'

Peter's mum, Nancy, glances at the pitiful, heartbroken father. 'Just go,' she says.

She turns her gaze on me. 'We don't wanna press any charges. Come on, Pete, get in.' She shoves Jenny and Peter into the house before spinning round towards the gathering. 'And you lot can fuck off, show's over.' She slams the door.

'Come on.' I touch Mark on the shoulder.

He flinches. 'I guess we're going to the station.'

'What for?'

'To book me.' He indicates my face. 'For that. I'm sorry.'

I believe him. Even so, I'm reluctant to let him go back home to Millie, not when he is so volatile.

'I really am sorry,' he repeats.

I sigh. 'I know you are. We aren't going to the station, Mark. You're going home to your wife and Sally. They need you. But this cannot happen again. Understood?'

He nods. I feel as if I'm handing him a beautifully wrapped but empty gift box.

'How did you get here?' I ask.

'On foot.'

'Come on then, I'll drive you.'

We make our way back to the car. The crowd parts like the Red Sea but they glare at me as though I'm a viper in their nest. They are practically programmed from birth to despise the police around here.

Mark sits in the passenger seat and looks out of his window, with the occasional surreptitious glance at my face. I hope he is sorry. If he's not, Millie really isn't safe in his home.

CHAPTER TWENTY-TWO

I pull up in front of the house and turn to Mark. 'I meant it when I said this can't happen again.' By now my face feels as though it has developed its own heartbeat.

Mark passes a hand across his eyes. 'I really am sorry. I didn't mean to . . . It won't happen again.'

'Come on then.' I open my car door and step out. Mark follows suit.

I notice Antonio's car parked behind Millie's. At least she won't be here alone. I follow Mark to apprise Millie and Ant of the situation. I doubt there will be any come-back on the part of Peter's family or mates but you never know. Millie and Ant need to be aware of the possibility, and Felicity too.

Felicity opens the front door before we reach it, Millie behind her. Felicity looks at my face and then at Mark. 'Tell me you didn't do that.'

Millie steps around Felicity to look more closely at my eye socket. 'Beth, what happened?' She turns to glare at Mark. 'Was this you?'

He nods, shamefaced and looks up at his wife. 'It was an accident. I . . . I was going for Peter, not her. I didn't mean to. I didn't even know she was there. I'm sorry.'

Felicity peers up and down the street. Curtains are twitching and a few people are standing outside, clearly listening in on our conversation. 'Just get in,' she barks at Mark.

He steps into the house like a reprimanded child.

'Where's Sally?' I ask.

Millie takes my hand. 'She's in her room with Ant, showing him her doll's house and books. She's taken quite a shine to him.' She peers at my face, frowning. 'You need to get that checked out at the hospital. Have you reported it?'

Felicity looks petrified. 'Have you?'

I shake my head. 'I haven't and I won't. However, if he does anything like that again, I *will* have to report him. I mean it, Felicity. I can't let something like this go twice.'

She nods. 'I know. The Lamberts, did they . . . ?'

'They didn't call the police. No one has. Go and be with him. He needs you. You need to lean on each other.' I turn to go.

'You still need to get checked out, Beth. You're in a state,' Millie says.

'Thanks, but I'll be fine. I'm not going to the hospital, there'd be questions.'

Felicity grimaces as though she is the one who's been hurt. 'I have a first aid kit. It's in the kitchen. Bottom cupboard beside the sink.'

'Okay, thanks,' Millie says. She takes my hand again and pulls me into the house.

Felicity goes into the lounge, where Mark is sitting with his head in his hands. She perches on the couch beside him. After a couple of beats, she pulls him into her arms. Millie leads me past them and through the double doors into the kitchen. She pushes me towards one of the chairs pulled up at the small table. 'Sit.'

'I don't need anything. I'm all right.'

'You're far from all right. It's a mess. You're a mess.'

After staring at me for a long moment she offers me a small smile.

'Wow, cheers, mate,' I say. 'I feel a lot better now.'

125

She retrieves a green first aid box from the cupboard and sets it down on the table. 'It's this or the hospital, you decide.'

'Fine.' I shrug.

She opens the box. 'So. What happened?' Millie lifts out a packet of cotton wool and a small plastic tub, which she fills from the kettle. 'Cooled boiled water. I need to get that cleaned up.'

'There's no dirt in it. It was his arm. I was trying to get him to let go of Peter. He had him by the neck up against the wall. He didn't mean it. This — it was an accident. He's grieving.'

'I know. But this . . .'

My face tingles as her fingers glide over my wound.

'Jesus, Beth, I'm so sorry.'

'Why?'

'I should have reported it, called it in officially. I would never have called you like that if I knew you'd be hurt. I'm really sorry, Beth.' Her eyes glisten with tears and it's all I can do not to wrap my arms around her.

'It was my decision to go alone. You did the right thing calling me. This family doesn't need to lose anyone else.'

She leans even closer to me and whispers, 'What if he did it, Beth? What if we're protecting the wrong person?'

I look past her to the lounge. 'He didn't. He's innocent.'

'How can you be sure?'

'Well, for starters he went after Peter to try and get Simon's identity out of him.'

'It could have been for show. A ruse. He could be playing us.'

'Do you really believe that?'

She shakes her head. 'No.'

I hold her wrist. 'Then trust yourself. You can read people better than anyone I know.'

'Well, you shouldn't have gone there alone. Anything could have happened.' She pulls her wrist free and continues to clean my wounds.

'I'm a DCI, it's my job.'

'Not to go in all guns blazing it isn't.' She touches my cheekbone. 'It's okay when you worry about me,' she says, 'but not when I worry about you. Why?'

I place my hand over hers. Our gazes are locked.

'Did you find it?' Felicity calls out.

I drop my hand quickly and smile sheepishly at Millie.

Felicity comes into the kitchen. 'I'm sorry Mark did that. He is too. This isn't him, you know. We're just ordinary people with normal lives. Well, we were. I don't know what we are anymore. But I know we aren't the kind of people to hurt anyone on purpose, we don't do violence. He's just, we're just—'

I turn to face her. 'I know. I understand.'

Felicity looks at me doubtfully. Still, I have given Mark a pass. Maybe this happening will help our relationship going forward. Perhaps they will start to trust me.

Millie puts a small plaster over a graze on my cheekbone. There's little she can do about the rest, and I refuse the packet of frozen peas she thrusts at me.

Mark doesn't say a word when I walk past on my way out. I hear the voices of Antonio and Sally upstairs. Millie follows me to the front door, opens it and steps back. She grabs my hand. 'Beth . . .'

'I'm okay.' I nod towards the lounge. 'You be careful.'

I turn to walk away, but stop. I want desperately to say something, but I don't know what. I struggle, and by the time I open my mouth to speak she's disappeared.

CHAPTER TWENTY-THREE

I wake up with a bruised cheek, a shiner and the headache from hell. I do my best to cover the damage with make-up and paracetamol then drive into work. I've been at the station a couple of hours when Detective Constable Aaliyah Kimathi rushes towards me with a blue folder tucked under her arm.

'Beth—' She looks at my face and does a double take. 'Shit, what happened to you?'

I clearly didn't do the best job then. Maybe I should invest in a better concealer.

'Oh, nothing. What you got?'

She hesitates a moment. 'That looks really bad.' She waits a beat and when I don't respond, she shrugs. 'Okay. Well, I was asked to bring you this.' She holds out the folder. 'It's everything the techies managed to get from Rose's mobile.'

'Thanks.' I grab it and plonk myself down at the near-est desk in the main office, eager to find out what they've uncovered. I am also actively avoiding bumping into any of the others, particularly Dillon. They'll ask what happened to my face and I'm not sure what I'm going to say.

Aaliyah hovers, peering over my shoulder at the print-out. I look up at her, squinting through my one good eye. The other is smarting like a bitch.

'Anything else?'

She rolls her hazel eyes, shakes her head then turns on her heel, aware I am getting rid of her. I find few things more irritating than having someone read over my shoulder, especially when I can sense they're full of burning questions that I'm not ready to answer.

I look through the contents of the folder and see they've emailed some photographs they found, plus a video clip. I log in to one of the computers and open my emails. The photographs show nothing unexpected — the usual selfies posed with two fingers in the air, lips pursed in the fish pout, something I will never understand. Rose and Jenny smiling, their arms linked, Rose's other arm outstretched to take the shot. They look happy, innocent. Seeing Rose like this fills me with sadness and utter rage.

Next, I open the video. The two-minute clip tells me exactly why Rose had been crying when her mum woke her up. It brings a whole new dimension to the case, one that has the power to obliterate what's left of an already crumbling family. It will also have every member of my team looking in the wrong direction. Because I don't believe Mark Danes killed his daughter. I don't believe he's the Brander. I didn't from the start, and after his attack on Peter Lambert, I'm even more certain of his innocence. But he *was* having an affair, and Rose not only found out about it, she recorded them. She had evidence.

For the team, for Dillon, that's motive. For me, it's a nightmare. On top of everything else, I failed to report his assault. He's demonstrated evidence of a volatile temperament and I have aided him in covering that up. I've even made Millie complicit in doing so.

If I go to the Danes and reveal his affair, the family will be ripped apart. Felicity was already struggling to look at her husband in the same way after what he did to me. She's barely managing to put one foot in front of the other. Sally needs her parents as a unit. I won't ignite the dynamite that blows their home apart. I refuse to damage them further. I know what that feels like. To be kicked while you're already scrambling around in the dark searching for your teeth.

Aside from everything else — and most importantly — I need the team focusing on Simon. If I let them in on this, admit he assaulted Peter and injured me, that he had an affair and Rose knew of it, the consequences could derail the investigation. Not unless I tell them about the phone and the messages I've received, which I can't do. I have no choice. I have to look the other way for now. I need to find out more about Simon, enough that this damn video won't fuck up the entire case.

I take the page informing us of the emailed video and photographs from the folder and slip it into my pocket. Dillon will get the same emails and they'll be uploaded to the system, but in the meantime I can play ignorant. The text messages are all typical for a teenage girl. There is nothing in them referring to the affair or anything else that could impact the investigation. If I make that page vanish for a while, it will hopefully buy me precious time before I am forced to deal with it. At some stage Dillon or someone else will flag it up, so I need to move fast.

If Dillon finds out I've failed to act on information about Mark's affair and Rose's knowledge of it, I'll not only be off the case, I'll be out of a job. If she finds out about Mark losing it with Peter, hitting me, and me saying nothing, I'll be done for here. If she finds out about the mobile I have tucked away in my inside pocket, it's all over.

I am breaking rules left, right and centre. The ice I'm skating on is so thin a falling feather could shatter it.

CHAPTER TWENTY-FOUR

I take a quick look through the door of the MIR. Heads are down, fingers hitting keyboards, phones clamped to ears. Quietly, I close the door again. I can't tell them where I'm going or about the video I have just seen. I don't want to lie, and neither do I want to bring attention to my injuries, not yet. If Dillon finds out that I'm about to go against her orders and approach Danielle, she will take me off the case. I have to speak to Danielle *then* convince Dillon it was worth risking a complaint of harassment. Sometimes it is better to beg forgiveness than to ask permission.

Rain with hail the size of small pebbles is hammering it down by the time I arrive at Preston's Riversway Docklands. The water level is high, the boats frantically bobbing up and down. There is a tall concrete wall running the length of the river to guard against flooding. If you look over the black metal railing alongside the path, there is a sheer drop down to the water, which is a murky brown. Today, it smells of blocked drains.

In summer the docklands are a beautiful place to spend an afternoon. I love coming here to have lunch at the riverside in the beer garden of the Ribble Pilot, to stroll the length of the docks taking in the scenery, admiring the array of sailboats. Today it feels oppressive, as though the weather is mirroring the storm in my mind, my thoughts churning like the water. I hold my hands over my head in a vain attempt to shield it from the fusillade of hail and hurry to Starburst House. I press the buzzer and wait, feeling sick to my stomach for more reasons than I can count.

'Yes? What?' Danielle sounds harassed. There's crying in the background, loud and insistent.

I rest my forehead against the wall beside the buzzer. I contemplate saying nothing and walking away.

'Who is it? If you don't speak, I'm going, and I won't answer if you buzz again.'

'It's Beth.' I stand up straight and take a steadying breath. 'It's Beth. Can I talk to you? Please, Danielle.'

'Are you for real? Seriously? You're still bothering me after we spoke to your boss?'

We?

'It — Celine — matters more to me than losing my case, even my damn job. Please, Danielle.' I'm begging. She's my best hope right now. 'Two years ago, I made you and your parents a promise. I made Celine a promise. I want to keep it. Please help me keep it.'

I wait.

The door buzzes.

I push through and dash up the stairs, reaching Danielle's apartment just as she opens the door. The baby's ear-splitting screams reverberate along the hallway.

She gawps at me. 'Jesus, what happened?'

I'd almost forgotten my face. Awareness makes it throb again. 'You should see the other guy,' I say with a slight smile.

Danielle shrugs and purses her lips. The screaming from inside the apartment intensifies. She turns to go in. 'I'm coming, Ava. Jeez, I'm coming, all right?' She stalks inside, leaving me to follow her into the kitchen, where Ava sits writhing in her highchair, banging her tray with her fists. With not a little difficulty, Danielle unclips Ava and carries her to the lounge. Ava's kicking, hitting, biting. This picture of the joys of motherhood makes me extremely grateful that I'm in no danger of falling pregnant.

Danielle sits Ava on the play mat. She stays on it for all of two seconds before throwing herself into a determined crawl and scurrying to her mother's feet to continue her tirade. Danielle lifts her up rather roughly and marches the screaming, purple-faced baby from the room. Four-year-old Erin, meanwhile, holds her teddy tight. She looks anxious.

Danielle comes back, looking flustered. 'She hasn't had a nap yet. She's shattered. I've put her down with a bottle. I know she should be coming off them now—' (as if I have the slightest clue as to what she should or shouldn't be doing) — 'but if it gets me an hour . . .' She spreads her hands help-lessly. 'So, what d'you want from me?'

'Your help. I think you might know something, even if you don't realise you do. I shouldn't be here because of the call you made. I'm sorry for upsetting you, I really am. But surely we both want the same thing — to get this person off the streets once and for all. I don't want anyone else to get hurt.'

'I don't know what you think I can say that would help. I've told you everything I know, over and over. I already feel like I've let Celine down because I can't help you. I want to, but I can't. And this—' she gestures to me — 'you showing up all the time, just makes everything worse. Tom is worried about me. *I'm* worried about me. I mean, look at the state of me.'

I have to concede that Danielle is a shadow of the young woman Millie and I visited only days ago. She'd been stylish, almost glamorous, organised. Her home had toys around, but it was clean and tidy. Today, her hair is in need of a wash, she's wearing no make-up, her clothes look thrown on and are creased to hell. The girls are the same. One child is screaming from her cot and the other looks on worriedly as her mum barely holds tears at bay.

Is this my fault? 'I'm sorry. I—'

'Wait. Can I say something else first?'

'Of course.'

Danielle looks down at Erin — a single tear slips beneath her glasses, tracing her cheek. A small smile plays at her mouth as she watches her daughter. 'I was angry that you'd let Celine down, not once but twice. First when it happened, then when you came with all these promises. You'd do everything you could, everything in your power, blah blah blah. It wasn't enough. And now you're here a third time because he's been free long enough to do it again. I was angry and hurt for Celine, and now for Rose and her family. I know what they have to go through. Tom was so furious that I'd been pushed back into it again. After last time I had problems, big problems. I couldn't deal with it. He's scared shitless of what will happen if you fail again. He's terrified he'll lose me. He *begged* me to make that call to your boss. He pleaded with me to put an end to my involvement. I couldn't say no.'

She takes a deep breath. 'I don't want to scare him. I don't want to lose myself again, but if I can, I'll help. I have to. She's my baby sister. Until you turned up today and said what you did downstairs, I didn't know how strongly you felt, but now I understand that I'm not alone. When you stepped back the last time, when you gave up—'

I go to speak, but she shakes her head and continues. 'Let me finish. I thought you'd stopped caring. I thought you wanted to move on from us, from a case you couldn't solve easily. At that point, I honestly believed that it had all been lip service after all, that I'd been suckered into believing you. I reckoned you'd seen Celine as a chance to boost your career, but it hadn't worked out. I was angry, completely fucking furious. But now I can see it on your face, and I heard it in your voice before. You care about this, about Celine. I know you want to help us. I want to, as well.'

Danielle looks at Erin, her tears fogging up her glasses. 'Their auntie should be playing with them, taking them to feed the ducks. But she's just a body in a bed, and my daughters will never get to know her. They'll never know who she was, who she should be now. I'll try to help as much as I can. Tom doesn't understand — how could he? He tries, but he didn't know Celine before. He hasn't *lost* her the way we have — me, Mum and Dad. He's thinking of me. I know it might piss you off, 'cause he's a detective and you think he should be on your side but he's my husband. He will always be on *my* side. He'll always do what he thinks is best for me.' She looks at Erin. 'For us. But I have to do what's right for Celine.'

I struggle to fight my own tears. 'Thank you, Danielle. I really do appreciate it. Thank you.'

'Tom isn't going to be happy about this,' she says. 'And I can't lie to him. We don't keep secrets.'

'I would never ask that of you. I can speak to him if you think it might help?'

Danielle shakes her head vigorously. 'God, no. I'll talk to him.'

'Fair enough. Whatever you think is best. But if you change your mind . . .'

'I won't. But thank you,' she says.

'Firstly, I am going to be passing on some very sensitive information. It's early days in this investigation. I'm trusting you with this. Please don't talk about it to anyone, it could compromise the case.'

'I won't.'

'We do have someone we are interested in speaking with. I'm going to describe him to you. I want you to think as far back as you can, before Celine's attack and since too. I want you to ask yourself whether anyone you can think of shares any of these attributes. It might be someone you knew, or even just saw hanging around. Remember, appearances change over time. It's been six years and he might look quite different now.'

Danielle takes a deep breath, as though she is preparing herself. She looks petrified. I wonder how bad her problems were after the last time I'd let them down. I could be throwing a grenade into a young family's home, one that is already plagued by tragedy.

The crying stops. Danielle smiles. 'Must have tired herself out.' Erin plays with her mum's hands. 'Okay, go on.'

'Right. He has brown skin, like mine. He's tall, over six feet. Muscular build. Shaved or bald head. He's handsome, apparently.' *Well fit* was Jenny Lambert's description, but obviously I won't repeat that.

Danielle listens impassively. I wish Millie was here, she would catch any flicker of a reaction.

'Any of that sound familiar? Anyone come to mind, anyone at all?'

Danielle looks to be mulling something over, deciding whether to reveal it. Whatever it is, it's something she didn't know before. She's made a connection. I see the very moment it dawns. I wait, wanting to shake it out of her.

Slowly, a veil falls across Danielle's eyes. She shakes her head. 'I'm sorry. I really can't think of anyone.'

She is lying through her teeth. If Millie's taught me anything, it's how to spot a liar from miles away. Danielle Spencer is bullshitting me. Why?

It would be futile to argue. That would only result in another phone call to Dillon. I'll have to find another way to get to the truth. If Danielle knows something, if she recognises the description of Simon, there's a chance her parents will too. There must be a connection between Simon and Celine. Something like that can be traced.

I leave, seething. How can Danielle keep it to herself? One young girl is already dead and Celine, her own sister, is in the state she is. How could she? What or who could be so important that she'll risk the life of someone else's daughter and sister and let the person who hurt Celine remain free? I storm down the stairs and dash to my car, oblivious to the hail. I have to get to the Wilsons' house before Danielle calls them — or Dillon calls me.

CHAPTER TWENTY-FIVE

I knock on the front door and stand fidgeting until John Wilson finally answers. At the sight of me, his eyes go skyward. 'You got him?'

'No.'

'Why are you here then?'

'Can I come in?'

'Diana isn't doing so good since your last visit. I think it would be best if—'

'Please? I just have a few questions. It — you — could really help.'

He kicks the door open with his heel. I brush past him into the narrow hallway.

'Who is it?' Diana calls from the lounge. She sounds as though she's just woken up.

When I go in, she is pulling herself up into a sitting position on the couch. She has a pillow behind her and an orange blanket is draped across her legs. She points to the armchairs. 'What on earth happened to you, Detective?'

I sit in the chair Millie sat in last time. 'Just an accident. I'm here because we have a person of interest.'

John's eyes light up.

'No name as yet, but a description of him. Now, this has to stay between us, okay?'

John nods. Diana's gaze seems to be going in and out of focus. Her movements are sluggish.

'You okay, Diana?' I ask.

John strokes his wife's upper arm. 'She's on medication for anxiety. She's been on it for years, ever since . . . Anyway, the doc upped her dose. It'll take a while for her to adjust.'

'Tell us.' She speaks very carefully. 'The description.'

I watch them closely while I repeat what I'd said to Danielle. This time there is no look of recognition. Only hope, followed swiftly by disappointment.

John takes hold of his wife's hand. 'I don't know anyone like that. No one comes to mind.' He looks at Diana. 'Can you think of anyone, sweetheart?'

She slowly shakes her head. They are not lying. They have no idea. Maybe someone will occur to them later, but for now, this is another dead end. Danielle, on the other hand, knows something.

I leave the Wilsons feeling like an utter shit. I built up their hopes only to shatter them. I've done it too many times. I'm not surprised they don't welcome my visits. They've yielded nothing but disappointment of the worst kind.

The rain and hail have vanished and the sun is edging through a thicket of clouds, a rainbow in the distance. I tread heavily back to my car and climb in. A loud ringtone in my pocket causes me to jump so that my knees hit the steering wheel. It's my own phone but for a second, I thought it was the other one. I pull it out, expecting the call to be from Yvette. It's Dillon.

'Ma'am?' Here we go. Danielle must have been straight on the blower after I left.

'We need you here. Now.' Her voice is urgent. I detect panic.

'What's happened?'

'Jennifer Lambert's been taken.'

I close my eyes. It isn't Millie, or Aunt Margie, or Yvette, or Amer. It isn't any of the people I expected it to be. I can't lie to myself, I'm relieved. But Jenny? Another kid?

'What? When? Where from?'

'Just get here, will you? 7 Salvador Street.'

'Is it him? He doesn't kidnap, what makes you think—?' Maybe it's someone else. Or better yet, perhaps Jenny has simply wandered off, run away.

'It's him. He left his fuckin' mark, the bastard. Get here, Beth.'

I drive like the wind, taking corners practically on two wheels. Jenny had seen him, but so had the lads. Taking her is another escalation.

He will kill her. If it *is* him, if Dillon is certain, then Jenny is as good as dead.

* * *

I swing the car into Salvador Street and squeal to a halt just ahead of the outer cordon. Dillon is waiting, her face like thunder. The press are beginning to gather, trying to catch photos of what lies beyond the police tape. Vultures, the lot of them. That the cordons are in place doesn't concern me, it only means the officer first on scene has done their job. But that the press has beat me here *en masse* seems off to me. Dillon would have contacted me as soon as she knew what this was. I have a sinking feeling I'm about to find out that this isn't a simple grab-and-snatch. Jenny Lambert is in real trouble, and judging by the activity around the house, she's already been hurt.

CHAPTER TWENTY-SIX

'What the hell's going on?' We've climbed into Dillon's car so as not to risk any of the vultures overhearing.

'What the fuck happened to your face?'

'Nothing. It doesn't matter. What's going on?'

'I'll let it go seeing as I don't have the time or the inclination to fucking do battle with you, Beth. But seriously — get that looked at. There's press crawling all over the show and I don't want them seeing my officers looking like they've just gone ten rounds with Mike Tyson.'

'Fine, but what the—?'

'You aren't going to believe this.' Dillon runs her fingers through her spiky blonde hair. It's a habit that crops up whenever she's under stress. Judging from the colour of her face, her blood pressure must be sky-high. 'Jenny Lambert left a note to say she was meeting Simon. He'd asked her not to tell anyone but she did anyway. You'd think a kid that had the sense to leave a note telling her family where she'd be would do so because they realised they were walking into a dangerous situation. I mean, fuck me, why didn't she just, you know, not fuckin' go? Stupid, stupid girl.'

I shake my head. 'How do you know he has her? Has he left a sign?'

'His mark. His fuckin' brand. He's gone off-the-charts psycho with this one.'

I feel sick. 'What do you mean?'

'He branded her like the others—'

'How do you know?'

'Give me a flaming second, would you?'

She holds up her hand. 'Sorry, sorry. I'm just up the wall with this sicko. He cut the brand from her and left it behind. Along with a polaroid. I mean, who even uses them anymore? It's proof I suppose, because you can see Jenny's face and the open wound on her shoulder. He left the brand, her skin, and the photo for us. He knew we'd be coming. Maybe he did it because she told him she'd left the note. Or he might have been planning to kill her but was worried he'd get caught in the act, I just don't know. I'm hoping you'll discern more, or that he at least got slack forensics-wise. Rush job, panic, maybe he left something useable. Right now, that's our best hope. Oh, and I take it you haven't checked your emails for a while? You should really be on top of them, Beth, but I'm guessing you've had other things going on.' She indicates my cheek.

I try my best to look puzzled. 'Sorry, I haven't checked my emails lately. Why?'

'Rose Danes recorded a video of her dad all over another woman. Amer checked her out. She has a solid alibi. Mark was looking like a possibility. We all know we're more likely to be killed by someone close to us than a stranger.'

'*Was* looking? You mean he isn't now?' I hope I'm disguising my relief.

'I was on the verge of calling you when Jenny was found. I was going to get you to bring him in, question him under caution. But Millie was with the Danes when Jenny disappeared. There's no way Mark could be responsible. The exercise book you found in Rose's room — she'd written how much she hated her dad. The kid was in turmoil.' Dillon looks down and shakes her head.

'Has anyone spoken to him about it?' I ask.

'No. That family are going through enough as it is. At this point, it seems more cruel than necessary.'

The inside of the car is lit up with a flash so bright I have to blink away white spots. 'What the fuck?'

I look out of the window and see a journalist retreating fast. He waves his camera triumphantly.

'Oh no you fuckin' don't, you piece of sh—' I jump from the car and leg it after him.

Dillon catches up before I can get stuck in. The cocky little git is standing in front of me, staring me down.

Dillon steps between us. 'What paper are you from?'

'I'm freelance. What of it? This is a public space.'

Dillon turns and points to her vehicle. 'And that is my car. *Not* public. This—' she points to the police tape — 'is a crime scene.' She jabs a finger in his direction. 'And *you* had better watch your step. *Never*, I repeat, *never* do anything like that again, or I'll have you arrested.'

'What the hell for?'

'Oh, there'll be something, I have no doubt about that. Now, stay out of our way. Do not show up at any of our press conferences. You will *not* be welcome. Are we understanding each other? I don't appreciate lack of respect or jumped-up little scumbags taking liberties.'

Dillon grins at me. 'Okay. I think we're finished here.' She catches hold of my arm. 'Come on. I want you suited and booted.'

We head towards the cordon, my footsteps heavy.

The house is dank, filled with a pungent stench of old onions and off mushrooms. Dillon and I are in full forensic gear. She wants me to see the scene first-hand.

Behind the fluttering tape are a few terraced houses. The house on the left is boarded up and looks long since abandoned. Our crime scene is empty. There are no curtains, nothing but a few pieces of old, falling-apart furniture. Peeling newspaper has sporadically and crudely been fastened to the windows with duct tape — a poor attempt at hiding what's going on inside. There are no bulbs in any of the light fittings, so the crime scene officers have had to set up lamps. This place was ripe for the Brander's purposes.

I follow the stepping plates into the lounge. 'Do we know who owns the house?'

Dillon's voice is muffled by her face mask. 'They're waiting on planning permission to knock down these houses and turn them into an apartment complex. They've hit various stumbling blocks, so they've been empty a while. This one was due to be boarded up tomorrow.'

We navigate our way to the area of red on the floor, our plastic shoe covers slipping on the stepping plates. It smells sickeningly coppery.

'Who might know they were due to board this one tomorrow?'

The flash of a camera makes us turn. I half-expect to see the journalist's face pushed up against the window, but it's Mick Reinhardt, one of the crime scene techs, busy photographing the scene.

His eyes peer over his mask. 'Am I disturbing you?' He's short and skinny, with long hair that will be in his usual ponytail underneath his hairnet and hood. His grey eyes gleam in the glare of a nearby tripod lamp.

Dillon waves a hand dismissively. 'No, carry on.'

Mick gives a small nod and continues taking pictures. Dillon is staring down at a polaroid lying on the floor.

In it, Jenny Lambert looks stricken. She is curled away from the camera, and most likely the person holding it. Her eyes are wide, her cheeks soaked in tears. Blood is pouring from her shoulder. He clearly forced her to pose for the photo. Terror is a powerful motivator.

I close my eyes for a moment before looking at what is on the ground beside the photo. Lying on the dirt-encrusted floorboards is a crudely cut piece of bloody, curling flesh, the dark shape of a raven seared into it. I can hardly imagine the pain and fear Jenny must have endured as he burned her and then sliced her skin away.

What would make him snap like this, so suddenly, so brutally? Why would he take this chance? And why Jenny? Why now and not then, when he killed Rose? He's mocking us, taunting us. He will kill and kill again, while all I have is a grainy image and a description that could fit any number of men. Who will he go after next?

For some reason, after all these years, he's just getting warmed up. I need to figure out why. I have no choice but to go back to Danielle Spencer and make her talk. Lives depend on it. Jenny's — if she isn't already dead — and everyone I love. Maybe my own, too.

I look at Dillon. She's waiting for me to say something.

'You said she left a note. Where? Who found it?'

'She left it on her bed, they aren't sure when. Peter Lambert found it and went after her. He trampled all over the damn place. We have him at the station now, giving his statement. Forensics have his clothes and trainers — again. Damn idiot rushed in here trying to save his sister single-handed. Doesn't trust the police apparently.' Dillon arches a brow.

'Is he a suspect?'

'Do you think he should be?'

I look down at the torn flesh, the polaroid, and sigh. 'Sadly, no. That would be too easy. We have him. Anyway, she's his sister.' Then I think of Danielle and what she's omitting to say. Perhaps those closest to us are the people we should most fear. After all, we'd never see it coming, would we?

'Simon, if that's even his name, is the mystery,' I say. 'He's the person not making himself known. I know you don't want me to get single-minded about it, but it's him, I know it is.' *And he's made himself known to me.*

Dillon glances at the torn flesh, the polaroid, and shrugs. 'I'm going to go with your gut at this point. We have nothing else worth shit right now.' Her mask has slid into her eyes, and she pushes it down. 'Millie is still with the Danes, isn't she? I need someone with the Lamberts. The mother is known to us — theft, prostitution, a couple of possession charges. Poor kid didn't stand a chance. Her stepfather,

Cormack O'Brien, is a waste of space. Mother doesn't know who Jenny's biological father is. Or she won't say. Peter's dad committed suicide when he was a baby. Tough house to grow up in. No wonder Jenny's a law unto herself.'

'I'll get someone round there. As far as I know, Millie is still with the Danes. She hasn't reported otherwise anyway. I'll get a message to her. Antonio Giovanelli is with her. Mark was being a little volatile. I was concerned for her safety.'

'Is that what happened to your face? Mark Danes?'

I shrug. 'It was an accident. It's been dealt with.'

'If you say so. I'm not gonna push the issue right now, there's no time. We're spread so thin, we might have to call on other departments. The Lancashire Force Major Investigation Team have said they are willing to step up.'

'You mean take over?'

'No, Beth. I mean help us. The only thing that matters is catching this guy. Stopping him before he kills Jennifer Lambert or anyone else. There's no room for egos here.'

I stare at my feet, feeling about three feet tall. I sound like a petulant child. But I don't want to risk the focus shifting from Simon. I need to be the one steering our ship to keep us on course.

'Yeah, I'm sorry. I know what's at stake. Call them in if you think they could help.'

'We should get out of here, we're in the way,' Dillon says.

The room has suddenly become crowded. Forensics are moving through it rhythmically, gathering evidence, photographing, videoing. Dillon and I edge carefully back along the stepping plates. We are both relieved to step outside and remove our suffocating forensic gear.

'See you back at the station then,' Dillon says.

'I have somewhere I need to go first. I won't be long.'

I hurry away, hoping beyond hope that Dillon won't ask me any more questions. I rush headlong to my car. Dillon did say she's prepared to go with my gut, but I can't be sure how far I can push things before she reins me in.

'Beth?'

Damn. I trudge reluctantly back to Dillon. 'Yeah?'

'Where are you going?'

I am simply unable to lie to Dillon's face and be believed. 'To speak with Danielle Spencer.'

'You're joking!'

'I have to, ma'am. She knows something that could save Jenny's life. I have to try.'

'After six years, what could she possibly know that's of any significance?'

'I went to see her earlier—' Dillon opens her mouth to speak. 'I know, I know. But I did. I gave her Simon's description, and she knew him—'

'She told you that?'

'Well, no, she didn't. She lied to me, but I could tell. She recognised his description. She clammed up after that, and she'd been chatty enough before. I left, and went to her parents—'

'Did they recognise him?'

'No.'

'Were they lying?'

'I don't think so.'

'But you're sure Danielle was. Why would she?'

'That's what I need to find out.' I look back at the house. 'When was Jenny taken? What time? How long ago?'

'We don't know.'

I grab Dillon's arm. 'Was it today? Was it this afternoon?'

'Possibly. Why?'

'I gave that description to Danielle. I went to see her parents. She had time to . . . She wouldn't have, would she?'

'What do you mean, Beth?'

The sounds — the chatter from the nearby cordon, the neighbours' muttering, the cameras clicking — all grow distant. This could have happened because of me. 'It's my fault. I did this.'

'What are you talking about? Beth, look at me.' Dillon grips my arm.

146

'Danielle must've . . . I think she might have told some-one — Simon, whoever he is. Danielle warned him, she must have, it's too big a coincidence. Something pushed him into making a move. It must be because I spoke to her. He knows we have his description. She told him. She must have.' My head is swimming.

'Beth, think about what you're suggesting here. Danielle's sister was attacked. She's been left in a vegetative state ever since. Why on God's green earth would she warn the person who did it? Why would she help him cover his tracks and hurt another kid? She knows he's killed. I don't buy your theory. You need to get yourself back to the station and go over it again with a clear head.'

'She recognised Simon's description, I know she did.'

'Then have a breather and then go and speak to her. I'll back you on that. You know I trust your instincts, I wouldn't have appointed you Deputy SIO otherwise. If you're saying she lied, then I believe there's a good chance she did. I'm prepared to go with your gut, but there are limits. As for Danielle warning Simon, I don't believe that for one minute. Speak to her. Find out what she knows, what she didn't say before. Be careful. You don't want her clamming up again. Go easy.'

'I will. Thanks, ma'am. For trusting me.'

I run to my car. The clock is ticking. Jenny might already be dead. But while there's a chance, I have to do whatever it takes to find her. Danielle *will* speak this time. Dillon doesn't buy into my theory, which means I'm in this alone. But I won't let another kid die if I can do anything at all to save her.

CHAPTER TWENTY-SEVEN

I've been leaning on the buzzer of 2B Starburst House for almost two minutes straight, muttering, 'Come on, Danielle, come on. Be home.' I'm on the verge of giving up when I hear the tinny sound of the speaker.

'Hello?'

'What?' Tom snaps. 'Who is it?'

'It's Beth. I need to speak with Danielle, urgently. Please.'

'Well, you can't. You need to leave her alone. Who do you think you are, coming here and upsetting my wife? And after she put in a complaint. She doesn't want to speak with you. Now, leave, or I'll be talking to Superintendent West. Hell, I'll go over her head if I have to. Go. D'you hear me? Go away.'

I grit my teeth. I refuse to let him prevent me from saving Jenny. Danielle knows something, and he might too. The photos on that blasted mobile flash through my mind. 'Why are you even home? I'm not going anywhere until I've spoken to Danielle.'

'Then I'm calling your superior. I'm going to lodge a further complaint. You want that, do you? And in answer to your question, I'm home because my wife needs me. You're putting her through hell — again. It's like you're frigging obsessed with her.'

'I'm sorry for any upset I've caused but Danielle wants to help. You can't prevent her from talking to me, Tom. I understand you're worried about her, and that you're trying to protect her, but this isn't the way. Come on, you're a detective, surely you want this case closed as much as I do? For the victims, for Danielle. Buzz me in, Tom, let me speak with her.'

I pause. 'Well?'

A long sigh reverberates through the speaker. 'I'll come down.' He clicks off before I can ask whether Danielle will be with him.

Tom Spencer appears at the bottom of the stairs looking dishevelled and sweaty in light blue jeans and a cream jumper. He peers at me through the glass pane of the door. Today, the cowlick looks scruffy rather than boyish. He yanks the door open and stands practically toe to toe with me. 'Danielle isn't here.'

'Where is she?'

'With Celine. Visiting. I told her she should spend some time with her sister. She needed to after you came here and dredged it all up again. Have you any idea how hard this is for her? Do you realise how fragile she is?'

'What about Celine? Doesn't she deserve some justice?'

His grip tightens on the door, his knuckles whitening.

'What are you so scared of?' I demand.

His shoulders slump. 'I'm scared of losing my wife, that's what. I almost did two years ago. She had a breakdown, you know. She became a stranger to me, to her family. We won't survive all that again.'

'I'm sorry for that, I truly am. But I'm here now because there's been a further development. I have to speak with Danielle. And this time she needs to be honest with me.'

'Are you seriously accusing her of lying? What do you mean, anyway? What development?'

'A young girl has been taken.'

'*Taken*? What's that supposed to mean?'

'Abducted, kidnapped. A teenage girl, and we believe it's the same person who hurt Celine and murdered Rose Danes. We need to find her before . . .'

I let the rest lie heavily in the air between us.

'How can you know it's him? I mean, he's never done that before, has he? He's never taken anyone.'

'No, he hasn't.'

'Then what makes you think it's him? This kid might have run away. It could be anything.'

'He let us know, that's how.' Everything to do with the Brander case is on a need-to-know basis and DC Thomas Spencer does not need to know, not if we don't want to hand the defence a conflict-of-interest argument should it ever get to trial.

'How?'

'That's not for me to say at this stage, but there's little doubt.'

Tom takes a step back and releases the door. 'I need to tell my wife.'

'Perhaps you can see why I need to speak with her. I take it she has the children with her?'

'What? No.'

'Then where are they?'

'Erm, her dad has them. He's taken them to the park, to run off some energy.'

'Come on then,' I say. 'I'll give you a lift.'

Tom pins me with his stare, his brown eyes unwavering. 'Oh no you won't. Don't even think about going to see Danielle at the home. She won't be there by now, anyway.'

'There's a girl's life on the line here, Tom.' I can't understand why he doesn't feel compelled to try and help. As a man, a brother-in-law, a husband, even more as a detective. How can he turn away and let another child die? 'Please, Tom, you must care.'

'Of course I bloody care. But I'll tell you what I care about most of all — my family, and you are a threat to them. So, for one last time, we have nothing more to say to you.'

He turns and treads heavily up the stairs.

CHAPTER TWENTY-EIGHT

My sleep last night was fitful, and my eyes sting with tiredness. Jenny has been missing since yesterday and it's as though I can viscerally sense the passing of every second. It's the Lambert press appeal this afternoon and I have barely anything to tell them. I'm in the hall, hesitating outside Dillon's office. The thought of informing her of my wasted trip to see Danielle yesterday and our lack of progress makes me want to turn tail and run.

A hand grips my arm. I jump and spin around, coming face to face with a smiling Aaliyah.

'Sorry, did I scare you?'

My first thought is that they've found Jenny. 'I'm fine, what's up? Have they found her?'

She shakes her head. 'Sorry, no, it's not that. I have something to show you though. CCTV has finally thrown a nugget our way.' She grins excitedly. 'I decided to cast the net a little wider. I mean, what the hell, right?'

'What have you got?'

'It's him. The Brander. I'm sure of it. Come on.'

We sprint along to the computer-lined room Aaliyah is primarily calling home these days. We sit down, so close our thighs not only touch, they rub together. Aaliyah points to the image on the screen in front of us. 'Look, the clever git. That's why no one spotted it till now.'

I lean forward. The image on the screen is a long shot of a man of the same height and build as Simon. It's time- and date-stamped the night of Rose's murder. He's standing outside a late-night shop wearing a dark anorak and trainers. I peer closely at the screen and can just about make out that the tell-tale Nike tick is there but that it's been coloured in. Aaliyah's right, he is a clever git.

'There's more.' Aaliyah's grin widens.

My lips twitch. 'He went in?'

'He did.' She moves the frames forward until we have our money shot square in front of our eyes.

He wasn't so clever after all. He must have thought we'd overlook him. 'Where is this? How far from Balfour Street?'

'An hour or so's walk. That's why it's taken us so long to find, and why he wasn't spotted the first time.' Aaliyah jabs a finger at the figure on the screen. 'You know what he's wearing? It's one of those pocket rain macs. He must have had it with him, plus a felt-tip or marker or something for his trainers.'

I'm impressed by Aaliyah's powers of observation. She's going to go far if she carries on like this.

'He thought it all through, though why he took the risk of going into the shop, I don't know.' She shakes her head. 'But there he is, right fuckin' there.' She prods the screen again and sits back, grinning in triumph. 'Good shot, eh?'

'How did he pay?'

Aaliyah's smile slips. 'Cash.'

'Great. Might've known. Did he touch anything? Rewind it, let me see it again, slowly. I want to see if he puts his filthy hands on anything.'

Aaliyah plays the entirety of the footage in slow motion. We examine Simon from every angle, but he doesn't touch a thing apart from what he buys.

'Did you see how carefully he picked it up?' I say. 'By the corner so he didn't come into contact with anything else? What was it, could you tell?'

She shrugs. 'Crisps, I think. Two packets.'

'So, murdering a fifteen-year-old kid gave him the munchies. He thought he'd stop for a snack on the way home. What a complete wacko. We need to get someone down there to speak to whoever was working that night. They might recognise him. Who knows, maybe he lives locally? Maybe we'll finally get lucky.'

'Amer already has someone on their way.'

'Ah, good.' I can't help but feel a little side-lined, redundant even. While I've been out achieving nothing, my team have been making strides without me. I'm pleased, but at the same time rather disappointed that they haven't needed me.

I scrutinise Simon's face and realise there's something familiar about him. I rack my brains, but I can't think what it is. He has a relatively long nose, which gives him an almost regal aspect. His eyes are dark, the exact colour indistinguishable from the image on the screen, fringed with long lashes. His lips are full — Aunt Margie would call them kissable. He's tall and muscular, handsome. He has olive skin much like mine, just as Jenny said. He could have any woman he wanted, so why would he do this? But then predators aren't about what they can and can't have, are they? They're about power. Taking what they want, when they want. I can understand why a mixed-up fifteen-year-old kid like Jenny would be drawn to him.

I can't make out his ethnic origin, I'd hazard a guess at him being mixed race like me. But Asian, Black? I can't be sure. Hell, I don't know my own ethnicity. My colour comes from my father, the father I've never met. Half of me is a mystery. As a teenager I would look in the mirror and try to trace the similarities to my mother. My mouth, my nose, for example, they come from my mum, as I've seen from Aunt Margie's photographs of her. My eyes, on the other hand, are nothing like my mother's. Hers were ocean blue, mine are brown. Aunt Margie calls them chocolate orbs. I'm taller than my mum too, my figure slightly fuller, breasts larger. I have family out there I've yet to meet. One day I'll find the time to look for my other half. Meanwhile, I have to find Simon, the Brander and Jenny Lambert, and keep the people I do have in my life safe.

I walk away with a few large printouts of Simon. The idea that he is somehow familiar niggles. Is that how Danielle felt? Like a word you can't bring to mind even though it's on the tip of your tongue.

I am about to open the door to the MIR when Millie careens into me. 'Beth, you need to come with me now!'

'What's happened? Is it the Danes? Jenny?'

'It's Yvette.' Millie's face is ashen. Her hand grips mine so tightly it hurts.

CHAPTER TWENTY-NINE

Millie pulls me out of the building. At the top of the steps overlooking the river she stops and takes both my hands in hers.

'For God's sake, Millie, what is it? Where's Yvette?'

Millie's grip tightens. 'We need to go to Preston City Police Station.'

'Why?'

'I stopped by with some paperwork and Yvette was there.' Millie looks intently at me. 'She's been attacked. She was messed up badly. She asked me not to tell you. I know as an officer I should respect that. Hell, as a woman I should probably respect that, but as your best friend I had to tell you. She needs you.'

'What happened to her? Was she mugged? Jumped? What, Millie?'

'She didn't tell me everything, but what she said was that she was working late a few nights ago—'

'Nights? Plural?'

'Yes. She was waiting for a late booking at the salon, she was on her own. Someone, a man, went in, and he . . . he . . .'

Oh, my God. Simon. 'He didn't . . ?

'She was physically and sexually assaulted. She wasn't raped. He tried but thank God, he couldn't.'

'He didn't mark her, did he?

'Mark her?'

'Was it *him*? The Brander?'

'There's no brand. It wasn't him.'

For a moment I feel immeasurable relief. It wasn't him. But someone hurt her, and I wasn't there to protect her. 'When, Millie? When exactly? Who did it?'

'The night before Rose Danes was murdered. They don't know who it was. They're looking for him.'

'She called me,' I say. 'She was upset. I told her she had no idea what real worries were. Oh fuck. I'm an asshole. A nasty, horrible, selfish—'

'Stop it, Beth. Stop it. You didn't know.'

'I didn't ask though, did I? I didn't listen. I didn't give her a fuckin' chance to tell me. That night I stayed at Aunt Margie's. I left her alone. She's been staying at her mum's ever since, I've barely been home. She needed me and I wasn't there.'

'You didn't leave her alone, she was with her mum. And you can be with her now. Come on. I'll drive.'

I turn and look back towards the station. 'The case . . .' I begin. I can scarcely believe I'm still putting work first. Even now, my first thought is of my case, just like Aunt Margie said. But this time it's pushing into my personal life in a potentially deadly way. It has to come first, for Yvette and everyone else.

Millie leads me down the stairs, and this time I let her. If only I could tear myself in two, or three, or four. I'm being pulled in different directions, drawn and quartered.

CHAPTER THIRTY

Yvette is sitting in the waiting room of Preston City Police Station, her head low, her red hair hiding her face. She doesn't look up when the door opens and closes, doesn't even look up when we draw near.

Some people would be hyper alert after being the victim of an attack. Yvette appears to have turned inwards. Consumed by guilt at my failure to protect her, I crouch in front of her.

'Yvette. Yvette, it's me. I'm here.'

Slowly, she raises her head to look at me. There are dark rings beneath her eyes and they're glistening with tears. Her skin is red and puffy. The assault of grief. It's waged a war on her.

He hasn't done a lot of physical harm, she hasn't any bruises. He gripped her hair, pulled her head back, forced his tongue against her neck. He shoved his hand between her legs and tried, and failed, to arouse himself. Then a man happened to pass by. An elderly man, apparently, no threat. He heard the commotion, heard Yvette yell out and dashed to her rescue. Her attacker fled instantly.

Millie shared all this with me on the drive here. It's what Yvette should have been able to tell me herself, if only I had listened.

Yvette looks past me. 'I asked you not to tell her. I might've known you would.'

'I'm sorry,' Millie says. 'But she needed to know. I think I should go now. Call me when you need picking up, Beth.'

'Okay, thanks.' I have to stop myself reaching for her. I can't help listening to Millie's retreating footsteps.

Yvette curls her upper lip into a sneer. 'It's always the same. You run to her, even now, when I'm here like this.'

Normally Yvette's jealousy over my friendship with Millie would rile me. Not now though. Now I feel nothing but guilt.

I sit beside her. 'I'm so sorry. I let you down.' I pull her head onto my shoulder and cradle her, rocking her like a child. I feel her tears on my neck.

She whispers into my shoulder. 'Yes, you're right, you did let me down. You should have been there when I needed you. I don't know if I can forgive you.' She pulls away, sniffling.

'I'll do anything,' I say, and take her hands in mine.

'Anything?'

Oh God, what did I just say? I was considering breaking up with her, and now guilt is ripping me to shreds. I think of Jenny Lambert still missing. Of the monster who has her, of his sickening trademark brands, of the threat he poses. Will I really do whatever she asks? Will 'anything' be my job? To commit myself fully to Yvette? I can't give up my job, walk away from Millie, or marry Yvette. I can't do any of those things. Even now, after what's happened, while clearly being in great emotional pain, Yvette will seize and latch onto this opportunity. She'll use my guilt to get what she wants, and she'll do it unashamedly. That's why our relationship won't work. But can I break her heart now, after this?

I hold her tight, trying to remind myself of how passionately I once felt about her. 'Anything,' I say.

* * *

Eventually we're led into an interview room so Yvette can look through a book of mugshots. She's shaking the entire time. She pauses momentarily over one picture. I stare at it — a twenty-something bloke with a birthmark under his right eye, floppy black hair and a dazed, drugged look about him. My hope lifts. If it's him, he can be located and brought in. But as with all the others, Yvette shakes her head. The book of mugshots reaches its end with her attacker's identity still a mystery.

The officers had offered to meet her at home so she wouldn't have to come into the station again, but Yvette had said she'd rather not let the bad stuff into our or her mum's home. She said it would make those places feel tainted. She tells me she doesn't know how she'll face returning to work. She hasn't been back since. Her clients are loyal regulars who'll wait for her, but only so long.

I hold her hand as I listen to the details. How he had worn gloves, the thick material rubbing her inner thigh as he'd shoved his hand where it didn't belong. How he'd rushed at her through the open door, moving too fast for her to react. How instead of fighting as she'd always assumed she would, she had frozen in fear. How she thought that if that passer-by hadn't heard her yell, her attacker might have killed her. There were sharp scissors lying around, plenty of heavy objects. He hadn't brought his own weapon. He hadn't needed to. The police thought it was an opportunistic crime. Lone woman in an empty building, the streetlamp outside blown. They'd had that fixed if it was any comfort.

Meanwhile, I watch the time ticking by, counting the seconds to the end of Jenny Lambert's life. I may already be too late. Yvette's fingers tighten around mine. My heart is breaking for her. She needs me. I watched the stress lines deepen across her face as mugshot after mugshot failed to offer an end to her nightmare.

We stand outside in the police station car park. 'I am so sorry, Yvette,' I say again. 'I really am. Please let me help you now.'

'Okay. We can try, I suppose.'

It's the first time Yvette has hinted that our relationship may not last. Relief and panic race through me. I want to push her away and pull her close at the same time. 'Where are you parked? Should I drive?'

'Brian drove me.'

So her waster of a brother brought her here and then left her alone.

'Before you say it, he offered to stay. I didn't want him hearing all of that.' She points at the station. 'He didn't need to.'

'I'm surprised you told him anything.'

She looks sharply at me. 'What else could I do? Mum was doing my head in. I went home, I thought you'd be there. You weren't, obviously. I was so scared. Terrified. I could hear every door opening and closing down the street like it was in our house. Every creak had me jumping out of my skin. I sat holding a kitchen knife. I was shaking so much I thought I might actually stab myself by mistake.'

'Why didn't you tell me? I'd have come home.'

'Are you trying to blame me? Really? I was upset, angry with you. You've been distant for ages. You said I didn't know what worries were or something like that. You said you had a dead fifteen-year-old kid on your hands. All I had was a failed rape. It paled in comparison. What was the point in telling you?'

As always, Yvette goes straight for the jugular.

'I didn't know. If I had . . .' It sounds pitiful. 'I messed up, I'm sorry. I'm glad you had Brian. Does anyone else know? Your mum?'

'What? Worried it might hurt your reputation as the avenging angel?' Yvette steps back. 'I shouldn't have said that. I'm just upset.'

'Forget it. I deserved it. Should I book a taxi?'

Yvette steps closer again, closing the gap between us. 'You're coming home with me, aren't you?'

Before I can utter a response, my mobile trills. I let go of Yvette's hand and pull the phone from my pocket. It's mine. I see the name on the screen and step away from Yvette.

'Ma'am,' I say. 'Tell me you've found her, that she's okay.'

'No. That's not why I'm calling.'

'Then why?'

'You're not here. Millie explained why and I do understand. It's obviously a very difficult situation for you and I want to be sympathetic. Normally I would tell you to take all the time you need. In this day and age, we have to be super sensitive. As a police officer and a woman, I feel deeply for Yvette—'

'But?'

'But this is a major investigation. We have a murderer out there, as well as a missing teenager who is in extreme peril. If you are to continue as my DSIO on this case, then I need you here, at the helm. I'm sorry if that makes me sound like a bitch. I apologise if it puts you in a difficult position, but right now I have to prioritise Jenny Lambert. As far as we know, she's alive and I want to keep it that way. She deserves to have our full attention. I understand if you can't give her that but you should tell me now so I can replace you. Beth, this isn't what I want to be saying to you right now, but I have no choice. It's the Lambert press appeal in a couple of hours. Can I count on you to be here?'

I shoot a quick glance at Yvette. 'I understand, and yes I'll be there. I'll be back as soon as I can.' How can I not be when along with so many other reasons, I'm the one he's chosen as his opponent?

With leaden steps, I walk slowly back to Yvette. 'That was Dillon.'

'I'll get Brian to pick me up. Can you at least wait until he gets here?'

'Of course. Will he stay with you until I get home? It, erm, it might get late.'

'You know what? I think I'll wait in reception. I'm sure they won't mind. Just go.'

'No, I want to wait with you.'

'You don't. You want to be back at work. You're practically squirming. Just go.' She stares at the phone in my hand. 'You'd better call Millie.'

Yvette stalks towards the station without a backward glance. I wait until she's inside before calling Millie, not because I'll be saying anything other than requesting a lift, but because I know the pain our friendship causes her.

It only occurs to me after she's gone that Yvette didn't ask about my face.

CHAPTER THIRTY-ONE

I wait for Millie outside on Lancaster Road by the corner of Bushell Street, not wanting to risk running into Yvette's brother. I'm being pathetic, hiding like this, but I can't face being harangued by him. The last thing I need is an earful from that jumped-up little numpty, even if I do deserve it.

The wind is picking up and my hair keeps getting in my face, irritating the hell out of me. Three kids sit on top of a green broadband box kicking their heels against it. The racket does nothing for my burgeoning headache. Another lad runs and launches a full can of pop towards them, splashing them all before legging it with a howl of laughter. He leaps over the railing around the garden of some flats and vanishes inside, the other three in hot pursuit. I contemplate saying something, stepping in, but I let it go. At least now it's quiet.

It's late afternoon and we've made no headway at all regarding Jenny's disappearance. I know I'm being spread too thin and I now have no doubt that Dillon knows it too. I'm dangerously close to being pulled off the case.

I watch the traffic trickle past, my chest tightening with each car. I'm itching to get back to work and guilt-ridden because of it. I look back towards the station and wonder if Brian's arrived yet. I'd hate him to see me avoiding him — he'd take great pleasure in that. A car full of teens passes, windows down, rap music blaring, leaving a plume of dark grey exhaust fumes in their wake.

Idly watching a gangly man jog past with a black Labrador, I lean against the wall. Come on, Millie. I take my phone from my pocket to check the time and almost have a coronary. I'm holding my mobile in my hand, but my coat is vibrating. The other phone is ringing.

My hand shaking like crazy, I extract it from my inside pocket.

Simon.

My mouth dry, I mumble, 'Hello? This is Detective Chief Inspector Bethany Fellows.'

There is nothing but heavy, laboured breathing in response.

'Hello?' My agitated voice gives me away. He'll know I'm unnerved and angry.

'Nice to hear your voice.'

It isn't nice to hear his. But it does sound normal. Like any other man. Deep, a little throaty, but normal. Nevertheless, goosebumps litter my skin. I've waited to hear him and now he's speaking, it sickens me. My muscles tighten, my jaw clenches — an involuntary physical reaction to the sound of his voice.

'Simon?'

'Of course. Expecting someone else?' He sounds amused.

'Is Simon your real name? Who are you really? Where are you?' He won't tell me, I know. But I can't not ask. I can't not try.

'I couldn't have known.'

'Known what?' What the hell is he talking about?

'I couldn't have known I'd be so lucky as to have you looking for me. I guessed, *hoped* you'd be involved, but to have you actually *hunting* me, well, it's a thrill. I feel very, *very* fortunate.'

'Tell me your full name. Where you are. Where's Jenny Lambert? Tell me, please.' I tighten my grip on the mobile.

He laughs cheerfully, as though he's regaling someone at a party. 'As if I would make it so easy. What would be the fun in that? But it's apt, don't you think? Fitting.'

'I have no idea what you're talking about.'

'Oh, you will. Soon enough. I've spent far too long hearing about you — Beth this, Beth that.' He sounds angry now. 'I got tired of it in the end. I did everything right.' His voice gets louder with each word until he is almost shouting. '*Everything*. Didn't matter. Didn't stop it from falling apart. What do I have to lose now? Why should I stop? Tell me, go on. Give me a reason to stop.'

I'm listening to the ramblings of a madman. I have no idea what he's going on about. 'How do I know it's really you? That you're the one. The Brander?'

He laughs. 'You get the piece I left behind? You're all poisonous. Especially ones like her. You come on the scene and the rest of us pale into insignificance. We become expendable. And I'm left alone, unloved. While you, you get to be loved, adored. Isn't it just grim?' The last word is a growl.

I can't make sense of what he's going on about. None of what he's saying resonates. I don't understand. 'Where's Jennifer Lambert? Is she alive?'

He laughs exultantly, and then stops. 'For now.'

I clutch the mobile so tightly, pins and needles prickle at my fingers. 'You've done enough now. No one else needs to get hurt.'

'But *I'm* hurting. Don't I matter?' He sounds whiny now, like a sullen child. 'Daddy always wanted me to take the jug to the well, send me away to the well with the jug . . . Save her, save her . . . But I failed over and over. Ever the disappointment.'

'What do you mean, Simon? You're making no sense.' He sounds insane. 'Who are you? What do I have to do with any of this?'

He laughs. 'Come on, who do you think I am? Have a guess.'

'I don't know. Give me a clue.'

I don't expect him to oblige, but he does, in a way. It sends shivers up my spine. The hairs on my arms stand on end. He begins singing, low, menacingly. 'If that mocking-bird don't sing . . .' He gives a final ringing laugh and the call ends.

I look down at the mobile, which I'm gripping so hard, it's shaking in my hands. Staring at the screen, I will it to ring again. I try to think back over what he said so I can attempt to untangle it, make sense of his craziness.

A horn blares. I drop the mobile, managing to catch it again just before it hits the pavement. My whole body is quivering. I look up and see Millie beckoning to me. I turn aside so she won't see me squirrel the phone away, back into my inside pocket. I walk over to the car and climb into the passenger seat without a word.

Millie touches my arm. 'What's happened? Did she recognise him? You look like you're in shock, Beth. What is it?'

'Recognise him? Oh, you mean Yvette. No, she didn't.'

'Then what is it? Has something happened? Is Yvette okay? Are you?' I'm shaking violently, rage coursing through me. 'Beth, say something. You're scaring me.'

I force myself to calm down. 'Sorry, it's just been a tough day and Dillon's pissed with me. Yvette's with Brian, she's going to her mum's. She's okay. I'm okay. Just take me back to work, please.'

Tears prickle in my eyes and I turn to look out of the passenger window. I can't tell her. I can't tell anyone, and it's killing me.

CHAPTER THIRTY-TWO

The drive to the station is uncomfortable. Millie knows I am hiding something from her and it makes us both awkward, our conversation stilted and humourless. It's a relief when we park and I can walk away from her.

Dillon makes a beeline for me as soon as I enter reception. 'Oh, good, you're back.' She lowers her voice to a whisper. 'How is she?'

'Shaken up, worried, scared. You know.' I am still pissed that she made me leave Yvette when I did.

Dillon pats my shoulder. It feels false. 'Yes, I can imagine. Still, I am sure her family is giving her support.'

I want to tell her to go fuck herself. I don't know what's got into me — I wanted to come back here, didn't I? 'Her brother is with her. He's taking her to her mum's.'

'Ah good, good.'

Having collected her things from the car, Millie pushes through the security door, almost hitting me with it. I move quickly out of the way, avoiding her baleful stare.

Dillon looks past me to Millie. 'How are the Danes holding up?'

'They're in pieces, but they're just about managing for the sake of the little one.'

'Poor bastards. Makes me glad I didn't have kids. Makes you vulnerable. They break your heart at the best of times. I—'

'Have there been any developments?' I say, cutting her off.

'Nothing substantiated. A witness who said they saw a man matching Simon's description with a young girl. Could be our guy, could be completely unrelated.' Dillon takes a mint from her pocket and pops it into her mouth. I hear it clanking against her teeth. 'They gave the witness no cause for concern.'

She withdraws the pack of mints again, as though remembering to be courteous and offers it out to me and Millie. We both decline.

'I get the feeling it wasn't them,' she continues. 'From what we know, Jenny had gone there under protest, so they'd hardly have been strolling along. But that's all we have.' She sighs. 'There is no CCTV in the area, no dashcam footage so far — we've appealed, of course, but there's nothing yet. He picked the perfect place for their rendezvous. I reckon it was a considered choice. The DNA came back on the piece of skin left at the scene. It's Jenny's. I just hope he's bothered to dress the wound but I'm not holding out much hope. To be honest, as time goes on, I think we're going to be lucky to get her back alive.'

The three of us walk into the MIR, which is energised, alight with the fervour of an active case. Amer's eyes meet mine and he gives a minute nod. It's one of understanding. We've worked together for so many years now that we don't need to sit and strategise, though we often do. We know our roles, how best to work together.

Millie heads over to the corner of the room. I can tell she's upset and wants me to tell her what's going on. She looks down at her notebook and furiously scribbles notes.

Amer approaches me. 'You okay? How's Yvette?'

His concern makes me want to cry. 'I'm fine. Yvette's frightened, hurt, all the things you'd imagine her to be.'

'I called a team meeting about an hour ago. I hope that's okay?'

He already knows my answer to that, he's just being respectful. I swallow. 'Of course. Thanks, Amer. I appreciate it.'

'Listen, if we can get out of here for about seven, you and Yvette are welcome at mine for supper. Zarah's cooking a biryani.'

My mouth waters. Zarah's the best cook I know, and for days now barely a morsel of food has passed my lips. Amer and Zarah have two gorgeous kids and a perfect little semi-detached in a quiet cul-de-sac. They lead the life most people aspire to. 'I'll ask Yvette, though I have an idea she might want to stay at home.'

'That's understandable. The offer's there though. If she's not up to it, I'll bring you a doggy bag for lunch tomorrow.'

'Thanks, mate. I'll ask her. Thank Zarah too.'

'Will do. You know how she likes to make sure you eat something decent every so often. It's her way.'

'Yeah, I know. She's the best. You're a lucky man.'

He winks. 'I know.'

'Right, I'm going to get set up for the press appeal.' I would have missed it if I'd stayed with Yvette — it's another reason I was eager to come back in. The Lamberts are in the middle of a living nightmare. I need to be here for them.

CHAPTER THIRTY-THREE

The press appeal is about to start. Nancy and Peter, along with Jenny's stepfather, Cormack O'Brien, are going in front of the cameras to plead for her safe return. They've been working on a statement with Millie and the force's press liaison officer, something Nancy will be able to read while being the proverbial deer in the headlights. It's a daunting task, not least for a mother whose daughter has been taken by the very man who killed her best friend. So far, Nancy's only contact with the police has been from the wrong side of the custody desk. She's been nicked for prostitution, theft and possession, and is as familiar with police procedure as many coppers. I haven't needed to tell her that she shouldn't mention what happened between Mark Danes and Peter. In mutual silent agreement, we are letting the matter lie. Nancy is a shattered version of the lioness who defended her son that day. The Brander is one adversary she can't do battle with.

I bring the family around the back, in order to avoid running the gauntlet of eager journalists. 'You holding up okay?' I ask her.

Her face is bleach white, her hair limp about her shoulders. She's wearing black trousers and a purple blouse. She's made an effort. I'm guessing she wants to look decent. But the black bags beneath her eyes, the quivering of her bottom lip, tell me that Nancy Lambert is as terrified as any mother would be.

'Just about,' she croaks.

I advise them of what's going to happen. Dillon will introduce them and explain what we have so far, investigation-wise. She is going to circulate Simon's description as a person of interest, someone we wish to talk to in order to eliminate him from our inquiries. We're beyond guarding our information about him so as not to tip him off about what we know or spook him. Nancy will then read her prepared statement. Dillon will tell the journalists that she herself will answer any queries they may have. I'll be sitting beside Nancy to be on hand should it all become too much, and be ready to read the statement on her behalf if she needs me to. They're going to beg the perpetrator to return Jenny to them safe and well. They'll ask for anyone with any information to come forward.

Dillon enters the back room, where we are all waiting to take the stage. She introduces herself to the Lamberts and explains that she will answer any questions that arise. The most important thing, she says, is to look directly at the camera and picture their daughter's face. The hope is that their appeal will reach her abductor, that they will be able to humanise her enough for him to keep her alive.

Dillon leads them out into the glare and whizz of dozens of camera flashes. Nancy's partner, Cormack, has to physically support her. She looks terrified. But it's Jenny's brother, Peter, who breaks down. The journalists immediately swing their lenses to focus on him. All his bravado has crumbled like a sandcastle in the rising tide.

Nancy just manages to finish her statement before she, too, succumbs to her tears. 'Please, I'm begging you, don't hurt my baby. She's just a little girl. Please let her come back to us.' She's gone off-script but her plea strikes home. The only person who seems unmoved is Cormack.

At a nod from Dillon, I lead the family away from the glare, while Dillon fields the questions.

'Is it true that Jennifer Lambert's disappearance is related to the murder of Rose Danes and the attack on Celine Wilson six years ago? Are we looking at a serial killer?'

The dots have already been joined.

CHAPTER THIRTY-FOUR

As soon as the Lamberts are gone, I return Yvette's call, but I just get voicemail. I leave a message asking her to call me back and try her mum. Same thing. I grit my teeth and call Brian. Just my luck that he's the one who answers.

'Hey, Brian.'

'All right?' I can hear him clattering about and imagine him under the bonnet of a car, mobile tucked between shoulder and ear. 'What can I do ya for, our kid?'

'Is Yvette with you?'

'What? Think it's bring ya sister to work day at the garage, do ya? No place for a bird, this.' I flinch at his comment but know better than to tell him how misogynistic he sounds. 'Look, Beth, try calling her, will ya? Leave me outta ya little girly dramas. Better yet, leave me sister out of 'em too. Why don't ya try supportin' her for once, instead of phonin' her all the time? It ain't right, you know. Now do one, will ya? I'm busy.'

He ends the call, leaving me wishing to hell I'd never called the eejit. I kick the wall in frustration.

'Whoa, what's got you so worked up?' Antonio Giovanelli is standing behind me, a Costa coffee I could kill for in his hands. 'Take your eyes off my Americano, will you? You'll have it blushing if you keep staring at it like that.'

172

I can't help smiling. 'Anything new your end?'

He shakes his head and takes a slow sip, eyeing me over the rim of his cup. 'Nah, not a thing. I'm heading back in now and taking my lovely hot coffee with me.'

'You're an ass,' I call after him, giving him my first and possibly last smile of the day. I grab my laptop from my desk and sit in a quiet corner of the MIR. I type everything I can recall of the things Simon said. I then search online for certain phrases, first trying, 'flying away', and 'ravens', for which I get a load of references to the Tower of London. Pet ravens, it seems, are loyal to their owners and *don't* fly away. I try coupling 'ravens' and 'extermination', which gives me pest control companies. I'm beginning to lose the will. Maybe he's doing this on purpose, sending me off chasing dead ends.

I look at the phrase, 'send me away, take the jug to the well'. It is totally meaningless to me but it stands out. I type in 'send away with a jug to a well', and get nothing again. But then I insert the word 'raven' and let out a gasp.

The first result comes from Wikipedia, which gives the reference, *Grimm 025: 'The Seven Ravens'*.

'Grimm', of course! He'd practically growled the word at me.

I read the fairy tale and realise it's what he's been referring to all along. I don't know why, but I finally understand what the raven represents: him.

CHAPTER THIRTY-FIVE

The buzz in the MIR has petered out. It's late in the day, not only according to the clock but also in the investigation. Our lack of progress has left a cloud hanging over the room. I stand staring at the whiteboards hoping for an epiphany.

Footsteps rush up behind me and a hand lands on my back. I gasp and turn. 'Jesus, Amer.'

'Sorry, didn't mean to make you jump. I just wanted to ask whether you're coming over this evening.'

I stare blankly at him.

'Dinner?'

'Oh shit, yeah. Sorry, Amer, I completely forgot. Yvette's at her mum's again. I was gonna stay at Aunt Margie's . . .'

His face falls.

'But dinner sounds spot on. What time do you want me? Should I bring wine? A dessert?'

'How about you follow me home now so you can see the kids for a bit before bedtime? And just bring yourself.'

I hang around in the corridor and wait for Amer to collect his jacket. We head out to our cars. He's in good spirits, considering. I can't drag myself out of my doldrums and I wonder whether this dinner is a good idea. I'm in no mood for small talk. I watch Millie get into her car and drive away, wanting to call out to her to be careful. I can't stop thinking of all the people I love who aren't currently in my sights and once more panic takes hold of me.

* * *

Amer and his family live in a little street directly opposite a green, the sort of place where cricket is played on long summer afternoons. Zarah's car will be in the double garage, cleaned to a sheen as always. Amer parks in the drive. I pull up alongside his car, get out and hear my name.

Eight-year-old Sara scoots towards me, calling, 'Auntie Beth, Auntie Beth!' She drops her scooter and rushes at me, grinning from ear to ear and wraps her arms around my waist, cuddling me tightly. Her long black hair is pulled back into a braid. She has the most flawless skin I've ever seen and big, soulful brown eyes.

Rayan appears around the corner. He leans his bike against the garage door and in a studied attempt at being cool, strolls casually towards us. 'All right, Auntie Beth?'

'Hey, Ray, how goes it, kiddo?'

'Ah, ya know, good. You?' He glances around, probably to ensure his mates aren't within earshot. 'We've missed you,' he says quietly.

It feels good to be around this normal family, reassuring. At the same time, I can't forget that Simon had sent me their images. What he did to Rose and Jenny demonstrates that Simon wouldn't baulk at hurting a child.

I follow Amer inside. The spicy smell of biryani fills the house. My stomach grumbles — I'm starving. Zarah's food has me salivating at the best of times, and right now I could eat the lot. We remove our shoes and go into the kitchen where Zarah greets us with two cold glass bottles of Coke Zero.

'For the worker bees.' She gives me a peck on the cheek. 'I'm so glad you came, Beth. The kids have been excited about it ever since they got home from school.'

Right on cue the kids open the glass-panelled back door. They take their shoes off and carry them through to the rack.

The kitchen is a delightful mix of old and new, with pans hanging from a rail above the breakfast bar, a custom-made spice rack and a sink that might have come straight out of an old country house. There is a framed picture of the Taj Mahal beside the fridge, which is one of those enviable American-style contraptions with a built-in ice dispenser. The cooker is an Aga, expensive but worth every penny, according to Zarah.

We head through to the dining room, where the kids are already waiting. Sara is holding a tattered box of Connect Four. 'Want a game, Auntie Beth?'

I smile. It's the last thing I feel like doing, but I can't possibly refuse those big, pleading eyes. 'Go on then, one game.'

Amer laughs. 'One day you'll learn to say no to her.'

'But not today.' I laugh too. I take a swig of the ice-cold cola and my mood begins to lift.

Ray slumps into the chair next to me, his elbow on the table. 'Boring game, that. How about cards instead? I know how to play poker.' He glances up at his mum, who's standing behind him. 'Just for fun like, not gambling.'

She taps him playfully on the back of his head. 'No poker for you, young man. Where'd you learn that?'

Amer's sheepish look isn't lost on Zarah.

'So, you've taught our twelve-year-old son to gamble, have you?'

'Oops, busted. Now about that greenhouse you wanted to buy . . .' Amer guffaws.

With a sigh, Zarah hands him a gardening magazine from on top of the hostess trolley. 'I've marked the one I like. For your convenience, dear husband, I've stuck a piece of card in too.' She saunters off into the kitchen, laughing lightly.

'I think I just got played.' Amer raises an eyebrow and opens the magazine.

I peer over his shoulder. The all-singing, all-dancing greenhouse is highlighted in yellow. The price tag is enough to make my eyes water.

'Crikey, I think you might need to remortgage.' He laughs again. 'What the love of my life wants, the love of my life finds a way to get.'

I envy these two their relationship and its easy togetherness.

The tablecloth is one of those fancy lace numbers, already laid for dinner with Zarah's polished best cutlery. Sara beats me easily at Connect Four, the snidey little sod. Mind you, I can't say my head was on the game. She probably thinks I've let her win. After a while, Zarah comes through and tells Sara to put the game away, which she does without demur. She'll argue to the ends of the earth with her father but never with her mother.

'I hope you're all hungry.' Zarah carries in a massive, steaming dish and sets it down in the middle of the table. I look ravenously at the huge pieces of chicken resting on top of fragrant rice. She brings the plates, warning us they're hot.

Everyone holds back so I can serve myself first. I take a good-sized helping, and wait for the others. I'm desperate to tuck in. I hadn't realised how hungry I was until I got here.

'Oh, I almost forgot—' Zarah goes to the kitchen and returns with a jug. 'I made a marsala gravy.' She puts it down next to me.

While I pour it, my stomach groans loudly. Zarah tuts. 'Dear me, you not been eating properly again?'

I sidestep her question and turn to Ray. 'So, you reading anything good at the moment?' He loves books and is always eager to tell me what world he's currently lost in.

'*The Island* by C L Taylor, it's really good.'

'Oh, I've heard of that one. I read her books too.'

'You read YA?' He looks surprised.

'She writes books for adults too.' I smile. 'What's it about?'

His face ignites as he relates the story so far. I hope adolescence doesn't take his passion for reading from him. There's something special about a kid his age being enthusiastic about something as innocent and magical as literature.

Sara cuts in to tell me that she's reading *Agatha Oddly*.

'It's about a murder investigation.' She looks at her dad, waiting for him to be impressed. He doesn't react and she looks back down at her plate, toying with the food. 'It's just a kid's book, I suppose.'

'Well, I think it's great you're both reading. Isn't it, Amer?' I nudge him.

'What? Oh, right, yeah, course it is. Sorry, I was just mulling over the case.'

'No work talk at the table,' Zarah says.

'Sorry, I hear you. It's just, this one's a tough one, ain't it, Beth?'

My lightness vanishes. I look at his gorgeous kids and remember the danger they're in.

CHAPTER THIRTY-SIX

I drive to Aunt Margie's on autopilot, without registering a moment of the journey. The garden of her bungalow is clearly visible under the outdoor security light, the colours bountiful. Rose bushes and carnations border a small tree in the middle of the lawn surrounded by a circle of multi-coloured stones.

The front door is open before I make it up the drive. Aunt Margie stands inside in her silk pyjamas and dressing gown. Her messy blonde hair is piled high on top of her head, her arms outstretched, ready to give me a hug.

'Come here, sugarplum. Oh, Beth, what on earth happened to your beautiful face?'

Tears prick in my eyes. I rush to her and fall into her embrace. 'I'm fucking everything up,' I sob, finally giving way to my tears. 'Yvette, work, everything.'

Aunt Margie gently ushers me into the kitchen. She sits beside me. 'Now, love, you do have a tendency to catastrophise, don't you? I'm sure it isn't as bad as you think. Come on now, my love, tell me all about it.' She touches my face. 'And tell me what happened to you. Who hurt you?'

I can't share everything with her, but I can lighten my burden a little, relieve some of the pressure in my brain.

'I'm fine, what happened to me was just a daft accident. But Yvette was attacked.'

Aunt Margie's mouth drops open. 'What do you mean? Is she okay?'

'Depends what you mean by okay. She's a mess. He tried to rape her, Aunt Margie.'

'Tried?'

'Yeah. Luckily an elderly man was walking by and went to help. It spooked him and he ran. It was days ago. I didn't know — or rather, I didn't bloody listen. I've been hiding out here with you while she's been going through hell.'

Aunt Margie places her hands on mine. 'Then why are you here now?'

'She's at her mum's. I only found out about the attack because Millie saw her at Preston Police Station. Yvette asked her not to tell me, but she did.'

'Christ, I bet that went down like a lead balloon.'

'She wasn't pleased. But I needed to know. Millie did the right thing.'

'Whatever you do, sugarplum, don't go telling Yvette that Millie was in the right.'

'Course I won't. I feel like a complete scumbag though. I should have been with her through it all. Even now I'm not. I know I should be. I want to be. But I'm being pulled in too many directions — the case, Jenny, Danielle.'

'Danielle Wilson?'

'It's Spencer now. She's married, remember. I went to speak to her again, I needed to speak to her.'

'I take it she didn't want to talk?'

'Her husband's a detective at the station. He works in the building but not on the case, obviously. You'd think he'd understand but he's putting barricades up left and right. He reckons I'm putting too much pressure on her. On the whole family.'

'He might be a detective, Beth, but he's also a husband. He's doing what any husband would if she's struggling. Is she?'

'Yes, she is.' Tears burn at the backs of my eyes.

She puts her arm around me and pulls me to her. I could stay there for ever. 'You, my dear, need some rest. You're getting worked up and exhausted, and you're losing perspective. Let me get you something to drink and then you can get your head down. We'll talk more after I've made you a nice hot drink.'

'Thank you, Aunt Margie. I needed this. I needed you.'

'That's what I'm here for, sugarplum, and don't you forget it.'

'I don't know what I'd do without you.'

She cups her hand under my chin and looks into my eyes. 'Good job you'll never have to find out.'

There's something comforting about sitting at Aunt Margie's little kitchen table having a hot chocolate. I always find my way back here when I'm troubled. It's my childhood home. The Brander is managing to spoil this too, because I'm listening for unexpected noises, waiting for him to attack.

Aunt Margie sits beside me with a mug of tea. 'So, my darling. Tell me what you're going to do about the Yvette situation.'

I drum my fingers against the side of my flamingo cup and take a breath. 'Support her, obviously. She's been through a massive ordeal. And her attacker is still out there. They showed her a book of mugshots earlier but she didn't recognise any of them.'

'You went with her?'

'Yes. She seemed to—'

'Seemed to what?'

'I could have sworn she hesitated over one image. It was as if she recognised him but then carried on. I'm probably reading too much into it.'

'Don't sell your instincts short. If you think she might have recognised someone, ask her.'

'I don't want to push her.'

'I get that, sugarplum. Maybe she's scared of reprisals. But if you think she's hiding something, my bet is you're probably right. My money is always on you, kid.'

A lump rises in my throat. This is why I come to Aunt Margie's when I'm uncertain or afraid. It's part of the reason I've been here the past few days and why I'm here again now. After all, she's the person who plucked me from the depths of disaster after what happened to my mum and nurtured me to become who I am today. My life isn't perfect, far from it, but if it hadn't been for Aunt Margie, I'm pretty sure I would have been one of those kids who fall through the societal cracks.

'I don't half love you, Aunt Margie.'

'I know you do, sweetheart. The feeling's mutual. Now, how's about we settle down in front of the telly and snuggle under the blanket until you nod off?'

It is a tried-and-tested method and right now, it sounds as close to perfection as I'm likely to get.

Aunt Margie takes the blanket from the hall cupboard. 'Tomorrow's a new day, sugarplum.'

'One that might cost me more than I can afford to pay.'

'What do you mean by that?' Aunt Margie covers me with the blanket.

'Yvette wants to talk, and I have a bad feeling she's going to ask me to walk away from something or someone.'

'I take it you mean Millie. Yvette has always had a problem with you two. Not that I blame her.'

I stare at her. 'What does that mean?'

'You two are so close. Yvette can't possibly compete. To be honest, I don't understand why the two of you haven't made a go of it yourselves. She's bi, after all — it isn't like she's never been with a woman.' Aunt Margie leans closer to me. 'Look, Beth, I know she hurt you when she dated that girl in college. I saw it, don't you think I didn't. I reckon that until that happened, you thought she was claiming to be bi to make things easier on you, or to—' she does air quotes — 'be "cool".'

I laugh. 'Don't be ridiculous. I was a confused kid, that's all. I'm all grown up now. Millie and I are like sisters. Best friends. You know, soulmates. Neither of us would ever risk that even if there was something there — which there isn't.'

'The lady doth protest too much.' She winks. 'Sisters?' Aunt Margie guffaws. 'Soulmates I'll buy, but sisters — no way. You two, there's something special there.' She waggles her finger in the air. 'You mark my words.'

I stare at her. 'You've never said any of this before. Why now?'

'Because I'm tired of watching the two of you dance around each other. The both of you going from one non-starter relationship to another. You're my girls and I want you to be happy. Together. When I die, I want to know that—'

'For God's sake, Aunt Margie, you ain't dying. Can we not? You're talking crazy.'

'Hey, don't be so cheeky.' She holds up our box set of *Wynonna Earp*, my go-to series for a giggle and a swoon. 'Season and episode please.' She grins.

'Season one, episode one. Let's start at the beginning.'

'Okay. Pop it in then.' She passes me the case with a grin. 'Got you thinking, though, haven't I?'

I kneel down in front of the TV to put the disc in. 'The last thing I need is more complications, or more thinking. So no, you haven't. Now, drop it, will you?'

I think of Yvette. I'm glad she's at her mum's. I'm even glad that Brian's there. Then my mind wanders to Millie.

'For now,' Aunt Margie says. 'But after this investigation is over, we'll talk again. And don't you dare go agreeing to any ridiculous demands of Yvette's. No matter what she's been through. I'm sorry about the attack, but she has no right to control you like that, no right at all. It's abusive to make those kinds of demands of another person. Now, you think on that, Ms Detective Chief Inspector. Think about what you'd say to someone else in the same situation.'

All I can think of is Millie.

CHAPTER THIRTY-SEVEN

I need to understand the meaning of the fairy tale and nursery rhyme he quoted. There's not only the tale about ravens, there's also, 'if that mockingbird don't sing'. Is it relevant that they're both about birds? Is it something to do with his childhood? Both the nursery rhyme and the story talk about parents, and fathers in particular. Is that it?

One of the mobiles buzzes in my jacket. But it isn't him. Yvette's name is on the screen.

It occurs to me that as soon as I'd spoken with Brian, I came straight here. I didn't try her again. Again, I feel guilty.

'Hey, Yvette, what's up?'

The line reverberates with her sobbing.

'What's wrong? Where are you? Has something happened?'

'I . . . I need you to come to Preston Police Station,' she says between gasps. 'I'm sorry, Beth. Please help me. I'm frightened.'

'I'll be right there. Don't be scared. I'll be as quick as I can. I love you.'

'I l–love you too.' She hangs up before I can say anything else. At least she's okay, she's at the police station. She's safe. He hasn't taken her.

On my way to my car, I send a text to Amer, Millie and Dillon, saying that I'm sorry but Yvette needs me. This could mean my time as DSIO on this case is over, just as I'm getting nearer to figuring it out. But I can't ignore Yvette's desperate call for help. I let her down before, I can't do that again. Not now I know what she's been through. At least I can trust my team to do everything in their power to save Jenny Lambert's life.

* * *

By the time I arrive at the police station, Yvette's in a state of collapse. I find her in the waiting room with her head in her hands, crying. There's no sign of anyone offering her care or support. They haven't even had the decency to put her in a side room. To say I'm furious is an understatement.

I sit down heavily beside Yvette and pull her close. 'What is it, sweetheart? Why are you here, like this? Have they found him?'

Yvette keeps her face hidden against my jacket. 'I'm so sorry. It was a mistake. I'm sorry.'

I try to pull away and get her to look at me but she holds onto my jacket and keeps her head low.

What does she mean, 'a mistake'? Why isn't there anyone with her? Another part of my brain is busy thinking of a way to explain to my team how I've made the connection between the Brander and 'The Seven Ravens' story, without mentioning his call.

Yvette's crying has subsided to hiccups. I try again to pull back, but she still refuses to look at me, keeping her face pressed against my jacket.

I'm asking her what she means when I see a pair of black loafers and look up. Detective Constable Neil James stands in front of us. He looks annoyed.

'Detective Chief Inspector Bethany Fellows,' he says, acknowledging my rank, which is above his. Perhaps he'll show me some respect and in turn act a little more humanely towards Yvette. 'Now that you're here, could you both follow me, please?'

'Where to? What's going on?' I ask.

Yvette starts crying again, sounding almost hysterical. I stand and pull her to her feet.

'Just to an interview room. Yvette wanted you with her for this.'

'For what?'

There's only two other people in the waiting area, a scruffy-looking middle-aged bloke and a scantily clad girl, neither of whom is showing the slightest interest in us. Nevertheless, Neil says, 'How about we get out of here to somewhere a little more private?'

I haven't a clue what's going on. Yvette loops her arm through mine and presses close to me.

In the interview room, Neil gestures to two seats and sits facing us but nearer Yvette. 'Miss Donovan, are you sure you don't want legal representation?'

She shakes her head.

I look between them. 'What would she need legal rep for? Would someone please tell me what the hell is going on?'

Neil sucks at his lip, setting his heavy moustache dancing. 'The gentleman who ran to help Miss Donovan when she was attacked has identified the man responsible. We brought him in and he admitted to what he did, held his hands up right away.'

'Well then, I don't understand. That's good, isn't it? Why would *Yvette* need legal help? She's the victim, for Christ's sake.'

Neil looks at Yvette, who is still crying but softly now. She is sitting low in her seat and squirming. A fog lifts from my brain and I see her clearly now, for the first time. 'What have you done?'

Yvette stares stubbornly at the floor. 'I'm sorry. Please, I didn't mean for it to happen. I didn't want it to go this far.'

I look to Neil. 'What is this?'

'Mr Arthur Lewis positively identified this man.' He reaches down to the chair beside him and retrieves a copy of the mugshot book that Yvette had looked at. A piece of paper is slotted between two of the pages.

I know which photograph he's going to show me. The one Yvette hesitated over, the one I could have sworn she'd recognised. 'Why didn't you say anything? You saw this picture — weren't you certain?'

She says nothing.

'There's more.' Neil snaps the book closed. 'We brought him in, he was easy to find. Petty thief, contact details up to date. Facebook, for God's sake. Pictures of where he hangs out, the lot. He's no master criminal, just a chancer.'

'But he tried to rape—'

Neil is shaking his head. Yvette begins to cry again. 'No. He admitted to attempted theft, but when Miss Donovan screamed and Arthur Lewis turned up, he ran off without taking anything.'

I stare at Yvette, sick to my stomach. 'Tell me this is a lie. He's making this up, isn't he?'

Yvette curls into herself, refusing to make eye contact with me or Neil, whose demeanour now makes complete sense. He looks at me with empathy and at Yvette with barely disguised revulsion. 'Miss Donovan admitted to lying. The scratch on her inner thigh, the one she said he caused, appears to have been made with a razor. Troy Keane is a piece of work but he's not known for sexual assault. Once he gave us his side of things, we spoke with Miss Donovan again and she confessed. She asked that we facilitate this conversation between you.'

I scrape my chair backwards along the floor. 'Why?' I stare at her, shaking with rage, hurt, confusion. 'Were you trying to make out that I'd harm you? Well?'

He holds up his hands. 'No, no, she hasn't said anything like that, don't worry. Normally I wouldn't have agreed to this, er, *chat* with you present, but you're a DCI, you know the score, so I thought on this occasion I could make a slight exception. She's already been charged with giving a false statement and wasting police time. She's been bailed.'

He looks at Yvette. 'You made a very serious allegation. This kind of thing can do real damage to an innocent man's life. It can also undermine genuine victims.'

'He's not innocent, he tried to rob me.'

'Why, Yvette? Why would you do this? It's disgusting.'

She is whispering but the malice is crystal clear. 'You didn't answer my calls. Then when you did, you told me I didn't know what real problems were. Your *victims* get your attention, I thought that—'

'What? You thought that if you were a victim, you could control me?'

'I thought you'd put me first for once. Didn't work though, did it? I never thought they'd find him. I didn't think anything would come of it, except maybe it'd make you give a shit for the first time in our relationship.'

'Pick up your things as soon as you can. I don't want to see you again. While I've been here a teenager, a *child* is missing, kidnapped and maybe dead. I did put you first. You don't deserve it. I'm done.'

I storm out and slam the door on Yvette's howls. She's done me a favour. I'm free. Free to give all my attention to bringing Jenny home and looking after the people in my life who matter.

CHAPTER THIRTY-EIGHT

Out in the car park I suck in huge lungfuls of air. Once in the car, I take out my mobile to call Amer. I want an update on the case, but I'm worried he'll ask about Yvette and I'm sick with shame.

At this moment, I can't remember why Yvette and I were even together. She feels distant from me, someone I've never really known. I summon up the courage to press 'call'.

'Any news?' I ask at once, not only because I want an answer but also to forestall his questions.

'Nothing yet.' His voice softens. 'What happened, you know, with Yvette, she okay?'

'I gotta go. I'll tell you about it later. Yvette's fine.'

I end the call before he can ask anything more. I glance in my rearview mirror before pulling out and see Yvette coming through the station doors, the wind blowing her red hair about her face. She sees my car and starts towards it. I pull out into Lancaster Road feeling nothing but relief. Aunt Margie will be losing her couch again tonight and only half so I can keep my eye on her. I need to be certain Yvette is packed and gone before I reclaim my home.

Halfway to the station a mobile rings. It doesn't come through the hands-free, which means it isn't mine. Swinging onto the kerb, I narrowly miss a bollard. I fumble in my jacket and bring it out, still ringing.

'Hello, Beth. Holding up all right?'

'I've been better. Is Jenny still alive?'

'Jenny, Jenny, Jenny. Yes, she's alive. But it's you I want to talk about. Jenny's just a pawn. You're the Queen.'

'Why can't you just say what you mean instead of all this cryptic crap? It's getting old fast.'

'Tut-tut.' I visualise him wagging his finger. 'No need to be rude now, is there? I simply want to get to know you.'

'Why? Why me? What's so special about me?'

'That's exactly what I'm trying to figure out.'

'I don't understand.'

'Like I said the last time we spoke, you will.'

'Why the ravens? It's "The Seven Ravens", isn't it? The Brothers Grimm fairy tale. Mummy and Daddy read it to you when you were a little boy, did they? Wait. You said Daddy sent you. So, it was Daddy who read it to you, that about right?'

His breathing is heavy, laboured. It sounds as though his mouth is pressed against the speaker.

'Come on, you can tell me. You hinted after all. Didn't you want me to figure it out? Well, I'll tell you. It's the story of a father who turns his seven sons into ravens, isn't it? A curse, after they fail to bring a jug of water back from the well. The father wanted to christen his sick baby girl before she died. He gave the brothers a jug and sent them out to the well for water and when they didn't return, he assumed they'd been playing and forgotten their mission. But in their eagerness to do as he asked, they dropped the jug. That's what you meant, isn't it? You were sent with a jug to the well, but you failed? Why? Why are you a disappointment?'

His breathing intensifies. I'm getting to him.

'Their father laid a curse on them that turned them into ravens. The parents were sad to lose their sons, but happier to have their daughter, who got better anyway and became more beautiful every day. The girl didn't know of the existence of her brothers, but when she found out, she set off to rescue them. She cut off her own finger to open the glass mountain they were trapped inside, and she saved them. Am I on the money, Simon? That the bedtime story Daddy read to you? What does it mean to you? Come on, tell me. Why is it so damn important?'

'You don't know shit.'

I've hit a nerve, he's angry. I think of Jenny and soften my tone. 'Then explain it to me. Please.'

He sighs. 'Not yet.'

I haven't even tried to have these calls traced. Most likely he's using a burner. It'll be untraceable. I hope I'm right, otherwise I'll have thrown away a chance to locate him.

'Why did you sing "Hush, Little Baby"?'

His silence lasts a few seconds. 'My dad used to sing it. He chose that book for me, to teach me how things work for us. Don't you see? Don't you get it yet? He was taunting me. He was always punishing me for not being enough, for being the wrong child, like in the story. He'd have sacrificed me if he could, and he'd have been happy doing it. He'd have lived happily ever after.' He laughs, mirthlessly.

'I don't understand what you mean, Simon. Come on, please. At least tell me where Jenny is, then we can stop all this. She doesn't have to die. Please, Simon.'

The line goes dead. I drop the phone on the passenger seat and slam my hand on the steering wheel with a scream of frustration. The windows are closed but an old lady walking by stares at me and shakes her head.

I get my notebook from the glovebox and scribble down every word of the conversation. I'll decipher it later, if I can. I start the car again and set off to the station.

CHAPTER THIRTY-NINE

I've been shaking since I found out about Yvette's lies, since the phone call from Simon. Work feels akin to a sanctuary when I get there. I park my car and head towards the station, already dreading having to field questions about Yvette. I can hardly believe my eyes when I spot her sitting on the bottom step, the main doors to the building just behind her. I can't fathom how she could summon the gall to show up here after the lies she's told. It's verging on the sociopathic. Does she have no shame?

I'm tempted to turn tail before she sees me, but she's clearly determined to talk to me. Besides, I won't let her hamper my performance as SIO any more than she has already.

She sees me. A nervous smile appears on her face. That phone call from the Brander gave her the chance to get here before me, and I wonder absent-mindedly whether she's been in and asked for me. Would she be that brazen?

As I draw near, she stands, her nervous smile transforming into a radiant one. Her red hair falls in waves around her shoulders, and I realise she's tidied herself up. What is she playing at?

'What are you doing here?'

'We need to talk.'

'Trust me, we really don't. You need to leave, now.'

'There's no need to be like that.'

'For Christ's sake, Yvette, are you serious? There's every need. Are you really so self-absorbed that you're oblivious to what's going on in the real world?'

She stares at me blankly.

'Well, I'll tell you then. There's a kid currently missing, we're pretty sure she's with a murderer. She's the same kid whose case you dragged me away from when she needed me. Do you recall why you did that? I'm a detective — you know that, you know what that means to me. For fuck's sake, what you did . . . it flies in the face of *everything* I stand for.'

She attempts to take my hand, and I yank it out of reach. 'Don't. Don't touch me.'

She steps uncomfortably close to me. I move back.

'You're not being fair,' she says. 'None of that stuff is my fault. I didn't hurt anyone. I made a mistake, that's all. You can't hold me responsible for everything. You're being unreasonable.' She sniffs and I wait wearily for the tears. 'You're upset, Beth. I understand, I really do. Look, don't worry, I'll give you some time, and when you're ready, we'll talk.'

'I'll never be ready. It's over, Yvette. Make sure you take your stuff from my house as soon as possible.'

She spins on her heels. Her cheeks are glistening. '*Your* house? It's our home, Beth. Please don't do this. Don't throw it all away because of one daft mistake. It's just . . . you were pulling away from me, you were always with Millie or Margie, and they both hate me. I'm not blind or stupid, I know they're always on at you to drop me. They'll love this. They'd do anything to come between us. I was desperate. That guy did try to steal from me, I really was terrified but if that old man hadn't interfered, there'd have been no harm done. No one would have ever known. The nosey old git just wanted some excitement. And now look what's happened.'

'Can you hear yourself? That "nosey old git" ran into potential danger for your sake, to help you. And what about "that guy"? What about his life after you'd labelled him a rapist? Just go, Yvette. And collect your things, or I'll have them dropped off at your mum's.'

She narrows her eyes. 'Can I hear *myself*? I've always been second best, haven't I? After work and Margie. *Millie*.' She sounds like a petulant child. 'I could never have been more to you than her. Or your work. Or your mad auntie. They all come before me. Go on, deny it, I dare you.'

I say nothing. I can't because she's right for the most part. I'm still seething though, hearing the way she talks about them. When we first got together what we had was great, new, and exciting. But I'll never be able to look at her the way I used to, not after what's she's done. If I'm being honest with myself, we've been over for a long time.

Yvette rushes away, her cries fading with the growing distance. I watch her go until I can no longer see her. Then I breathe a sigh of relief.

CHAPTER FORTY

I'm bracing myself to face the team when Millie steps out of the station. 'Oh, hey. How did it go? Is Yvette okay?' She misconstrues my expression of distaste and adds, 'Sorry, daft question. Of course she isn't.'

I slump down onto the step Yvette has recently vacated. Millie jogs down the stairs and sits beside me. 'What's up, Beth? Can I help?'

'I'm not sure anyone can help at this point.'

'Beth.' She takes my hand into her lap. 'You're worrying me, what's going on?'

'She lied.'

'What do you mean? Who lied? Are you talking about Danielle?'

It takes me a moment to realise she's referring to my belief that Danielle knows something but isn't talking. I shake my head. 'No, not Danielle. Yvette.'

Millie's mouth opens in a silent O.

I nod. 'Yeah, you heard me right. She lied. She was never assaulted. Some chancer tried to rob the salon — that part was true, but he ran off when the old man disturbed him. He didn't even steal anything, much less put his hands on her like she claimed. I can't believe she's done this.' I shake my head. 'I'm so embarrassed. What are the people in there—' I look up the steps — 'going to think?'

'It doesn't matter what anyone thinks, but in any case they won't think badly of you. This isn't down to you, Beth. It's her. What the hell was she thinking? I mean—'

'Yeah, I know. It's disgusting, vile, revolting, I could go on for hours listing every damn thing it is and the damage she could have done. It turns my stomach.'

'I get that. Did she say why she did it?'

'You don't wanna know.'

'Try me.'

'She was jealous, felt pushed out by work, Aunt Margie. You.'

Millie blanches. 'Me?'

'Yes, it's ridiculous. She's a bloody child. She wanted my attention, so she played up. Told one of the worst lies she could possibly tell to get me to go running and I did, like a complete idiot.'

Millie squeezes my hand. 'Hey, you're not an idiot. You're a good person and you did what anyone would have done. I believed her too.' She shakes her head. 'If I hadn't told you, you never would have known.'

'That's not true, Mills, she would have told me one way or another. Then she would have made me feel like crap for not listening, not asking. It's why she did it in the first place. You did her a favour, lucky for her that you happened upon her like you did. She knew you'd tell me. It gave her something else to use as a weapon.'

'You have to let this go. Jenny needs you, we all do.'

'I know. I feel like I'm failing at everything right now. Maybe Dillon should have picked someone else as DSIO. I'm clearly not up to it.'

'What a load of rubbish.' She sounds almost angry. 'You have incredible instincts, a great investigative mind and fucking hell, Beth, do you care. You're exactly the person she should have picked.'

'What if I can't do it? What if Jenny dies?'

'You're doing everything you can to bring her home safely. Whatever happens.' She looks thoughtful. 'Of course we're all hoping for a good outcome but you can only do so much. Are you hearing me?'

I look away.

'I said, are you hearing me?' Millie holds both of my arms and stares into my eyes until I nod. 'Okay, good. Come on, let's grab a Costa and walk into the station together. I got you.'

'There's one stop I want to make first. I'll text Dillon and Amer, let them know. You coming?'

'Where to?'

'The shop, the one that captured the Brander on CCTV the night Rose was murdered.'

'Why? Uniform have already visited the store. The owner couldn't help us, nor could the staff. What do you think you can glean from going there? Dillon won't be happy if we don't get back to the station sharpish.'

'Amer has it covered for now. I just want to tread in the Brander's shoes for a minute, connect with him if you like.'

She takes a moment. 'Okay then, if you think it might help, I'm with you. Come on.'

The drive doesn't take long. The traffic has eased somewhat and for once the lights are on our side. The shop is rundown, the windows smeared. The dismal concrete wall is covered with graffiti. It isn't much better inside. The shopkeeper looks up as we enter, probably checking to see if we look like the type of people he'll need to keep his eye on. We must pass muster because he goes back to reading his newspaper spread across the counter.

I follow the same route as the Brander, footstep for footstep. I've absorbed every possible detail from the CCTV, and it's imprinted on my mind. I might not have been able to see his face clearly but I know the way he moved his arms, how he shuffled his feet when he stood in front of the crisps and sweets. He had stared at them for a while until he made his selection. Two packets of crisps.

At least, that was the assumption. I look at the metal bars with the various packets hanging from them and realise we were wrong.

Until now, no one had checked. There had been just too many packets. We couldn't possibly take them all in the hope of finding his DNA or fingerprints, the expense of such a fishing expedition would never have been authorised. By the time we'd located the CCTV it had been far too late to strike lucky in that regard anyway, not to mention he'd only touched the corners of the packets he took. That's why no one had noticed that he hadn't been buying crisps at all. He'd purchased two packets of milk chocolate buttons. I stare at them hanging there, my mind whirring.

I grab a packet, hurry over to the till and hold them up. The shopkeeper looks up from his newspaper. 'Yes?'

'Have you changed that display? Have these been moved at all? Are they in the same place as usual?'

He shrugs. 'Same. Always the same. Been like that for a year or more. You wanna buy?'

'Yes.' I fish a two-pound coin out of my jacket pocket and drop it into his outstretched hand. 'Thanks. Put the change in the charity box.'

Outside the shop, I hold the packet of chocolate buttons up to Millie. 'Turns out he bought these, not crisps after all.'

'And? Does that mean something to you?'

I look at the packet in my hand then glance around to make sure no one is within earshot. 'He murdered Rose, then bought two bags of these.' I stare expectantly at Millie.

'I don't get what you mean, Beth. What difference does it make whether it was crisps or chocolate?' Millie stares right back at me.

I lower my hand. 'When I was with Danielle, her kids went mad for these things. They're a child's treat, don't you think?'

'Maybe.'

'So,' I scowl, 'this sicko murders a teenager then buys chocolate on the way home for who? His kids? Is he sitting at home right now with his wife and children, reading bedtime stories and watching cartoons? Is that what we have here? Someone capable of switching roles just like that?' I click my fingers.

Millie opens the passenger door and holds it wide for me. 'Come on, get in.' She smiles. 'Everything could mean something, even if we haven't figured out what that is yet. Maybe he is a father, a husband. These people appear normal, in some ways they are. They usually have more than one version of themselves. The regular Joe and the killer. Much of the time they can exist in the world without standing out. He wouldn't be the first murderer to go home to a family.'

CHAPTER FORTY-ONE

On the drive back to the station my secrets are smouldering inside me. I finally let them catch fire, I can't keep them from her any longer.

'Mills,' I say at last, 'will you pull over please?'

Millie looks at me worriedly and indicates — the clicking of the indicator feels like a timer on a bomb. I worry my hands in my lap and wait until she finds a spot to pull up kerbside.

She turns to look at me. 'What is it, Beth?' She's staring with those wide eyes that know me so well. I am about to confess something that could change the way she views me as a detective and her best friend. 'Come on, Beth, what's wrong?'

I take a breath. 'Shit, I don't even know where to start.'

'Now you really are freaking me out. Is it Margie? Yvette?' I shake my head and she gasps. 'Is it you, are you ill?'

'I wish.' My gaze keep diverting away from hers, flitting about the car, through the window — anywhere else.

'What the hell is that supposed to mean?' She looks so concerned it makes me feel sick.

'I mean this is so much worse than that and a lot fucking harder to tell you.'

She tries to take my hand, but I pull it out of reach. 'Don't,' I say. She looks hurt but doesn't try again. 'If you're nice to me I won't be able to tell you and I have to tell you, I really do. I can't keep this to myself any longer. I should have been honest from the start.'

'Whatever this is, Beth, you're my best friend, that won't change. And you're a damn good detective.'

'I wouldn't be so sure about that.' Confusion is evident in her eyes. What I don't want to see is the hurt, the anger, but I'm guessing I soon will. 'Not long after this investigation kicked off, I received something. A parcel.' I hold my hands out as if it's sitting in them right now.

'A parcel?' She stares at my hands, then looks up at me as I let them fall.

'Yes. It was delivered to the station by a courier. I tried to trace it but I couldn't. It was a mobile.' I hesitate, running my tongue around my dry mouth. 'It was from him, the Brander.'

Millie sits back from me, distancing herself. 'The Brander? How do you know?'

'Because the bastard let me know, that's how.' I spit the words out. 'He warned me not to tell anyone and he sent a stream of picture messages. They were of all of you. You, Aunt Margie, Yvette, Amer, everyone I love. He was threatening you all.' I can feel the anger rising inside me, edging into my tone and making my body stiffen. 'He said I couldn't protect all of you all the time and he was right. He sent a photo of Rose to prove his identity. Then he sent one last photo. It was me, sitting in the office holding the fucking mobile. He was there somewhere, watching me.'

'Fuck me. Someone at work? That can't be right.' She shakes her head but I can tell by her expression that she's doing what I did — what I'm still doing. She's mentally assessing everyone we know.

'I hope not. I don't know what to think. How else would he have taken that photo? I couldn't trust anyone after that.' I pick at my nails anxiously and note her watching so stop, but the compulsion is hard to resist.

She arches a brow. 'Not even me?'

'That's not why I didn't tell you, of course I trust you. I trust Dillon and Amer too, but there was someone watching me that day. Someone close enough to take that photo, to know when I was holding that phone in my hand.' I take it from my pocket and hand it to her and she begins looking through it, at the messages, the photos. 'I know I danced to his tune, I know I kept this from you, from Dillon, from everyone. I made a mistake, but I did it for the right reasons, Mills, you have to believe that. I was trying to keep you safe the only way I could. He made it clear I wasn't to tell anyone, or . . .'

'Then why are you telling me now?' She spots the image of Rose and gasps.

'Because he's taken Jenny. I played his little game and he's fucking with me big time . . . But now I think I've figured something out.' I hold out my hand for the phone, she hesitates then relinquishes it.

'You know he was always going to carry on, right? He wouldn't have stopped because you played by his rules. You do realise that, don't you?' It shocks me that she's being understanding, but I'm grateful for it.

'I do now. I was scared,' I say as I put the phone back into my inside pocket.

'I am pissed though, Beth, really fuckin' pissed. You put yourself in danger, you jeopardized your career with this case.'

'I know,' I sigh, 'you're right. Hit me with it, I know I deserve it.'

'Regardless, I do get it,' she shrugs, 'kind of. You've acted like a prize idiot, but if he was threatening me in that way, I might have made the same call.' She sees the eagerness on my face. 'Might have,' she clarifies. 'There should be nothing you can't tell me, nothing at all, I mean we're meant to be best friends, aren't we?' I nod, she shakes her head. 'I would have listened; I wouldn't have judged you or the decisions you made. I would have trusted you in the way you haven't trusted me.' She looks wounded. I flinch.

'I do trust you. I'm sorry.'

'You don't trust me enough or we wouldn't be having this conversation now. We wouldn't need to.'

'I really am sorry.' I look down at my lap, contrite.

'It still stings. I thought we were better than this.'

I want to make it up to her, but I'm at a loss as to how. Then there's everyone else I've been as good as lying to. 'I hate that I kept this from you, from everyone. I didn't think I had a choice. I didn't know what else to do.'

'Are you going to tell Dillon?'

'I guess I have to.'

She shakes her head. 'It could end your career. You need to think about this. What's done is done.'

'You're advising me to reconsider telling the truth?' I'm shocked. Millie is normally the most ethical person I know.

She puts her hands to her face. 'Maybe I am.' She closes her eyes momentarily then focuses on me. 'But I don't want this to end your career, it would destroy you. You don't deserve that. You can't change what's already happened. What if you don't need to tell her? What if she never has to know?'

'It will come out eventually.'

'It might not,' Millie counters. 'But if you tell her then there's no question.'

'I love that even now you're trying to do what's best for me, but I have to do what's right, no matter what the cost.'

'Just promise me you'll think about it some more first?'

I nod. She seems placated by this, and switches subject, business-like once more. 'You said you'd figured something out? What?'

'He's called me too, dropped hints about the raven's meaning from what I can gather. I used what he said, and I did some research — he was referencing "The Seven Ravens", I'm sure of it.'

'The Grimms' fairytale?'

'You know it?' I say, surprised. I'd never heard of it, not until I followed the breadcrumbs he'd dropped. I talk her through everything he said that led me to this conclusion and she nods in understanding, agreeing with my deductions.

'And he sang "Hush, Little Baby",' I add.

'What do you think that means?'

'He said he was always hearing about me, Beth this, Beth that. That he was the wrong child. I don't know, Mills, but it's clearly personal. He chose me for a reason.'

Her eyes widen. 'You don't think . . .' Her sentence trails off, because we both know exactly what I'm thinking, and I can tell from Millie's horrified expression that she's thinking it too.

CHAPTER FORTY-TWO

Before we go anywhere near the MIR, there's something else I have to do. I've had Simon's words going round in my brain endlessly, taunting me. Until now I couldn't see their meaning — or didn't want to. The time has come to see if my theory holds water. I head downstairs and run to the Forensic Unit, Millie following me. It's one of the best assets of our building, our very own science department.

'What are we doing here?' Millie asks.

'I have a favour to call in.' I need to get this done fast — I can't keep disappearing from my team, from Dillon. Simon has been dealing the cards and so far, the game's been rigged. Now it's time for me to loot the deck and reshuffle it.

Millie follows my lead without any further questions, and I couldn't be more grateful for that. She knows about the mobile and I can't expect her to cover for me, I can't risk her career too. So I have to do this before I face Dillon, before I'm ripped from the case and put on forced leave. I know what's coming, it has to. I need to act fast before that happens.

Caroline Walters practically walks straight into us. 'What are you doing down here?'

'Hey, Caroline,' I say, my voice low. 'You remember when your brother was jumped, and I helped you out? You told me you owed me one in return.'

When Matthew Walters was attacked by a group of known thugs who were going to walk on a technicality, I stepped in. I did something I'd never done before, and probably won't do again. Matthew was sixteen years old. He was a good kid. He'd done work experience with us, for Christ's sake. After the attack, he ended up with a broken leg, a cracked skull, three broken ribs and a punctured lung. He was lucky to live. He'd been planning on joining the force. He'd looked up to me and Amer, keen to become one of us, one of the team. Instead, he became a shadow of himself, afraid to set foot outside his parents' house. What I did was plant his DNA on the head honcho. I'm not proud of it but it ensured their conviction. They were guilty as sin, everyone knew it. Now they're off the streets and Matthew can sleep again. Neither Caroline nor I ever expected me to call that favour in.

I lead her into the women's toilets and check all the stalls to make sure we're alone.

'What do you want me to do?' Caroline asks. She looks like a cornered animal.

'I need a DNA test running on some old evidence.' Millie's eyes are unwaveringly focused on me.

'I can't do that. It needs to go through the official channels.'

'Look, Caroline, I know this is asking a lot. I risked a lot when Matty was hurt, but I wanted to help. Now I'm asking the same of you. Please.'

'What evidence?'

'Celine Wilson. You remember the case?'

Caroline appears worried. 'Everyone remembers that case. Why does it need to be done this way? I don't understand. With everything that's happening, if you have a suspect, surely—'

'I need you to check the DNA that was found against mine.'

She stares at me, bewildered. 'Your DNA? But why?'

Millie's eyes widen, understanding now why we are here. I focus on Caroline. 'I want you to do a familial DNA test.'

The father bought a mockingbird for his daughter in the rhyme. In the story, the brothers were sent by their father to get water from the well for their sister's christening. It all leads to the same conclusion. We're family. Maybe it's time to explore my roots, discover the identity of a long-lost sibling. The thought turns my stomach but if that's what links me to Simon, if it's the reason he's coming after me, then I have to know.

'Are you serious? You think you're related to him? The person who . . . ?' I nod. 'Wait here.' Caroline looks from me to Millie and walks out.

Millie says, 'I see why you've come to this conclusion, I'm wondering the same thing. But are you sure you want to do this, Beth? In this way? Once you know something you can't unknow it.'

'I have to.'

Caroline comes back with a swab and a plastic tube.

Millie leans against the sinks, watching the door while I open my mouth.

Caroline scrapes the inside of my cheek and puts the swab into the tube. 'Okay, but I don't know how I'm going to explain it if anyone asks.'

'Don't give them a reason to ask then.'

'You think it's that easy? Come on, you're a cop. You know I can't access evidence from a crime scene without leaving a trail.'

'Sometimes you have to break a few rules.' I'm being an asshole, a prize bitch. I swallow my guilt, thinking of Jenny, of them all. 'How long will it take?'

Caroline shrugs. 'Five, six hours maybe. I'll do it as fast as I can. Believe me, I don't want to take any longer than I have to. But I need to get hold of it first. It won't be easy to get into the system without alerting anyone.'

'I'll call you later. Come on, Millie.'

I'm walking a fine line here, dangerously close to the wrong side of it. It makes me wonder if me and the monster

I am now sure is my brother are more alike than I thought. It's not a pleasant notion.

Millie touches my hand, her fingers grazing mine. 'Like I said, I won't judge you and I will trust you. I do trust you.'

'Thank you, Mills, it means everything. Jesus, I hope to God I'm wrong.'

'And if you're not?'

'Then I'll deal with it.'

'You won't be dealing with it alone.' She puts her arm around me. 'I'm here, I'm not going anywhere.'

I nod. I am doing the right thing.

We dash upstairs. I'm ready to face the music. Finally, Dillon will know the truth.

CHAPTER FORTY-THREE

Millie and I walk out into the main office. 'I'm going to tell Dillon, about the mobile,' I say.

Millie grabs my arm. 'What?'

'I have to, I can't drag you down with me.'

'But—'

'Exactly. You can't think of another way either.'

'What about his threats? Don't you think he'll make good on them? After all, he had the mobile delivered here.' She looks up and down the office. 'He could have eyes on us even now.'

'I know that, Mills, and I'm bloody terrified. I don't know which way is up anymore. I'm so far over the line I wouldn't be able see it with binoculars. At some point I have to do the right thing.'

She looks around again, her gaze lingering on Dillon's office door. 'Let's go outside, get some fresh air, talk. Then you can do whatever it is you need to. I won't try and stop you.'

I hesitate. 'Okay.'

I press the green release button to open the door to reception. Outside, the wind smacks me in the face, cold and brisk. The thought of coming clean to Dillon leaves me feeling nauseated. There's zero likelihood of me staying on the case afterwards, and the chances of me keeping my job aren't much better.

In silence we meander to the riverside and sit on a bench. The water is high and moving fast.

After a few minutes, Millie looks at me. 'Don't tell her.'

'I have to.'

'I know, but just don't. This job, your career, it's everything to you, Beth. It's your identity. What good will come of telling her?'

'What if they can trace it, his phone?'

'That's not going to happen. He's far too considered.'

'But what if they did? What if all this time I've been harbouring this secret for him? It might be a way to get to him and I've said nothing, not even to you.'

'Well, you have now.'

'Yeah, that makes it worse. Now you're part of the deception. I can't do that to you.'

'You're always trying to protect me, to save me. I don't need you to, but you do it anyway.' She takes my hand. 'Let me protect you this time. Don't tell her.'

'I'm fucking everything up. Celine's case, Rose's. Now Jenny's been missing for days and we're no nearer finding her. Yvette did what she did. I'm sleeping on my aunt's couch. It's all such a mess.'

She squeezes my hand. 'That's why you need to take a moment. Don't do something you can't take back. Just think about it for a while. And, Beth, you aren't fucking up. You're doing the best you can with what you have, you're running around like a madwoman trying to find answers. There's nothing more you can do.'

'What if it's true?'

'What?'

'What if Simon, the Brander, what if this sick creep is my brother? What does that make me?'

'Oh, for Christ's sake, Beth, it doesn't *make* you anything. You're a detective, you do good. He's nothing to do with you. Sharing his DNA doesn't make you the same as him.'

'Can you give me a minute? I need to clear my head.'

'You won't do anything without telling me, will you?'

'I promise.'

'Okay.' She stands but looks at me worriedly. 'You're sure you won't go straight to Dillon as soon as I go in?'

I smile. 'I won't.'

'I'm going to check out HOLMES 2, see what new enquiries it's thrown up. Then I'll be in the MIR. See you there?'

I nod. 'See you there.'

Millie walks away. I stare out at the water, watching the white froth swirl over the rocks. I close my eyes and listen, focusing on the sound of the water, the call of the birds. I'm grounding myself in the moment. Breathing slowly. In. Out. Concentrating on the rise and fall of my chest. Gradually I feel myself growing calmer. I almost fall off the bench in shock when the mobile buzzes against my chest.

I pull it out of my jacket. 'Simon.'

'How's your day going, Detective?'

'So, it's "detective" now, is it? I'm not up for your games today, Simon. Where's Jenny?'

'Tut-tut-tut, how rude.'

'Jesus Christ, would you do something decent for once in your miserable, disgusting existence and tell me where she is. She has a family, people who love her. You must have seen them on TV. Please, Simon. I'll do anything, whatever you want.'

'Miserable, disgusting existence? That's not very nice, now, is it?'

'Where is she?'

'Somewhere you'll never find her, at least not in time.'

'Why are you doing this?'

'Because I can. Because I want to watch you suffer.'

'Why? Why me?'

'Do you really want to save Jenny?'

'Yes.'

'And you'll do anything?'

'Anything.'

'Okay. Stand up from that bench you're sitting on.' I jump to my feet and look around frantically. I can't see anyone on a mobile. He could be sitting in or outside the bar, he could be in Costa, Greggs. He could be in the station. 'Where are you?'

'Simon says get in your car and start driving. Alone.'

'What?'

'I won't repeat myself. Do it, now. Trust me, her life depends on what you decide to do.'

I run to my car and roar out of the parking lot, fumbling with the phone to set it on speaker. 'What now?'

'Just drive. Take the A6, then head towards Lostock Lane. Continue onto Farington Road and then pull over. I'll call you. Trust me, you don't want to be late.'

'Late for wh—?' The line has already gone dead. I drive around the outside of the Capitol Centre retail park, following his orders but not the rules of the road. I'll most likely be getting a few speeding tickets after this.

I reach Farington Road, park and wait. A couple of minutes later, the phone rings.

'I'm here.'

'Good. Now before you go any further, take your mobile and throw it out of the window.'

'What?'

'What did I say about not repeating myself?' he says.

'Okay, okay.' I look at it and see a load of missed calls. I promised Millie I'd see her in the MIR. I throw my mobile, watching it hit the ground and the screen splinter. 'It's done.'

'Next, you're looking for Leyland Lane. Don't mess this up. No phone calls, no alerts, no deviations.'

Before I can respond, he hangs up. I set off, driving as fast as I dare — the roads are clearer here. When I'm there I pull over and wait again.

It's a good five minutes before he calls and by the time he does, I'm sweating profusely. 'What took you so long?'

'Now now. Simon says keep driving and look for Feathery Lane.'

'Then what?'

'Just go.'

I speed along Leyland Lane, slowing down to check the various side roads and dirt tracks leading off. Eventually I find it, a narrow road full of potholes, which cuts through fields. At the top of the lane, I park up and look around. There's no sign of life anywhere. There is a copse to my left and shadowy woodland up ahead. I shudder.

The mobile rings.

'I'm here,' I say.

'Get out of the car.'

My heart pounding, I spin round to look behind me. There's no one in sight. 'I'm out.' Though I think he already knows that.

'Start walking up the lane.'

I pull my jacket tight. It's freezing. The wind is whipping the trees. Some of them are skeletal, others crowding the sky with their mass of leaves. The further I go the more vulnerable I feel. His breathing resounds down the phone but he doesn't speak.

'How much further?' I ask.

'Keep walking.'

I've been going for at least fifteen minutes. The woodland is casting a shadow across this end of the lane and the farms. Then I look to the right, just beyond the trees, and I know where he's leading me. I see a rundown shack hardly visible in the shadows. From what I can make out, half the roof is missing and the walls are crumbling.

His laughter rings in my ear. 'And there it is, Jenny's current home. Off you pop. Better hurry. Oh, and you'll lose signal once you hit the treeline. Remember, no phone calls, not until you have her. Those are the rules, Beth. And I make them. I wouldn't break them if I were you. Now go. And, Beth, good luck getting her out.'

I don't give myself time to think, I run like Mo Farah, and I don't stop until I'm there. My feet squelch and I sink to my ankles in the marshy ground. Staggering through the rotten doorway, I slip and grab the wall. It crumbles beneath my hand. I hit the floor half in, half out of the building.

'Shit!' I struggle to my feet. I call Jenny's name repeatedly but all I hear is my own voice echoing back.

I stumble through the first room — nothing but bare stone walls covered in ivy that winds across the ceiling, or what there is of one. Weeds and dirt cover the floor. It's dark. The shack is surrounded by trees and there's little light. Further in, I have to tread carefully, guided by the odd glimmer of faded sunlight that manages to seep into the rooms. It's all the light I have. I check the mobile and sure enough, there's no signal. I don't know how to switch on the torch or whether it even has one, and I'm not about to waste time trying to find out.

I navigate my way through the rooms, calling out to Jenny. At least there's no upper storey. As it is, I'm half-expecting the whole building to fall on top of me. Maybe that's his plan. Is Jenny even here?

There's a gap in the wall at the end of the third room. It doesn't lead outside — I can see another room beyond it. I call her name again. Still nothing.

I look for a door, some way in. There isn't one. I crouch until I am almost on my hands and knees and hear the unmistakable sound of rodents scratching. It wouldn't take much to overpower me in this position. My heart feels as though it's about to burst through my chest.

There's a bang behind me. Still crouched, I turn around as fast as I can and squint into the blackness. 'Who's there?'

Nothing.

'Simon?' My voice is shaking. If he is here, no doubt I'm a source of entertainment.

I crawl through the hole, grazing my knees and hands on the splintered surface, then get up carefully, feeling around in the pitch dark. I'm surprised to be able to stand. With my arms outstretched, I turn in a slow circle and don't come up against anything. My heart sinks. I'm pretty sure this is the last room.

There's an odd whistling sound. I shuffle cautiously towards it, hitting a button on my phone. The screen gives off a dim light. It's just enough for me to see her.

'Oh my God. Jenny.'

CHAPTER FORTY-FOUR

Jenny is slumped against the far wall. I use the crap light from the mobile to attempt to at least catch a glimpse of her face. My hand trembling, I feel for a pulse. It's weak, but it's there. I breathe a sigh of relief. It's Baltic in here — she should be ice-cold but she's on fire.

I'm not sure I'll be able to get her out. I can't carry her. There's no damn signal and I have no idea where Simon is. He could be anywhere.

'Jenny, it's going to be okay.'

She groans, so quietly I barely hear her. She's almost unrecognisable, not because of the darkness but because of what's been done to her. What Simon has done to her.

I run through my limited options in my mind — try to get her out myself and risk hurting her more, or leave her here and run until I get a signal. Once I make that call, it's over for me. I won't be able to explain how I knew to come here. Right now, however, the only thing that matters is saving Jenny. If there's any way I can.

I put my arms around her and pull her forward. Her scream is so piercing that I let go and she slumps back against the wall. I can't move her. Shit. I have no choice.

Her head lolls to one side. 'Jenny. Jenny, listen to me, okay? I'm going to get help.' She stirs, trying to catch hold of me I think, but she hasn't the strength. 'I'm going to get help. I will come back, I promise. I'm not leaving you.'

Leaning forward, I kiss her gently on the top of her head and carefully wrap my jacket around her. I crawl back through the gap. This time I won't bow to fear, I won't hesitate. Endlessly tripping and righting myself, I run back through the rooms.

Finally, I crash out into the open air. He wasn't inside — not as far as I could tell — but he might be lying in wait for me out here. As I run, I hold the mobile up in front of me, watching the screen until the bars appear. When they do, I skid to a stop and tap out Dillon's number.

'Detective Chief Ins—'

'Ma'am, it's Beth.'

'Beth! Where the fuck are you? We've been trying your mobile, you can't just—'

'Ma'am,' I shout. 'I have Jenny. She needs an ambulance, and we have to find a way to get her out of a small space. She's hurt really bad.' I reel off the details of how to find us, then hang up and run back. Dillon can reprimand me later. There's no time now.

I get back and find Jenny shivering violently.

'Help is coming, sweetheart, you're going to be okay.' I try to hold her hand but she yelps, so I let go. 'I won't leave you.'

When they finally manage to get her out and I see her properly for the first time, I'm almost sick. He's destroyed her. She's shaking almost to the point of convulsing. Her teeth are chattering and she's mouthing words soundlessly, though only the occasional groan is audible. She's covered in blood and her face is almost destroyed. Her eyes are inflamed, the skin bulging around them, blood-soaked. If I hadn't spent so much time studying her photograph I might not have recognised her. But it's her, all right. She's here, alive, if only just.

Both of her ankles are bent at impossible angles, as are her wrists. She would never have been able to get herself out of that room. No wonder she couldn't even touch me and yelped when I took her hand. She has a busted lip and a blood-encrusted, probably broken nose. Her hair is soaked, her dirty clothes plastered to her skin. She's got one hell of a fever.

Some police officers have arrived but so far Dillon isn't here. The paramedics load Jenny into the ambulance and before anyone can stop me, I jump in.

The ambulance blue-lights us to the hospital, siren blaring intermittently. They rush her through to resus. I only just manage to keep up. When we get there, I am barred from entering. Pacing the corridor, I look up and see Millie coming towards me.

She breaks into a run and pulls me into her arms. 'Beth.' Her voice is thick with tears. 'I knew something had happened. I didn't know what, but I knew. Are you all right? Is Jenny?'

'I'm okay.' I don't say anything about Jenny, too scared to hope. 'How come you're here and not—?'

'At the scene? I knew they'd bring her straight here and I knew you'd stay with her if you could. I take it the ambulance left before Dillon arrived?'

I nod. 'I couldn't leave her. Fuck, Millie, she's not in a good way.'

'I know. I saw them wheeling her through as I came in.'

'Her mum?'

'She's on her way.'

Millie's mobile rings. She looks at the screen then to me. I can tell from her face who it is.

'Answer it,' I say.

'Ma'am?' Millie listens, frowning. 'Yes, I know but—'

I hear the murmur of Dillon's voice interrupting.

'I'm here now. Yes, Beth is too. No, they haven't said, we're still waiting. I'll tell her. As soon as I know anything, I'll call. Okay, yes. Yes, I will. Bye.' Millie lowers the phone from her ear and looks at me. 'She's pissed.'

'I gathered.'

'I had to tell her you were here, I'm sorry.'

'Mills, it's fine, of course you did. It doesn't matter now anyway.'

'Why not?'

'Because my career is done. I have no choice now, I have to tell Dillon about the phone. There's no possible way for me to explain how I knew where to look. Besides, I'm sick of the lies. This isn't the kind of detective I want to be. He's turning me into someone I don't recognise. I refuse to give him that power anymore.'

She holds my hand. 'Tell her I knew.'

I shake my head. 'No, this is all on me. I won't take you down with me. In any case, by the time I told you, it was already too late. There was nothing you could have done.'

'I could have come forward. I told you not to tell Dillon and look what happened to you. He could have killed you.'

I smile. 'But he didn't. Nothing happened to me except we have her back. Jenny's through there.' I indicate the door to resus. 'She has a chance now.'

'Dillon is staying at the scene for now, so you have some time to think it over,' she says.

'I won't change my mind.'

Nancy and Peter Lambert burst into the corridor. Nancy runs towards us with Peter in tow. Her face is ashen. I peer round them but there's no Cormack.

'Where is she? Where's my baby?' Nancy cries.

'They're doing everything they can,' Millie says.

'What do ya mean? Is she . . . She's not gonna die, is she?' Peter's voice breaks.

'I'm going to ask for a family room, somewhere quiet for you to sit and wait,' Millie says. 'The best thing you can do now is let them do their jobs. I know it's hard. I'm so sorry.'

Millie talks to a nurse, who leads us into an empty side room. We sit on red padded chairs. Both Nancy and Peter look ravaged from lack of sleep and stress. I notice them staring at me and realise with a jolt what I must look like.

I'm covered in muck and probably a fair amount of Jenny's blood as well as some of my own.

'You found 'er?' Nancy says.

I nod and clear my throat. 'Mrs Lambert—'

'Nancy,' she says.

'Nancy, I . . . I'm sorry it wasn't sooner.'

She looks at me expectantly. 'What 'ave they said? What are her chances? What'd he do to her?'

Shaking my head, I look to Millie for rescue.

'Nancy,' Millie says. 'Jenny is very poorly. We don't know the extent of her injuries yet but the doctors are doing everything they possibly can to help her.'

'You mean to save her, don't ya? Just be straight wi' me. It's life and death, ain't it?'

'We just don't know. Not yet.' Millie's voice is soft, reassuring.

Peter gets up and goes to the door. 'Want a drink, Mum?'

She nods. 'Thanks, son.' I doubt she's bothered but like me, she realises he needs to do something practical. He's trying his best to hold it together.

When he's out of the room, Nancy gives a weary sigh. 'I ain't slept right since she went. I try to stay awake in case I miss 'em if they come in. They mightn't wake me.'

'I'll stay for as long as it takes,' Millie says. 'So, if you fall asleep here, I'll wake you, I promise. Maybe give into it and have a nap, you need to stay strong.'

'No, I ain't takin' the chance.'

I sit next to Millie. The seats in here are comfortable, designed for long hours of waiting.

Millie leans forward. 'Okay, I understand. This room is reserved for you, no one else is going to be using it. The hospital want to support you in any way they can.'

'All I want from 'em is my daughter, alive and well.'

Peter returns carrying two cardboard cups. 'Sorry, I didn't think to ask if youse wanted one. I can go back, no problem.'

For some reason his offer moves me to tears. I won't let them fall, however. This is not about me.

'Don't worry about us, we're fine,' Millie says.

Peter hands his mum her coffee and sits beside her. We wait in near silence for a good couple of hours before a doctor comes in.

She introduces herself as Dr Geski and sits down, her white coat billowing. 'Mrs Lambert, before I begin, I'd like to make it clear that what I'm giving you is just my initial findings. I haven't yet written my report. If at any point you find it too difficult to listen to, ask me to stop. Okay?' She sounds kind, gentle.

Nancy sits forward. 'Okay.'

'Yeah,' Peter says.

'Firstly, I would like to let you know that my colleague, Dr Vickers, is with Jenny now. She is being constantly monitored. Now, if you're ready?'

Nancy nods.

'Jenny has suffered a number of injuries. She has severe damage to the lateral and medial areas of both ankles as well as damage to the plantar surfaces of both feet.'

'I don't understand wha' that means,' Nancy says in a small voice.

'Can you, erm, dumb it down for us, please, Doc?' Peter says.

Dr Geski offers a small nod, blushing slightly. 'Sorry, yes, of course. Jenny underwent repeated blows to her ankles and feet with a blunt instrument. Both her wrists have been broken. There is a lot of damage, multiple fractures. She has been hit in the face numerous times. Both eye sockets have sustained fractures.' Nancy lets out a sob. 'Sorry. Do you want me to continue?'

She nods.

'As you already know, her shoulder was burned, and a piece of skin removed. She is severely dehydrated. Now this will be very upsetting to hear.' She looks pointedly at Peter and then Mrs Lambert. 'Are you sure you want me to continue?'

'Was she, er, I mean, raped?' Peter blurts out.

'No.'

Nancy glances at her son. 'Just tell us. Everything.'

'At some point her eyelids were stitched open.'

Nancy pales further. Peter looks like he might be sick.

'She couldn't close them, which has created a lot of damage. It appears she hasn't eaten or had anything to drink for a long time. We immediately began giving her fluids intravenously — that's through her veins,' she clarifies. 'However, what we are most concerned about right now is—'

Tears are streaming down Nancy's face. She clutches a scrunched-up tissue. 'About what? How can it be worse than . . . ?'

'When the skin was cut, the wound was left open and untreated. Jenny has developed what is known as a cellulitis infection as well as severe sepsis. We are treating both aggressively with intravenous antibiotics. We're doing everything we can. The hope is that if we are able to stabilise her enough, she can be moved to Intensive Care. However, I do have to be honest with you. Jenny is an extremely poorly young girl, and you need to prepare yourselves. Her situation is critical.'

Nancy breaks down in floods of tears. 'My baby,' she keeps saying. 'My poor, poor baby.'

Another doctor enters the room quietly. Her face says it all. Nancy and Peter see it too. They turn to each other. Everyone is silent. We all know what she is about to say.

'I'm so sorry.'

Nancy Lambert's wail sounds like the cry of an animal in distress. Peter doubles over and vomits on the floor. Watching the scene unfold is like witnessing a car wreck in slow motion. Looking down, I see patches of blood on my clothes and it's all I can do not to wail myself.

Jenny Lambert is dead..

CHAPTER FORTY-FIVE

.We leave the Lamberts to grieve in private and sit in Millie's car. Neither of us speaks.

Millie starts the engine. 'I'm going to drive us to Aunt Margie's. Dillon texted and told us not to come back in. We need a break, Beth, we both do.'

'I can't.'

'Why not?'

'Because I'm the DSIO. I need to be at work.'

She looks at me sideways. 'Dillon wants to see you in the morning.'

'I'm off the case, aren't I?'

'She didn't say that.'

'We both know I am though. I should go to the scene.'

'You can't. Amer has it covered, Dillon is there. Beth, you need to rest for a bit before this case kills you. You look ill. I'm not taking no for an answer.'

She sets off. I stare out of the passenger window, tears rolling down my cheeks. We both know that if I did turn up, Dillon would have me removed, forcibly if necessary. There's no way out of this. Jenny is dead and whatever way I look at it, I'm to blame.

Millie glances at me and pulls over. She takes hold of my arm, trying to turn me to face her. 'Beth, please . . .'

I remain looking out of the window. After a while I give up struggling. Millie gazes into my eyes.

'Millie, I—'

'You keep getting hurt,' she cuts in. 'I can't lose you. I can't.' She, too, is crying now.

'Why did he go to such extremes with Jenny? He didn't do that to Rose, he didn't torture her. Why, Mills?'

'I don't know.'

'I can't figure him out. I've tried everything I can think of to get inside his head but it's like breaking into Fort Knox. Whenever I think I've got a handle on things, he usurps me.'

'Then how are we going to stop him?' she says.

Her question hangs in the air. I know she's right. I need a break. Exhaustion is yanking me into its depths. I need to sleep, no matter how much I ache to keep going. My need to catch this fucker is visceral. But I won't be any use to the investigation if I become delirious. So, I will take the night then I will be back tomorrow fighting fit. I won't be the weaker opponent. I'm going to nail him to the wall.

'You're right, we both need some time out. We'll do what you say. You're going to drive us to Aunt Margie's and we're gonna drink hot chocolate in front of a shit movie. Tomorrow you'll get back on the horse and I'll face whatever I have coming.'

She gives me a weak smile. 'Okay.'

* * *

Aunt Margie welcomes us with open arms — literally. She must have seen us drive up and is standing at the door. 'Come here, you two.'

Millie and I step into her embrace and the three of us stand together in a huddle. 'Oh, how nice it is to see you

223

both. My beautiful girls, come in, come in.' She steps back and looks at me, frowning. 'What on earth happened to you?'

I break down. Aunt Margie pulls me inside, Millie following.

'We couldn't save her,' I say. 'Jenny Lambert, she's dead.'

'Oh.' Aunt Margie covers her mouth with her hand. 'Oh no. That poor child. Her family . . .'

'I found her, that's why there's all this.' I indicate my clothes.

'You need to have a hot shower, get into some clean pyjamas and let yourself be for a while, sugarplum. Come on now.'

She ushers me through to the bathroom and passes me a towel. 'I'll grab your PJs, won't be a moment.' She touches my face. There are tears in her eyes. 'So much pain, Beth. This career. I know what it means to you but . . .' She lets her sentence trail off. Well, she may not have to worry about it for much longer, not after I see Dillon tomorrow.

I shower and, wearing warm, fabric-softener-scented pyjamas, head straight for the kitchen, knowing that's where they'll be. I hear the low murmur of their voices, which stop when I walk in. Aunt Margie and Millie turn to me, their faces etched with concern. Millie is sitting where she always does, a mug of hot chocolate in front of her. There's one for me too.

'I heard the water go off.' Aunt Margie nods at the mug. 'It's hot. Sit.'

It reminds me of years gone by, the hours Millie and I spent in this kitchen. There's an enormous amount of comfort to be found in familiarity. Some things never change. Whenever one of us is in need of solace, a cup of hot chocolate is Aunt Margie's first port of call. Next will be the blankets and a DVD. I already feel some of my stress ebbing away and can breathe a little easier.

Aunt Margie dips a biscuit in her tea and tips the cookie jar towards me. I shake my head and she tuts. 'Millie wouldn't have one either.' She looks between us. Millie sits on one side of her, me on the other.

'My girls. I worry about you both so much. It's such a relief to have you both here, with me.'

We have our drinks and go through to the lounge. Aunt Margie insists we watch a tearjerker — by her reckoning, we need to get it out of our systems. I might have argued that it'll probably finish us off instead, but I keep my counsel. We watch *John Q* and have a good cry, which, to my surprise, does actually help. I sleep with Aunt Margie and Millie takes the couch.

Restless, I hear Millie up and about in the early hours. I am tempted to go to her and talk things out the way we usually would. But I stop myself. I can't keep leaning on her. Since Aunt Margie told me she'd always thought we should be together, I've felt awkward around Millie. While everything was going on, I could push it from my mind. Now, in the quiet of the night, I can't stop thinking about it, about her. About the way my heart starts to race whenever she's nearby. I'd thought I'd buried those feelings as we grew older, but since Aunt Margie's revelation they are back, stronger than ever.

I stare at the ceiling, going over everything that has happened, wondering if I could have changed the outcome. I picture Jenny in agony, terrified, and am overcome with rage. Lying rigid beside my sleeping aunt, I wait impatiently for daylight to shine through the window. All I want is to continue my search for the Brander and make him pay for what he did — if Dillon will let me.

CHAPTER FORTY-SIX

I wake up to the scent of bacon and make my way to the kitchen, where Aunt Margie sits watching the door like a meerkat, her Mad Hatter teapot in pride of place in the centre of the table. Millie walks in right after me.

'Morning, girls.' A smiling Aunt Margie pulls out chairs for us. 'Sit, sit.' She pours tea into a couple of flamingo mugs and presents us with two full English breakfasts.

I look at my plate. My stomach lurches in revolt but I eat what I can. We say goodbye and set off to work. I'm dreading having to face Dillon. Once I speak to her there's no coming back. I won't be allowed anywhere near the case.

I spend the drive staring out of my window, watching the fields and trees whip by. The sight of them makes me think of Jenny, yet I can't avert my eyes. I watch the scenery and ruminate. Guilt has become a passenger in my life, and I want nothing more than to get rid of it. At the same time, it's necessary. After all, I deserve it.

As soon as we arrive, Millie reluctantly leaves me and goes to the MIR. I head to Dillon's office feeling like I'm en route to the gallows. I raise my hand to knock, and her door opens. I drop my hand.

Dillon's face is thunderous. 'Not now, Beth. I want you back here at 10 a.m. Thanks to you, I'm running around like a blue-arsed fly. I have people to answer to as well, you know. You've created a right stink.'

I nod, my throat closing around any words of apology. I step back.

Dillon glares at me. 'And don't even *think* about going near the MIR. Don't talk to anyone. Don't touch this investigation. You understand? I want you out of the building, sitting on your hands until 10 a.m., okay? I can't trust you. I had your car towed back here, it's in the car park. Sit in it and don't move.'

Anger is coming off her in waves, smacking me in the face. I rush from the building, out into the biting cold. My hands are shaking. I grip them together, but the tremors won't abate.

I race down the steps and dash over to the bench. I'm sweating, my heart is pounding and I can't catch my breath. I know what's happening. Sitting down, I close my eyes and take slow, deliberate breaths.

When I was a teenager and mum's murder was haunting me, I received therapy for debilitating panic attacks that came upon me almost daily. It felt like I was losing control of my life, consumed with pain and anxiety. Poor Aunt Margie was overcome with worry. Now, after all this time, it's happening again. I fight to push the feelings down, as hard and deep as I can. The Brander, everything he's done, and the fear of what he could yet do is threatening to devour me. Well, I won't let it.

I take the Brander's mobile from my jacket and dial Aunt Margie's number. She'll be able to talk me down from this cliff edge. As soon as I have a chance, I'll get a replacement for the mobile he made me throw out the window. I listen to it ring, then hear the click as it switches to answerphone. I try three times before letting out a frustrated shriek. It's early, no one is around to hear my cry.

After I've been sitting for around half an hour, the mobile rings. I'm naive enough to expect it to be Aunt Margie. My stomach drops when I see his name.

Hatred pulses through my body, I'm alive with it. 'You bastard.'

'Well, that's not very nice, is it?' He chuckles. 'I think it's time we had a little tête-à-tête, don't you? You keep asking me to put a stop to all this, well, maybe *you* can.'

'I don't trust you.'

'And I don't see what choice you have. You should be receiving a picture message, right about . . . now.' He laughs. 'Have a gander.'

Filled with dread, I open the message. On some level I think I already know what I'm about to see. It downloads slowly, then there she is, and my pulse beats loud in my ears.

'When? Where?'

'Now. Get in your car and I'll text you the details. Just me and you. Do not do anything stupid.'

'Okay. I'm setting off now.'

'When you're in your car, wait for my text.'

I locate my car by clicking the keys and watching for the lights. There it is. I jump in. He's getting exactly what he wants again but I have no choice. My heart is in a vice, I'm shaking from head to toe. I focus all my rage on him. I'll wrap my hands around his throat and squeeze. I'll put a knife through his heart. I'll do whatever it takes.

I start the engine and look at my phone. The promised text materialises. How the fuck does he always know where I am? The odds have been stacked against me from the word go.

* * *

We are to meet in a bistro not far from here. He's booked us a table under the name Grimm. Thinks he's a comedian, the sick bastard. I drive there like one possessed, park and go inside. The table is ready and waiting. The waitress leads me to it, casting a disapproving eye over my slightly dishevelled appearance.

I count the patrons — there's more than ten of them. I contemplate telling them to leave, but then I consider Simon's likely reaction and take my seat, my heart hammering. There is a glass bottle with wax around the neck and an unlit candle stuffed in the top, next to a small silver basket containing condiments. The table is set for two. I've been here less than five minutes when the phone buzzes with a text.

I've arranged a very special delivery. I'm outside watching, so no heroics. I see anyone attempting to leave and I pull the plug. By now you must know I always have eyes on you. So, believe me when I say I'm WATCHING YOU. :)

I'm still trying to understand what he means when the waitress who seated me comes over to my table. She's carrying a box disturbingly similar to the one the phone came in, only a little larger. She is smiling, no doubt assuming it's a birthday surprise or something romantic. It can't be another phone — I already have one. I turn it over in my hands, open it and peer hesitantly inside.

Staring up at me is a dead raven. I take it from the box and see the necklace made of thread around its neck, a homemade pendant bearing the word *BOOM*. Then I hear the ticking.

I look around again and know he's telling the truth. He'll be watching me. I have no choice. I'll let the bomb explode if that's what it takes. I can't let the people I love die. My Aunt Margie, my lovely, kooky, precious auntie. She was wearing those clothes this morning, so I know the photo he sent me was taken today, that it's genuine. I've lost one mum, I can't let another die. But if I do nothing, I, and everyone here, will be blown to bits.

The door opens. With a smile and a wave, he heads in my direction. I clutch the raven to my chest. I know what I have to do.

CHAPTER FORTY-SEVEN

I watch him cross the room towards my table. He looks taller in person, at least six foot three. He sits down opposite me, smiling. His dark eyes are so like mine. His head is completely smooth and hairless — Aunt Margie would call him a skinhead. The thought of her brings a lump to my throat. If I can save him, maybe I can save her too, because he's the only person who knows where she is. He dies, so does she. He's also the one who can deactivate this bomb. Once I have what I want, I'll take pleasure in destroying him. Whether that's locking him or up or seeing him dead, I don't care. I want him wiped from the earth. I want to end him.

'Lovely to finally get together, isn't it?' He beckons to the waitress and orders two Americanos.

She gives the raven a look of utter distaste. I am making no attempt to hide it. 'You really shouldn't have that in here, you know. There's no animals allowed for hygiene reasons.'

Simon laughs. 'It's dead. Stuffed. I wouldn't worry about hygiene. It's probably cleaner than your undercarriage. Now, about that coffee.'

She stalks away. I'm half-expecting her to come back and demand that we leave. Instead, she plonks our drinks onto the table and with a sniff, marches off.

'Great service, I must say.' He stirs his coffee, takes a sip and grimaces. 'Urgh. Vile. Tastes like fag ash.' He's being loud and obnoxious. A few of the other customers glare. He raises his index finger and motions for them to turn back around.

'Where is she?' I say.

'All in good time. First, I'd like to get to know you a little better. When I was a boy—'

The waitress, still scowling, comes to take our order.

Simon waves her away. 'We're not ready. Now, if you don't mind?'

'We have customers booked in for brunch.' She looks around. The place is fairly compact. 'I'll give you a couple of minutes.'

'Are you deaf as well as butt ugly? Go away.'

She snaps her notebook shut and turns on her heel.

'When I was a boy,' he says, 'I lived with a mother who had a chip on her shoulder the size of Europe. She blamed my dad for the mess her life had turned out to be, and she blamed me for being his son.' He pouts.

The waitress comes back with a man in a chef's uniform. He looks ripped, and she stands with her hands on her hips, grinning at Simon.

The chef towers over him. 'Belinda here says you were rude to her. We don't stand for customers mistreating our staff. I'd like an apology right now.'

Simon raises an eyebrow.

The chef waits for him to respond. Simon looks mildly irritated, as if the man is an annoying child. After a few seconds of this, the chef has had enough. 'Right, that's it. Get out. Go on.'

'Simon,' I say, 'Please. Don't.'

He smirks at me. 'Say that again, it makes me all tingly inside.'

The chef frowns. The waitress looks disgusted.

'Simon,' I say. 'Leave it.'

The chef prods Simon's shoulder. 'Out.'

He gets slowly to his feet and stares at the chef. The waitress is looking on, smirking, probably expecting him to get a pasting. If only.

He feels around behind him, searching his back pockets. When I realise what he's about to do, it's too late to act.

He pulls out a knife and plunges it deep into the chef's throat. He follows this up by snatching a fork from the table and thrusting it into the chef's eye. The chef screams in agony, while the other customers rise from their seats in horror. Someone screams.

I cannot believe this is happening.

Simon smashes the bottle on the edge of the table and, laughing maniacally, rams the broken bottle into the chef's stomach. Amid the chaos, I place the raven on the table with as much care as if it was a newborn baby. I have no idea what will trigger it.

Simon stands looking around him wildly. People are running for the exit. 'Stop!' he shouts. 'Stop now, or the bomb will go off and you'll all be soup.'

They freeze, then stare, horrified, at Simon. I see one woman in a business suit eyeing the door, probably calculating her chances of making a run for it.

'He's telling the truth,' I yell. 'See this?' I point to the raven. 'There's a bomb in it.'

The waitress holds her hands out, staring at them, as if she can't believe she carried a bomb through the restaurant. Then she vomits.

Simon snarls at her. 'Dirty bitch.' He looks at the petrified customers. 'I want you all to take a seat. Go on.'

Incredibly, the chef is still showing signs of life. Blood bubbling from his lips, he makes a gurgling sound. I make a move towards him but Simon holds his hand up. 'No, you don't.'

He reaches down and pulls the knife from the man's throat. Blood spurts from the open wound and the man's eyes roll into the back of his head. I can't do anything, or Simon might detonate the bomb.

Only I know he has Aunt Margie, and only I can save her — if he hasn't already killed her. Yet again, I am forced to play by his rules.

In silence, the other customers take their seats. Simon turns to me and I too sit. 'Now, no one move while I continue my family reunion. I'll let you know what happens when we're done.'

So, I was right. This animal is my brother. While he fusses with his chair, I hear the unmistakable sound of sirens approaching. Using a white napkin, he fastidiously cleans the knife. I watch in disgust. He must know there's no getting out of this, but what does it mean for Aunt Margie? What the hell has he done to my lovely auntie? If he's already . . . I'll have nothing left to lose. I'll kill him. I pull the raven closer.

'Now, where were we? Ah, yes, I was telling you about my mother from hell. You see, we don't all have some exotic aunt to come and rescue us. I was stuck with my mum, and I hated her. I mean, you go on dates with a partner to see if you're suited, why remain stuck with a parent just because you happen to have been born to them? It's absurd,' he scoffs. 'Well, despite my evil mother's best attempts to keep me from him, I managed to find out who my dad was. I met him and found my family, somewhere I could finally belong. I wanted to stay. When I met Celine—'

I lean forward. Am I finally about to learn the truth?

'—I was still living with my mum. You know what that bitch named me? Sigmund, after her old dad. I hadn't even met Grandpa Sig, he was long dead by the time I came along, so why lumber me with a name that made me a fuckin' laughing stock? The sadistic bitch. My dad gave me the name Simon. I told him I hated Sigmund, and why. He even gave me a nickname — Money. I thought that was pretty cool. Sounds kind of gangster, don't ya think?' He laughs.

'Well, at first, dear old Dad was great. I wanted to be just like him, to have a relationship with him like the one he had with my—' he does air quotes — '*amazing* brother. But it was never going to happen with my mum around.'

'What does all this have to do with Celine?'

'I'm coming to that. Dad was always telling me I should be more like my bro. A proper lad. Well, Celine was friends

233

with him. I couldn't understand what he saw in her. She was a sprog, just fourteen and not the best-looking girl I'd ever seen. I didn't get it, to be honest.' He looks wistful for a moment. 'But she was nice, I suppose. I got talking to her and she listened. I told her I needed to get away. Said my mum treated me really badly. Then along *he* came. Dear brother. Just as I was getting close to Celine, he moved in for the kill. Not long after that, my dear mum passed on. So tragic.'

'Was it him then? Did he hurt Celine?'

'In a manner of speaking,' he says. 'I went to that house, their little meeting place, and caught him in the act. He was raping her. I could never be with her after that, he'd defiled her. And I had no choice but to protect him. He was my brother. I liked Celine, I genuinely did, but family's family.'

'You sick fuck. You're both twisted, evil.'

'That's not a nice thing to say to your brother, is it?'

'You're not my brother.'

'Oh, come on, how many clues do you need? You're supposed to be some hotshot detective.'

'Even if it's true, DNA doesn't make you my brother. You mean nothing to me. Less than nothing. Who is your brother, *Sigmund*?'

He glowers at me.

'Who is your father?'

He strokes the raven's head. 'Let's not forget who holds all the cards, shall we? Play nice.'

'Why the brand?'

'You've already sussed most of it out. Come on, you're supposed to be intelligent. Can't you put the rest together?'

The sirens have stopped some way beyond the restaurant. In the near distance I see a swarm of flashing lights. The immediate vicinity is eerily deserted.

'"The Seven Ravens". You were jealous of me. That's what all this is about, isn't it?'

He claps his hands slowly. 'Finally, she gets it. I thought it was bad enough that I had my perfect brother to contend with. Dad idolised him but he adored you even more. Once he told me about you, that was all I heard. He never, ever fuckin' stopped going on about the daughter he had with the love of his life.'

I swallow my rising bile.

'You know, he used to sing that shitty lullaby all the time — the one about pappa buying his baby a bird and all that. Drove me mad, though I wouldn't have minded if he'd been singing it for me. No, it's what he said he'd have sung to you. I was the consummate disappointment. I could never live up to you. You weren't even there to compete with. You were a story, a fairy tale.'

He flicks the bird's beak. I jump out of my skin.

'*And if that mockingbird don't sing,*' he trills. 'Well, that bird ain't likely to sing, is it?' He laughs. 'Well, as you know, having *finally* figured it out,' he smirks, '"The Seven Ravens" is a Brothers Grimm fairy tale. The father turned the sons into ravens because he thought they'd cost him his only daughter. She lived but it was too late, the sons were doomed to their fate. He used to bang on at us, saying he'd swap us in a heartbeat if he could have his girl. Told us we should up and fly away. No matter what we did, how far we went to prove ourselves, it was never enough. But do you know what happens at the end? The brothers are trapped in a glass mountain, living as the ravens the father turned them into, a curse to avenge his precious daughter. The sister — that's you by the way — takes a ring that had belonged to her parents and sets off to save her brothers. Like you, she hadn't known they existed. She was presented with a chicken bone by the morning star so she could open the glass mountain and save them. But the daft girl loses it.'

He reaches out and strokes my finger, making me shudder. 'Well, what was a loyal, devoted sister to do after that but cut off her own finger and use it as a key?'

I curl my hands into fists.

'She owed them, after all. They'd lived in exile their whole lives while she'd been loved and cosseted by their parents. It was a happy ending, I suppose — apart from the missing finger, of course, and all those lost years. But do you know what really,

really riles me? Even after everything the brothers suffered, the sister comes off as the heroine.' He scowls at me. 'You still win.'

'You really took your bedtime stories to heart, didn't you, Simon?' I say.

'Dad told me to read that story and to "take from it what you will". So I did and I understood perfectly well what he was getting at. I would always be second — no, actually third best. Bottom of the pile. I would never be anything more. Daddy was very cross after Celine. But he understood that I was protecting my brother. The only thing I did wrong was not finishing the job. Turns out I didn't need to, though. She's as good as dead. You see, though Daddy despised me, he did teach me a few things over the years.'

I glance at the raven. 'Is this thing ever gonna go off? You're beginning to bore me.'

'That's not very nice. Well, the thing is, it never was going to go off.' His grin widens. I watch in horror as he picks up the raven and takes a serrated steak knife from the table. He saws its neck open and pulls out a little clock. 'Tick-tock, tick-tock.'

I've had enough. He's too far gone. There'll never be any reasoning with him. I stand up.

In one swift movement, he is beside me. He takes hold of my arm and twists it up behind my back.

'Run!' I yell out to the room.

Some do, others hesitate.

'When you go out, hold your hands in the air. Go on, run!' I twist, which only serves to intensify the pain. I was wrong to believe I could save him, he's insane.

He whispers in my ear, 'Don't forget dear old Aunt Margie now. Stay still.'

Desperation drives me to hope, despite myself. I daren't risk making another move.

'Where is she? Is she hurt? What have you done to her?'

'Come on, we need to take a little trip.' He sets off at a shuffle, holding the knife to my throat. I look down at the chef, who is lying in a pool of blood and I picture the gaping wound in Rose Danes' neck. 'I saved this beauty for you. It's a special knife. My father and I used it to gut fish and a few other things.'

Even though Simon had wiped it off, I can still smell the metallic tang of the chef's blood. He shoves me towards the kitchen. It's empty. Anyone who was lucky enough to be in here and not out front has long since scarpered.

I'm hoping the police have some sort of plan in mind. Maybe they have a sniper in place. But if they kill Simon, I may never find Aunt Margie. He pushes me ahead of him out of the back door. I have become a human shield.

'Don't shoot!' I scream into the bright lights. I see the shapes of coppers everywhere, and overhead the *thwack, thwack, thwack* of helicopter blades. Wind rushes brutally at us. A cordon has been put up to keep pedestrians and press at bay. It is flapping ferociously.

'He has a hostage somewhere,' I shout. 'If you shoot, we won't find her.'

I know they will still consider taking him out. It isn't my call. I can only hope they listen. Blinded by the lights and the low winter sun, I can't see what they're doing, if there are indeed snipers in position.

The knife is cold against my neck. I wonder what it will feel like to die. I might even be happy to go. Then I won't have to face up to my monumental fuck-up, or the insurmountable grief of losing someone else I love.

Then I see them, their familiar shapes against the light. Dillon, Millie. *Aunt Margie*. They're standing watching me, us, from behind the cordon. He laughs, his breath warm at my ear. 'It's so easy to doctor a photograph these days. And you fell for it, too. Some detective. So, I guess I won in the end, didn't I? My last move. I think it was worth it.'

He takes the knife from my throat and kisses my cheek, raising the blade aloft. 'Been great meeting you, sis.'

A small crack resounds through the air. He slumps to the ground, pulling me with him. I struggle to my knees and look down at his beautiful brown eyes staring back at me, lifeless. Blood is pooling, spreading around the back of his head and there's a neat little entry wound on his forehead. I look down at him, feeling complete and utter relief.

CHAPTER FORTY-EIGHT

I'm at the hospital being checked over. I'm in deep shit about the mobile, about going after him alone. I don't know what I was thinking. I wasn't, only that I didn't dare risk the lives of those I love. That doesn't stop me worrying that I might have been wrong, though it turned out the phone he was using was an untraceable burner. We'd never have got to him that way. It's some solace at least.

I'm still there when they let Millie and Aunt Margie in to see me. Aunt Margie's sweet face has me in tears. She rushes towards me. 'Oh, sugarplum, I was so scared.' She covers my forehead, the top of my head, my cheek, with kisses.

'All right, all right.' I smile. 'I'm okay, just a bit battered and bruised. You've no idea how good it is to see you.' I won't tell her how he used her to get at me. I refuse to burden her with that.

Then it's Millie's turn. Her eyes are shining. 'Fuckin' hell, Beth, I thought he was going to kill you right in front of us.' She takes both my hands, raises them to her lips and slowly kisses them.

'I'm so sorry,' I say. 'I didn't know what else to do.'

Millie is shaking her head. 'Don't ever, ever, put me through something like that again, Beth. I couldn't lose you, I wouldn't survive it.'

I don't know what to say, I've never seen Millie like this, so completely shattered. My hands are trembling in hers. 'I'm sorry.'

'There's something else,' Millie says. 'Peter Lambert has finally admitted that Jenny spiked Rose's drink after they fell out. She confessed it to him the day she vanished. She felt like it was all her fault, which is why she took the risk of meeting Simon. He must have got to her somehow, worked on her guilt. And she must have thought she could save the day, make things right, that nothing bad could ever happen to her, not like Rose.'

'Poor Jenny. She certainly suffered for what she did. She made a juvenile mistake, and the price she paid was far too high.' If only she hadn't gone to meet him. I can feel nothing but pity for the poor, mixed-up girl.

The door opens and in walks Caroline Walters. 'Can I have a minute with Beth, please?'

Aunt Margie and Millie look at me, then back at Caroline. No one moves.

'It's okay,' I say. 'Give us a moment.'

Millie kisses my cheek. Both she and Aunt Margie look back before closing the door behind them.

'I have your results. You won't tell anyone how you got them, will you? My job, I—'

'I'm so sorry I asked that of you. I won't say a word, I promise.'

'It was a fifty-six per cent match. The Brander is your half-sibling. I guess they've got him now, anyway.'

'The sample wasn't from the Brander.'

She looks confused. 'I don't understand. Like you asked, it was the sample from Celine Wilson's rape kit, the semen, that I tested.'

'Yes, I know. My other half-brother deposited that sample. Some genetics, eh? He raped her, and then Simon — the

Brander — cleaned up after him. He told me the gory details in the restaurant. If he was lying and he did rape Celine, we'll soon know, but I think he was telling the truth.'

She gapes. 'Fucking hell.'

'Tell me about it.'

'He happen to tell you who his brother was, or is?' she asks.

I shake my head. 'No, he kept skirting around it. He didn't tell me who his father is either.' I won't call him my father, not until I find out whether he is a monster like his son. According to Simon, he knew about Celine. He was an abusive father, too. If all that's true, he created the Brander. Even if it turns out he's innocent, I doubt I will ever think of him as my dad.

'They'll get a full identification now they have his body. It's only a matter of time.'

'I know.' It's a relief in one respect, but it will also open a Pandora's box and I'm not sure I'm ready. I'm not sure I ever will be.

'I'm gonna go.' Caroline stops by the door. 'I'm glad you're okay, Beth.'

'Thanks. And, Caroline?'

'Yeah?'

'I really am sorry.'

She offers me a small smile and leaves.

CHAPTER FORTY-NINE

Dillon visits and gives me what for, telling me how stupid I've been and that I put myself and everyone else at risk. I deserve so much more than what she dishes up — she's clearly holding back. It's going to hit at some stage though, and I'll have to take it on the chin when it does. I am put on suspended leave with full pay while an investigation into my conduct and ability to do my job is carried out. I'll be lucky to keep my career afterwards, we both know it, and it's out of Dillon's hands. When she leaves, she touches my arm and wishes me well. It means a lot. She's incensed but she still cares. Maybe she'll fight my corner, which might give me a chance of salvaging my career.

I've been cleared for discharge and am waiting for Millie to arrive. She's been back to the station. I begged her to go in, to see if there'd been any news. Dillon won't be impressed if she finds out that Millie is feeding me information, though I'm sure she'll expect her to.

When Millie finally walks into my room, I am sitting up in the chair, dressed and eager to leave.

The look on her face frightens me. 'What's happened?'

'We have an ID on Simon. His real name is Sigmund Edwards. He had his mother's surname.'

'Right . . .'

'His father was noted as his next of kin.'

'Who is he?'

'Stanley Baker.'

I shake my head. 'Means nothing to me, I've never heard of him. What about the brother?'

Millie shrugs. 'Nothing. We're not even sure he exists at this stage.'

'He has to. Caroline told me the DNA test was a hit. It was my half-brother who raped Celine, but Simon says it wasn't him. Why would he lie?'

'When they test — I don't know whether to call him Simon, Sigmund or the friggin' Brander.'

'Let's go with Sigmund.' The name he hated.

'Okay, when they run the test, it could be his DNA. I don't know why, but he could have been lying to you.'

I shrug. 'It's possible I suppose.'

'But you don't think he was?'

'No.'

'There's something else . . .'

I sigh. 'When isn't there? Go on, what now?'

'Sigmund had stage four terminal lung cancer. He had nothing to lose when he . . . I guess he wanted to go out in a blaze of glory or something.'

'He was diseased long before he got cancer. He really hated me yet he didn't even know me. The things he did to those kids . . . he's right where he belongs.'

'Come on, let's get you out of here,' Millie says.

'Do you have an address for him?'

'No, Beth. Not now. You need to rest.'

'I *need* to do this, Mills. I can't not. You must understand.'

Millie reluctantly drives me to 5 Albert Road in Kirkham. Stanley Baker has been notified of his son's passing and will be interviewed in due course. I'm nervous, and have no idea what to expect. When the news was broken to Baker, he apparently accepted it with little reaction then demanded that they leave him to grieve. When they asked if he had another son, he shut the door in their faces.

He lives in a red-brick Victorian terrace with a neatly trimmed hedge running along the front of a tiny concrete yard. The gate is missing, so we walk straight up to the blue wooden door and press the bell.

'Can I help you?'

He approaches us from behind, casually swinging an Aldi carrier bag. He's wearing a grey flat cap, a dark duffel coat and workman's boots with steel toecaps. He addresses himself to me, ignoring Millie. He doesn't look like a grieving father. 'You here to see me?'

'Mr Stanley Baker?' We show him our IDs, though he only looks at mine. I shudder.

'That'd be me,' he says with a smile. 'What can I do ya for?'

'Is there anyone at home apart from you?' I ask.

'Nope, just me. Why?'

'Can we come in?'

He continues to smile. 'Sure.'

He has olive skin and dark hair. He looks very much like Sigmund. I can see some similarities to me but not many. I cringe inwardly. It's all too real. I notice that his hand trembles when he turns the key. He gestures us in.

The hallway is decorated in neutral tones. There's a small table at one end with a spider plant on it. A glass-panelled door leads from the hallway into the lounge, which is furnished with a brown couch and matching armchairs, all adorned with red cushions. A throw is laid across the back of the settee. In the corner of the room is a red cuddle chair, and in front of the fire a brown rug. Care has been taken, down to the way the numerous plants are arranged. The ornaments range from a beggar on a bench holding a sign reading 'hungry and homeless' to a man with a cigar. When I look closer, I realise it's actually a joint.

He gestures to the couch. 'Please, sit down. Would you like a drink? Tea, coffee, juice?'

I shake my head. 'Nothing for me, thanks.'

'Nor me,' Millie says.

He moves to the cuddle chair, never taking his eyes off me. He didn't even look at Millie when she refused his offer of a drink. He's scrutinising me. He must know who I am. My skin crawls. He puts the carrier bag on the floor beside him.

'Do you live alone?' I can't help but glance at the carefully arranged vases of flowers, the plants. They look like a woman's touch.

He sees me looking and laughs lightly. 'Erm, yes I do. I have an allotment. I like flowers, they brighten the place up. All I have here is a small concrete yard that I can't do much with. I like having flowers around the house, they make me breathe easier somehow. Sounds odd, I know.'

I do the same thing. How similar are we? He's staring at me intently. I glance at Millie and see that she's watching him closely. I can't read her expression.

'How many children do you have?' Millie asks.

His eyes narrow. 'I had two until today.' It's the first time he looks at Millie, and the look is bitter. 'But you already know that.' He turns to me and smiles. 'A son and a daughter. I'm ashamed to say they have different mums and I don't have a relationship with either of them.'

'Your son, Simon,' I say, careful to refer to him by his chosen name. 'He claimed to have a brother.'

'Well, he didn't.' His eyes widen. He nudges the carrier bag with his foot.

'Did he have children, a partner?'

He frowns. 'Never even came close, poor lad. He just wasn't built that way.' That blows my earlier theory out of the water, not that it matters now.

'We understand that Simon came to live with you when he was a teenager. That his name then was Sigmund?'

'Yes. He was fifteen. His mum died in a car accident. Mechanical failure. Poor woman. And the name . . .' He smiles. 'Well, Sigmund was a pompous name for a kid, he hated it. He used to get picked on at school. His mum named him for her dead dad. I just opted to make life a little easier for the boy.'

'Had you seen much of him before he came to live with you?'

'Well, once he knew I existed, yes. From time to time. He would come and see me on occasion. He always was a bit messed up — case of angry teen complex. Not surprising when his mum landed him with a name like Sigmund. He was always gonna have issues.' He laughs again. It jars.

'Why didn't he know you existed?' Millie asks.

Still looking at me, he says, 'Because his mum didn't tell him about me. But he was a resourceful lad, found her diary, some old photos and tracked me down.' His face lights up with pride. 'One look at him and I knew he was mine. His personality was another matter. He was a nasty little so and so. But he was mine and I tried. You've got to do your best, haven't you? Try to help shape them into the people you want them to become.'

'You said you have a daughter?' I ask.

'I do.'

I bite my lip and stare straight at him. 'What is the name of your daughter?' I'm assuming he knows, but what if I'm wrong?

I feel Millie's eyes boring into me.

'How about that brew now?' He reaches down, picks up the carrier bag from the floor and lifts it into his lap. 'I have the milk right here. It would be quite something, wouldn't it, to finally share a cup of tea with my daughter.' He gets to his feet, smiling broadly.

The room spins. Millie stares at me, her mouth open. Neither of us knows what to say. He knew who I was right away. Maybe he's always known.

Millie is kneeling in front of me and taking my hands in hers. I hadn't even registered her getting up. I stare at her, struggling to catch my breath.

Stanley saunters back in carrying three cups. 'I made two teas and a coffee. That's what you prefer, isn't it, Beth?' He sets them down on the coffee table, each one on a coaster with a picture of a farmyard animal.

What he says next fills me with foreboding. He knows my date of birth, my mother's name. He knows about Aunt Margie. He knows where I grew up, what schools I attended. When I joined the police. How fast I climbed the ranks. Hell, he even has a photo from my passing out parade. He retrieves it from a drawer of the French dresser and shows it to me. All the while he's smiling, like this is an everyday occurrence. He's been in the shadows of my life this whole time.

Simon said my mum was the love of Stanley's life. She couldn't have loved someone evil. Maybe Simon was just a bad seed. But there's something dark about Stanley Baker. I see it, I feel it and I can tell by Millie's demeanour that she does too.

Everything Simon did was because Stanley favoured the daughter he'd never met over the fucked-up son who craved his love.

'Did you know what he was doing?' I say to him. 'Tell me the truth.'

'Of course not. I did my best with him. He was damaged before he ever came to me.'

I can't stay any longer. Sitting in his living room, talking about Simon, Stanley's knowledge of every detail of my life, it's too much. Millie was right, I can't deal with this now. I will when I'm ready, but not yet.

By the time we get back in the car, I'm shaking. Millie drives around the corner then pulls over and takes my hand.

'Beth, look at me. You are not a product of that man. You are your mum's, you're Aunt Margie's, you're mine. You are not his. Do you understand me? You're not his, you're not Sigmund's. You aren't tainted by them.'

Tears roll down my cheeks. 'Simon, no, *Sigmund* said my mum was the love of that man's life.'

'It doesn't mean he was hers.'

'What *does* it mean?'

'I don't know.'

'It changes everything I thought I knew about myself, about my mum. I often imagined my father, the family I didn't know but wanted to. I always thought that one day I'd find them, or they'd find me. I never thought—'

'Why would you? We don't know who Stanley is yet. Just because his son was—'

'Millie, don't do that.'

'Do what?'

'Protect me with falsehoods. You're always honest with me, don't stop now.'

She shifts in her seat. 'Okay, it didn't sit right with me that he had no emotions about his son's death, about the crimes he'd committed. There wasn't any shock or revulsion, just acceptance, like a shrug. It was as though he already knew, like he'd known for a long time. I know he'd been informed earlier but still, he was emotionless.'

'Do you think he had anything to do with it?' I ask.

'I hope not. There was something disturbing about him though. Put it this way, I wouldn't want you going back to see him alone.'

CHAPTER FIFTY

It turns out that being on suspension gives you a lot of thinking time. I've spent the past week reading, spending time with Aunt Margie in her garden, walking along St Anne's Seafront and Fairhaven Lake. I've been to the Harris Museum in Preston for the first time in years. However, my attempts to cram all my time with activities have done nothing to slow the cogs in my mind.

The DNA test they ran against Sigmund using the sample from Celine's rape kit wasn't a match. He'd claimed he had a brother and I believed him. Stanley Baker was insistent that he has one son and me, his daughter. I can't tell Dillon about the DNA test Caroline ran. Doing so wouldn't just end my career, it would end Caroline's too. I'm in a bind and, right now, I can't see a way out.

It is tormenting me daily that either Stanley is lying about having another son, or . . . what? Was it him? Did he rape Celine, and Sigmund was protecting him to the end? I'm not going to contact Caroline to ask questions or beg more favours — I apologised to her and I meant it. I won't compromise her or anyone else again.

Millie's been reprimanded and ordered not to reveal anything further to me regarding the investigation. Amer is also under strict instructions to give me a wide berth when it comes to the case. This time I'll obey the rules. I've caused enough problems.

Amer and Dillon will wrap up the investigation. They'll get the answers eventually. I trust them to do what needs to be done. If Stanley Baker is guilty of anything, they'll prove it.

Aunt Margie was shocked when I told her Mum was supposedly the love of Stanley's life. She said that mum was shy, a bookworm and not one for dating. Her pregnancy had come as a shock to Aunt Margie. Mum had claimed the father was someone she had no ongoing connection with. It was a one-off and she'd been caught out. It didn't sound like the sister she knew but Aunt Margie stood by her. And once I was born, my grandmother came round too. They'd all adored me.

I know Mum loved me. Aunt Margie's recollections and the boxes of photos we pore over regularly are a reminder of that. I was four when she died, so I never got the chance to know her. My memories are eclipsed by the horror of her death.

It's nighttime and I'm at home, despite Aunt Margie's offer to clear out my old room for me. Yvette is gone and the house is mine again. I've reclaimed it.

My phone buzzes with a text. It's from Danielle.

I need to see you. I've been thinking and there's something I should have told you ages ago. Please meet me. I'll ping you the place. I don't want to say this in front of Tom. I made a mistake, I don't want it to cost me my marriage.

An uneasy sensation swims in my stomach. I recall Danielle's reaction when I gave her Simon's description. I'd felt in my gut that she knew something, that she recognised his description but wasn't telling me. I still can't understand why. She'd already essentially lost her sister. If she thought revealing whatever she knew would threaten her marriage, I could almost understand her reluctance. But it may have cost Jenny her life. There's no excuse for that.

249

I get into my car, trying to calm my angry thoughts. My phone pings with the address. I try to call Danielle, but she cuts me off. I'm guessing Tom is at home. He must be on leave.

The light drizzle transforms into sheets of rain. The hail that hits the car like bullets reminds me of the day I visited Danielle's flat and she held something back. I wonder what she will say now. I lean forward in my seat with my beams high, my windscreen wipers going at full speed. It does little to improve my view.

The sky rumbles. Flashes and streaks of lightning are followed almost immediately by a boom of thunder. It's unrelenting. Not surprising, then, that as I turn into Orb Street, my tyres aquaplane. My heart in my mouth, I grip the steering wheel and wait to feel them gain traction again.

At last I park the car. Breathing a sigh of relief, I peer through the windscreen to take in my surroundings. It's a small, rundown street. I'm guessing Danielle's using a friend's house so she can offload in private, away from her family.

I wriggle out of my leather jacket and cover my head with it to shield myself from the hail, shove my keys into my back pocket and make a run for it. I knock and the door swings open.

The hallway is uncarpeted, the bare floorboards creaking beneath my footsteps. I close the door behind me. The house is in darkness, the only light that of a streetlamp just outside.

Hesitantly, I move toward the first door I see and push it open. 'Hello? Danielle?'

The room is in pitch darkness. I look for a window and when my eyes have adjusted a little, I realise it's covered in cardboard and black tape. This isn't right. I turn to run.

Too late. Someone clamps a hand over my mouth and I'm unable to scream. They grasp my waist. I kick backwards and connect with their shin — there's a yelp and I know it's not Danielle. This is a male. His grip on my mouth tightens, his fingers digging into my cheeks and jawbone. I try to yell but all that comes out is a grunt.

I wriggle from side to side trying to loosen his grip, but he grasps me harder, closer, until I can feel his chest against my back. His groin presses against me. He's aroused. I want to be sick.

His hand still covering my mouth, he slides his arm from my waist. I hear the rip of tape being unrolled, bitten off. He puts it over my mouth and presses it in place. Then he slings me to the floor, where I lie on my stomach. He kneels on my lower back, twists my arms behind me and binds them tight with tape.

He pulls me up and roughly spins me around to face him but I still can't see his face. It is just too dark. He shoves me backwards, hard. With a crack, my spine hits the wall and I go down on my knees. I look up, straining to see him, but he's invisible in the blackness.

I wait for what is coming next, my hands clammy, dread in my gut. When nothing happens, I twist my body in an attempt to reach into the back pocket of my trousers and get at my keys. After a few desperate tries, they are in my hand, and I saw at the tape.

His laughter reverberates around the room, but he makes no move to stop me. I continue working at the tape but in my panic, I drop the keys. He must have heard them clatter, yet he makes no move. My back to the room, I feel around in the dust, until my hands touch metal. I pick them up again.

I turn, struggle to stand and brace myself against the wall. It's marginally easier to hack at the tape from this position. I stop. My heart leaps into my throat. He is coming towards me.

There is a click and suddenly his face is illuminated in the beam of a torch.

My eyes widen. How could I not have known?

CHAPTER FIFTY-ONE

Tom grins evilly. The beam of the torch pointing up at his face causes his eyes to gleam. How could I not have seen the similarities between us? He has the same nose as Simon, the same full lips. I look at him aghast, because I see, so clearly now, just like Simon and myself, he gets his olive skin from Stanley, our father. I stare into his brown eyes, a perfect reflection of my own. I feel sick.

'There's no point screaming, no one will hear you. We're in another Salvadore Street.' He's referring to the place his brother kidnapped Jenny from. 'It's almost like Preston wants to make things easy for us.' He laughs, reaching towards me. I flinch.

He rips the tape from my mouth. It feels like the skin has gone with it.

'Why, Tom? Is that even your name?'

'Don't be dense. Course it is. Do you think the good old British police didn't run checks before I joined?'

'Then how? Why is there no record of you?'

He rolls his eyes, shaking his head. 'Oh, come on. Are you really that dumb? Like Simon, I had my mother's name. Dad was careful about that. While I was with him, I didn't go to school. I wasn't even registered with a doctor. To all intents and purposes, I never left my mother's care. Truth is, she was more than happy to take handouts in exchange for custody. She was even able to claim for me. Never got found out either. Perfect set-up for a woman like her. She was a waste of oxygen, but keeping her in the background worked for Dad, so that's how it was.'

'And Simon?'

'Sigmund. Let's go with that, shall we?'

So, he despises his brother too? 'Okay. Sigmund then.'

He grimaces. 'That pathetic little shit cost me everything. Not once but twice. First, he attacked Celine. She was my friend, and he may as well have killed her.'

'You raped her,' I shoot back.

'Rape, sex, call it what you like. I wouldn't have killed her though — she'd have kept quiet. He didn't need to go that far, not with her.'

'If she was your friend, why did you hurt her?'

'I loved her. She was the only person I ever cared about. When you're raised the way I was, it shapes you.'

I remember Stanley talking about trying to shape his child. 'That's a pathetic excuse. You chose to do it, you weren't forced to.'

He pushes his face against mine, nose to nose. 'I didn't know any different. You'll never understand. The things we did, our little family. We weren't like other families. We didn't go bowling or fishing together. There were no trips to the cinema or days at the beach.'

'What did you do then?'

He moves back a few steps and smiles. 'What didn't we do? Dad taught us to be just like him. From eleven years old for me, fifteen for Sigmund.'

'Is that why Sigmund was jealous of you, because you'd been *shaped* earlier? Couldn't he compete?'

'Compete? He wanted to *be* me. Until he realised we had a worse enemy in common.' He glares at me. 'Dad always loved you best. And he made damn sure we knew it. You came from the woman he loved, the only woman he'd *ever* loved.'

'Did he hurt my mum?'

He shrugs. 'Like father, like son.'

'He raped her, didn't he?' My whole body shakes with rage.

He grins. 'Then, four years later, when he realised there was walking, talking evidence of what he did, he killed her.'

My mind explodes. 'What?'

'That's right, he raped her and then he murdered her. He killed her because of you. If you'd never been born, he'd have let her live.'

I fight back tears. 'What about Danielle?'

'She was my chance to change. I'd already joined the police by then. I wasn't what you'd call committed, but, hey, we all need to earn a crust.'

'You like the power.'

He laughs. 'Anyone who says that they don't is a liar. But when I met Danielle . . . I loved her from the moment I laid eyes on her. I was almost glad about Celine then. If Sig hadn't done what he did, I wouldn't have met Danielle.'

'What do you mean, *loved*? Why are you using the past tense? Have you hurt her?'

He slams his fist into my solar plexus, I double over, gasping for breath. 'She's my wife and you fucked us over. So did he.'

Slowly, I manage to stand up straight. 'Sigmund?' My voice is little more than a whisper.

'I cut Dad and Sigmund off after I met Danielle, I had no further contact with either of them. Then fucking Sig thought he'd butt into my life, didn't he? He contacted Danielle behind my back and begged to see his nieces. She kept it from me. What kind of a wife would do that, eh?'

'She let him see them?'

'Yeah, she did. Sneaking him in while I was at work, cosying up to him when I was out paying our bills. They spent evenings curled up on the couch while I worked into the night.'

His arm shoots out and he grasps my throat. I can't breathe. With my hands bound, I'm powerless to push him away. He stands with the length of his body against me, my legs trapped between his. After a few seconds, he lets go. I cough and splutter and gasp for air.

I think of Danielle and those kids, my nieces. Has he hurt them? Killed them? I recall going round after Rose had been killed and watching Danielle with the girls. They were a handful, Erin whizzing round with her doll's pram, both full of energy. Then I remember what calmed them down.

Now I know why I felt that I was missing something at the shop. I knew that Simon buying milk chocolate buttons was significant, though I didn't realise how significant. He was buying them for the kids. He killed Rose Danes and then he went to see his nieces. My nieces. I feel sick.

'She started asking questions after you came round and fed her that description of Sigmund. I told her it meant nothing, it could have been any number of men. It was a coincidence. I went on about how upset I was about her going behind my back.' He clenches a fist. 'But then that selfish pig of a brother of mine goes and gets himself killed on purpose. Just because he was dying, didn't mean he had to take me with him. His photo was everywhere after that. She doesn't bother with the news, but even she didn't miss the stories everyone was sharing on fuckin' Facebook. I couldn't keep it from her anymore. When she figured out I'd been involved with Celine, it was over. My life is over.'

He reaches around his back. At the same time, my key cuts sever the last bit of tape. I swing my arm and stab the key into his cheek.

He yells and brings out a knife and raises it, ready to strike. I hold my hands up, crossed at the wrists, blocking his attack, then knee his groin and, as he doubles over, shove him hard. He stumbles backwards and falls, dropping the knife.

I kick it away and before he can get up, lay into him, raining punches and kicks down on his head and body. I don't let up for a second, or he'll come at me again. I pummel him with everything I've got and I keep going until he's no longer moving. Racing to the door, I run to my car, peel away from the kerb and scream out of the street.

CHAPTER FIFTY-TWO

Parking outside Starburst House, I leg it to the door and hit the buzzer. The rain is lashing down. I'm bruised, battered and soaked to the skin. A man is jogging down the stairs. He opens the door and before he can stop me, I run past him and take the stairs two at a time, my heat hammering.

I pound on her door. 'Police! Open up, Danielle.'

I'm losing my shit. I pummel the door, giving vent to all my pent-up anger.

A couple of the neighbours peer out of their doors. I flash them my ID and am about to yell at them when an old lady holds out a key. I snatch it and jam it into the lock. 'Call the police,' I tell her.

The sound of a child crying brings tears to my eyes. Not dead. I race into the house and follow the cries into a pink room. For a moment, I can't move. Then I break into action. The kids are in a cot, imprisoned beneath a bed sheet fastened across the bars to stop them getting out. Erin is pushing at it and both girls are crying.

I battle to loosen the knots. The stench of stale urine and faeces fills the room. They must have been trapped here for days.

Danielle is bound to a chair, a gag over her mouth. I hesitate, move towards her, but she nods to the cot, her pleading gaze telling me to help the children first.

* * *

Danielle and the girls have been checked over at the hospital. They were all a little dehydrated but other than that, they're physically okay. The emotional and psychological effects of their ordeal will take much longer to heal.

Expecting to get some sort of admission from Danielle, I'd set my phone to record and put it into my pocket before I ran into the house where Tom attacked me. I wasn't expecting to record the despicable truth about my paternal family, the half of me I had always wondered about. The knowledge that I'm not only related to them but that I am also the product of rape makes me physically ill. I'm the reason for my mum getting killed. I'm the dirty secret Stanley Baker wanted to keep.

I'm in hospital yet again, this time with injuries inflicted by my other brother. I sent Millie the recording, along with the address I'd been lured to and an SOS for Danielle's apartment. I'd done it on the move, driving through torrential rain at speed. It's not an experience I would recommend to anyone, or ever want to repeat. I'd been desperate. For all I knew, Danielle and the girls were on borrowed time.

The police arrived just as I was untying Danielle. Two ambulances turned up shortly afterwards, one for her and the kids and the other one for me. I'd left Tom unconscious, and had assumed he'd be incapable of getting far, but by the time they got there, he was gone. There's been no sign of him since. It's as though he's evaporated.

Millie walks into my room. 'Jesus, Beth. What were you thinking?'

'I'm sorry. I've been saying that a lot lately, I know, but I mean it. I'm sorry.'

She rushes to me and pulls me into a hug. The door opens again and Aunt Margie crashes in. Millie lets go and Aunt

Margie puts her arms around me. Her tears wet my cheek. After a few minutes, she puts her hands on either side of my face. 'Oh, sugarplum, what a mess.'

'Stanley Baker has been arrested,' I begin. 'He's being questioned about—'

'I know,' Aunt Margie says. 'DS West told me. My poor, poor sister.'

I'm fighting not to break down but it's useless. A sob bursts out of me and the tears won't stop. 'I'm sorry.'

'Hey, hey, you didn't do anything — except go and get yourself hurt again.'

'I did. It's my fault Mum was killed. Because of me you don't have a sister. If I hadn't been born, if she'd never had me—'

'Don't you dare,' Aunt Margie says. Her gaze softens. 'Your mum loved you more than anything. I love you the same way. You are not a product of that disgusting man. You are ours. Do you hear me?'

I nod, and she embraces me again, keeping hold until my tears run dry.

CHAPTER FIFTY-THREE

It's been four days. I'm at Aunt Margie's, sitting on the couch with a blanket over my knee, Millie beside me. Aunt Margie is busying herself baking, which is her latest hobby. If I stay much longer I'll be leaving here at least a stone heavier.

The doorbell chimes and Aunt Margie emerges from the kitchen, patting flour-covered hands against her apron, leaving a trail of white on the floor.

She returns with Dillon and Amer in tow. The expressions on their faces send me cold.

'What's wrong?'

They are silent, as if neither of them knows what to say.

I switch off the TV. 'Something's wrong. I can see it on your faces. What is it?'

All three of us look at them expectantly, frightened of what else there could possibly be.

Dillon looks at me sympathetically. 'The DNA tests have confirmed Stanley Baker to be your biological father and Sigmund Edwards and—' she hesitates — 'Tom Spencer to be your half siblings.' She looks from me to Aunt Margie. 'I'm sorry. I know this must be very upsetting for you. But it does mean we can build a strong case against Stanley Baker.'

I nod. I can't tell them I already knew. They can never find out what Caroline did for me.

'There's more,' Dillon says, and my stomach drops. 'Forensics have been searching Tom's home. They found an item tucked away in the crawl space above their apartment. The upstairs apartment had no access to it, so it was essentially pretty well hidden. What they found there, well it was extremely disturbing.'

'What?'

'A book.'

'I don't understand.'

'Some sort of scrapbook . . .' Her voice trails away.

Amer looks stricken. Whatever this is, it's really bad.

'Just tell me, please.'

'It's brands. Twenty-eight of them.'

'What do you mean, brands?' Though of course, I know exactly what she means.

'Pieces of skin with brands on them, cut from people. Preserved between the pages of a fuckin' scrapbook, like those pressed wildflowers people used to keep.'

I spring to my feet. 'What the fuck? Are they dead, the people they cut them from? Why did they leave Rose Danes to be found then? What . . . ?'

Amer steps forward. 'Sigmund was taunting you, playing with you. When he found out his condition was terminal, it freed him up to come after you. He didn't care what happened. In the process, he got to bring down the brother he hated and the father he could never please. It was calculated. All of it.'

I sit back down. 'So, Rose, Jenny . . . He murdered them, brutalised them, to get some sort of twisted revenge?'

Dillon nods. 'It appears that way.'

'But the book was in Tom's home?'

I notice Dillon is digging her fingers into her thighs. 'He was clearly very involved in it all at some stage. He kept the evidence. Who knows why. But some of the brands predate Simon and Tom as adults. Some brands predate their birth.'

'They're dated?'

'Oh yes,' she says. 'They were meticulously stored and catalogued. There's no information about where or who they were from, just the year.'

'Do you think they're all dead?'

'I think if they weren't, we'd know by now. They must have chosen their victims carefully so they could remain under the radar. Plus, the brands were removed, so even if they were found—'

'There wouldn't be a brand to link them. If the bodies were decomposed enough by the time they were discovered, whoever did may never have known skin had been removed.'

'Exactly.'

'And it seems the only time they were careless about DNA was leaving semen in Celine's attack, otherwise I would imagine something would have been flagged. But of course we will look into it all. We'll cover every possible avenue.'

'You said some predate Sigmund and Tom?' I ask.

Dillon nods. 'We found a print in the book beside one of the earlier brands. It belongs to Stanley Baker. We're looking to charge him, though we're not sure what with yet. It's still under consideration. We currently have no proof that these brands are from murdered women. He's claiming he knows nothing about the book. We're anticipating his lawyer putting forward that he handled his sons' property in all innocence, before the brands were put in there. But the years are clearly marked. We have a good shot at keeping him in custody for the foreseeable. At the very least for your mum, while we compile more evidence.'

'Tom?' I ask.

She shakes her head. 'We won't stop looking.'

Dillon and Amer don't move, and I know they have something else to reveal. I'm on tenterhooks.

Dillon takes a breath. 'On the last page of the scrapbook are the words, "to be continued" with Tom's signature underneath, along with a smiley face. He's a detective, Beth. He knows how we work. He'll know how to hide. It's not over yet.'

I'm aghast. Tom's on the run with nothing to lose but his freedom. He clearly has an axe to grind with me. He's a killer, like Stanley, like his brother. He won't stop.

I'm still suspended from work, waiting to learn my fate. If they sack me, I'll go it alone. But one way or another, I'm going to end this. I'm going to get to the whole truth, whatever it takes. Even if it means I have to dance with the Devil. Me, Tom's sister. I won't let him win.

THE END

ACKNOWLEDGEMENTS

Huge thank you to my editor Emma Grundy Haigh for her belief, support and hard work. This book would not be what it is without her. Special thanks to my agents at Northbank Talent Management, in particular Hannah Weatherill, who has been a wonderful champion of my work, given the best advice and guidance and is always encouraging.

Thank you to the Joffe Book team, who are all absolutely brilliant. Thanks to the judges with the best taste, who unanimously voted my book the winner of the inaugural Joffe Books Prize for Crime Writers of Colour. In all seriousness this book would not be in your hands without them. So, thank you, Jasper Joffe, Emma Grundy Haigh, Susan Yearwood and one of my all-time idols, Dorothy Koomson. Also, thank you to Dorothy Koomson for the advice via our Zoom chat — you are one of the very best in this business.

I am thankful for the wonderful opportunities I have had, such as winning mentorship and guidance from two incredibly giving and hugely talented women, Nadine Matheson and Harriet Tyce. Thanks as well to the lovely and talented Awais Khan (check out the online courses he runs) and Sean Coleman at Red Dog Press, whose sponsorship allowed me to undertake one such course.

An enormous thank-you has to go out to my unofficial writing mentor, who has been there from the start, Diane Chamberlain. You amaze me and I value your friendship and support.

Thank you to Alexandra Sokoloff for showing me the way when it comes to planning and storyboarding. Anyone who struggles in these areas or just wants a little helping hand, check out her online courses.

Thank you to my writing friend, working CSI and fellow author, Kate Bendelow, for your guidance, advice, support and friendship. It's not often you meet someone and know right away you will be friends for ever, but with you that's exactly what happened. I am so grateful to have you in my life.

Thank you to Nicole Cowan for your friendship and to you and your family for the red wine, shared love of crime books (Mo) and for welcoming me into your home on so many occasions while I was at university. I'll never forget all the times we should have been studying and you dragged me kicking, screaming and protesting into the bar — at least that's how I remember it. Or Louise and Renee catching and chastising us!

Thanks to ex-detective and author Graham Bartlett for being on hand to answer my questions. Thank you as well to ex-detective Steve Page for answering my questions. Thank you to scientist and fellow author Brian Price; the scene we discussed didn't make it into the book — for good reason. I am grateful to him for saving me from myself. You are a gent.

Thank you to editor and friend Ian Skewis, for your advice and on-going support and friendship.

Thank you to the team at UK Crime Book Club and the ladies at the Book Lover's Companion podcast. Thanks to Jacky Collins and Kelly Lacey, for all your wonderful support and for your friendship.

Thank you to the team at the Capital Crime Writing Festival and all the authors who attended its inaugural festival — you made me believe I could do this, and I have! Thank you especially to festival director Lizzie Curle — your support and friendship means the world.

Thank you to the people on the Preston Remembers Facebook group, who have always been on hand to answer questions and show support.

Thank you to the many wonderful crime authors whose work inspires and entertains me. And who have been so wonderfully encouraging and generous with their time. Special thanks to Jenny Blackhurst, Caz Frear, Amer Anwar, Mari Hannah, M.W. Craven, Lisa Jewell, Rob Parker, R.C. Bridgestock, Lesley Kelly, Tana Collins, Vaseem Khan, Trevor Wood, Howard Linskey, David Fennell, William Shaw, Liz Nugent, Sharon Bairdon, Noelle Holten, Michael Malone, Sarah Stovell, Sarah Bonner, Marion Todd, Stephen Booth, Olivia Kiernan, Fiona Cummins, Amy McLellan, Heather Fitt, Ann Bloxwich, David Mark, Roxie Key, Rosie Walker and Douglas Skelton. Thank you also to the wonderful Karen Sullivan of Orenda Books who has been a great support and inspiration. I apologise if I have missed anyone from the list — but please know I am eternally grateful to you all.

Thank you to the book-loving community in general, in fact, to the entire book and writing community — on Facebook, Twitter and Instagram — you are all the most fantastic people.

Thank you to my amazing Crime and Publishment family — the group attend a yearly weekend in Gretna Green run by Graham Smith. Special thanks to Irene Paterson for reading early versions of my work and giving insightful feedback.

Thank you to my Swanwick Summer School family. I may have only attended one summer with you so far, but I was welcomed with open arms and will return.

Thanks to Berwick Library in Northumberland, for your support, especially Katy Wedderburn, Diane Wright and Gerard Young. Libraries are so very important to communities; they are the beating heart for many, and they offer a place of sanctuary and learning. Please support yours.

Thank you to the *Lancashire Evening Post* and *Blog Preston* for running stories about my writing journey. Preston is my home city, so it is lovely to have them follow my career. It is also where these books are set.

Thank you to the team at Guys and St Thomas', the Royal Victoria Infirmary and Freeman Hospital who all look after my complex health issues. I literally wouldn't be here without them.

Thank you to my hairdresser extraordinaire, Cheryl Gill, who manages to do wonderful things with my otherwise terrible mop. The character of Yvette and Beth's remarks about her career are in no way a reflection on you. You are the best hairdresser I've ever had, and I would recommend you to anyone.

Thank you to my life-long friend Antonio Giovanelli — especially for giving me permission to steal your name.

Thank you to author and friend Amer Anwar, for also allowing me to steal your name.

Thank you to the wonderful writing groups I have been a member of, such as South Shields Fiction Writers who meet at the Word and Kelso Writers.

Thank you to Gilly Becket, Linda Wright and Angi Plant, for your friendship and support.

Thank you to my readers. It has always been my dream to see someone lost in a world I have created. I hope you were lost there for a while and that you enjoyed the trip. I'd love to hear from you and see photographs of my book in the wild.

Now for the BIG thanks to my friends and family. I hope this book and the ones to follow make you proud. My parents, Paul and Dawn Newport — I love you both dearly. My sister, Kerry Newport, thank you for always supporting my writing and reading early versions of my work — love you loads. My cousin, Cherie Ali — you are one of life's treasures, lots of love. My nephews Brandon Forde and Bradley Whittle — I love you both very much. Massive love to the rest of my family, aunts, uncles, and cousins. I would be remiss if I was not to say thank you to my writing companion, my Labrador, Laddy — I love you, my fur baby.

A sincere thank you to those I have loved and lost, who will always be with me including, but not exhaustively, my Nanna, Grandad, Nan, Uncle Stephen Newport, Chantelle Jeffries, Auntie Bet, Auntie Maggie Walker, Joshua Holgate, Lee Giovanelli, Sara Tennant, Lynette McLaughlin, Barbara Redman and Peggy Dunn — I miss you all every day.

Enormous love and thank you most of all to the person I choose to spend my life with — she reads everything I write, supports me every day, carries my books, comes to writing festivals and events and is the one I laugh with the most — my incredible wife, Amy Newport. You are my person.

Thank you for reading this book.

If you enjoyed it please leave feedback on Amazon or Goodreads, and if there is anything we missed or you have a question about, then please get in touch. We appreciate you choosing our book.

Founded in 2014 in Shoreditch, London, we at Joffe Books pride ourselves on our history of innovative publishing. We were thrilled to be shortlisted for Independent Publisher of the Year at the British Book Awards.

www.joffebooks.com

We're very grateful to eagle-eyed readers who take the time to contact us. Please send any errors you find to corrections@joffebooks.com. We'll get them fixed ASAP.